# "WHERE IS YOUR FAITH IN GOD, RABBI?" ASKED SHELLY.

The rabbi glanced over glumly from behind the jail bars. "My faith in God is fine," he said. "It's people I'm not so sure about."

"You'll have your turn on the witness stand—your chance to explain your side of the story," said Shelly. "Don't you think your goodness will shine through?"

"Is that what I have to depend on? To keep me out of the electric chair?"

"They don't use the chair anymore."

"That's a relief. So what will it be? Hanging by my neck from a noose?"

"An injection."

"Good Lord! A shot! I hate needles. . . ."

**Books by Richard Fliegel**

The Next to Die
The Art of Death
The Organ Grinder's Monkey
Time to Kill
A Semi-Private Doom
A Minyan for the Dead

Published by POCKET BOOKS

# A Minyan for the Dead

## Richard Fliegel

**POCKET BOOKS**

New York   London   Toronto   Sydney   Tokyo   Singapore

This book is a work of fiction. Names, characters, places, and
incidents are either products of the author's imagination or are
used fictitiously. Any resemblance to actual events or locales or
persons, living or dead, is entirely coincidental.

An *Original* Publication of POCKET BOOKS

POCKET BOOKS, a division of Simon & Schuster Inc.
1230 Avenue of the Americas, New York, NY 10020

Copyright © 1993 by Richard Fliegel

ISBN: 0-671-74449-6

First Pocket Books printing March 1993

10  9  8  7  6  5  4  3  2  1

POCKET and colophon are registered trademarks of
Simon & Schuster Inc.

Cover art by Tristan Elwell

Printed in the U.S.A.

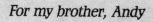

*For my brother, Andy*

My thanks to Dr. Philip Schwarzman, and to Rabbi Jeffrey Marx, for their advice and information on the contents of this book. The mistakes are of course my own. And a special word of thanks to my editor, Jane Chelius, for her clear head and kind heart.

# 1

"No mystery here," said Patrolman Felipe Montoya to Detective Sergeant Homer Greeley as the blond plainclothes officer kicked aside a dented beer can before it could nuzzle the soft leather of his tasseled shoes. Beyond the damp spot where the can had been, a trail of garbage like the spill from an urban horn of plenty led back to a sideways trash can, over which hung the inert arm of Rocio Lucero, draped in the universal gesture of comrades to the end.

It was the angle the police photographer had liked best, squatting in front of the corpse and the can as if taking a shot of two buddies. The deputy coroner was late, but the rest of the technical work had already been done—including the photographs, which meant that Homer was free to kick the can without worrying about disturbing the scene of the crime. Then he reached over the long, skinny body and rubbed a hole in the wooden fence behind it, which had evidently held the bullet now bagged by the Crime Scene Unit's ballistician.

"Furies?" Greeley asked.

Like a blind man reading braille, Montoya passed delicate fingers over the *placas* sprayed over the splintery boards in which the gang scribbled its ownership of this miserable alley, half a block from an IRT subway platform in the Bronx and a million miles from the rule of law.

"These are Furies," he said, indicating two blue signatures on the upper edge of the fence that read Poquito 6 and El Toro, the *T* of which had been crossed with a horizontal line twisted at both ends in a deft suggestion of horns. But these two noms de guerre had been effaced by a defiant spray of red paint that had also scrawled another signature, twice as large, that read in a rounder, less angular script, Die! El Gato.

Montoya tapped the big red swirls. "Los Diablos," he said, "here."

"Then this is . . . El Gato?"

The patrol officer glanced at Lucero and lifted the corner of one eyebrow. "Must'a run out of lives."

Greeley squatted alongside the corpse and inspected the right index finger without touching it, confirming his memory of a peculiar red semicircle that had caught his eye earlier. A few moments later he found it—the punctured can of paint—in a clump of weeds under the hinges where the fence met the bricks of the tenement to the south. With his handkerchief Homer gripped the can by the raised ring along its bottom and dropped it into a plastic bag, which he initialed and dated.

"They caught him in the act," Montoya said.

Greeley nodded. "Standing here, writing, with his back to the street. He hears the car—"

Montoya raised a square, thick-fingered hand, and consulted the pad in his belt.

"A Celica, according to the token seller in the

subway. At least, one drove away about ninety miles an hour after the shooting stopped."

"He hears the Celica enter the alley, turns, and tries to crawl behind the trash cans. But there's no place to hide, and they shoot up the cans too. This one goes over and he falls on top."

"Looks right to me."

"Anything else on the car?"

"We didn't get a license. One of those yellow fastbacks—you know, seventy-eight or -nine—with the thin red racing stripes."

There were only about fifty of those in the four square blocks of the neighborhood around them. So they wouldn't find the shooter's car, unless someone came forward. They both knew that no one who could help would consider doing so.

"Did you know him?"

"El Gato?" Montoya shrugged, a gesture between I-don't-know and I-don't-care. "I've seen his name around. Had to be a Diablo, of course, overwriting the Furies. But I couldn't've connected it to this face before, or even to his family name until I saw the library card in his wallet."

Greeley nodded, tugging the white cuffs from the sleeves of his linen suit jacket. It was getting cold for linen already, the last week of September. His mind wandered to the hangers in the back of his closet, and then to the spattered windbreaker over which the face of Lucero still seemed to wince. It was too often like this—the name, the face, and the gang affiliation came together only when the card had to be stamped DECEASED and removed from the precinct gang file.

Gang killings were never particularly interesting to Homer, because there was so little opportunity to exercise his skills at detecting clues to the criminal. They would have the bullet, of course, though the gun might be dumped by now; the opportunity was nothing more than a chance encounter with an enemy painting a name on a wall; and what could you say about motive? Even his former partner Shelly would've been stuck for something to wonder about here, Homer thought, turning up the collar of his suit jacket as an ill wind whistled down through the fire escapes overhead. Two patrolmen were already going door to door, asking if anyone who lived there had seen anything useful. But if they lived there, the most useful choice was not to have seen anything at all.

"Here we go," said Montoya.

Greeley looked up as a five-year-old station wagon turned into the alley with only its parking lights on, despite the gathering darkness. It was seven ten, two hours after Homer had taken the call at the precinct house. He could have turned it over to the night shift and punched out, as his partner had already done. But he had nothing planned for the evening, and nowhere in particular to go. So he had taken it—a decision he regretted now, as the deputy coroner's Volvo rolled right up to them, braking violently inches away. Its headlights went out and then on again, full force, when a thatch of brown hair poked out of the driver's window.

"I know—I'm late," said Ray Davidson, dismissing their objections before they could be articulated. He seemed to feel a confession of lateness was as good as being on time, preempting their grounds for a complaint.

Montoya said, *"He's* not going anywhere," flipping his thumb toward the corpse.

Davidson shook his head. "Always the same jokes. Don't you guys ever watch the new cop shows?"

As the deputy coroner knelt and settled down to his work—briefly inspecting the corpse, cutting and staining an insertion to take the liver temperature—

Greeley turned away, unable to maintain his usual interest in the proceedings. Montoya was right: There was no investigation here, since, even before rigor mortis, the victim had already transmogrified into a statistic, an increment in the record of gang-related crimes in this area during this period of time—a part of an abstract phenomenon that was no longer personal and individual. Lucero's family, if he had one, would be weeping alone, while the rest of the community bewailed the rising murder rate or consoled themselves with the thought of one less gangbanger in the neighborhood.

"Well, he was shot," said Davidson. "No doubt about that."

Greeley scrutinized the remains and found them difficult to imagine as a threat to the city streets: skinny wrists, narrow shoulders, and a slender neck with an Adam's apple protruding like a chunk of debris in his throat. Who was this Rocio Lucero, a fifteen-year-old boy who had been shot for writing his name on the fence? Was he really a soldier, a fighter for his gang who might have driven around with a shotgun on his lap, cruising for Furies on their turf? Or was he mostly a writer, a kid with a can of paint who in another part of town would have been enrolled in arts-and-crafts classes after school?

He turned to Montoya. "Any rap sheet?"

"Never been to Juvy."

"He had a library card?"

The patrolman nodded, blinking in something like sympathy. "The bad ones I know," he said finally. "So he must'a been all right." Now a shrug—which meant something in particular, Homer understood, the big shoulders rising and falling as if to say, There's nothing we can do about it anyway, is there?

"Can you give me a hand here?" Davidson said, looking from the corpse to the Volvo as if the distance between them were more than any man could be expected to manage by himself.

"He doesn't look that heavy."

"Heavy enough."

"They're all heavy enough when they're dead," said Montoya, gripping the lifeless ankles.

Davidson had the left shoulder, but when he tried to lift the right as well, the head fell backward. "Take the other side here, will you?"

Greeley was not squeamish and couldn't understand his own reluctance to lend a hand. And yet, when he squatted beside the deputy coroner so they could lift together, the shoulder felt frail in his hands. "Not exactly buff, is he?"

Montoya grunted. "As buff as he's ever gonna be."

It was something Homer might have said himself to a partner whose curiosity about the victim seemed to exceed any possible utility it might entail, and it annoyed him to realize he was asking those questions himself. But now, as he helped the deputy coroner carry the limp head and shoulders into his station wagon, Greeley wondered whether anyone would be asking those questions if he didn't ask them. It seemed to him they needed to be asked. Homer cleared his mind and settled Lucero's shoulder against a blanket in the back when Montoya dumped the lower half of the body and bent the knees to squeeze in the legs.

"All right," said Davidson, shoving in a shoulder, "let's just get it closed now."

Some part of Lucero must have been leaning on the mechanism inside the car, because they met with resistance in closing the rear door. Homer put his weight against it, and it closed behind him with a *thump*. It was the sound of an ending, all questions answered. But Greeley's mind was just beginning to work.

A MINYAN FOR THE DEAD

"Need a lift?" asked Davidson.

Greeley had an unmarked Reliant; Montoya, a black-and-white. So they parted company, concluding the investigation, which only their report would continue. The case of Rocio Lucero was just about closed.

Homer tried to shake that thought as he turned the key in his ignition and gunned the engine, which was not his custom. A fifteen-year-old victim and no perp was not the way he liked to leave a case.

But he could not shut it out on the subway ride home, after he had driven the Reliant back to the precinct house, punched out, and caught his train at the el, from where it snaked through the burned-out tenements of the south Bronx, dipped under the Harlem River, and reemerged at 149th Street, continuing down the length of the island under Seventh Avenue. His subway car also carried a black mother with a five-year-old son who stared across the aisle at Greeley until they got off at 125th Street. What sort of life was waiting for him on the streets above the subway? Ten years from now would he be creeping along the tracks of a train yard at night with cans of spray paint in his belt? And if he's caught in the act by a rival gang . . . ?

The graffiti on the walls and the doors and the ads seemed to jiggle with laughter as the train pulled out, heading south. Greeley shut his eyes as if trying to sleep and concentrated on where he might eat his supper. Italian food sounded right to him—should it be Pontevecchio for a veal chop or Casa di Pre for cutlet parmigiana? But as he thought about packing away his summer suits and bringing out the winter ones, the image of Lucero kept returning. And, as he got off at Fourteenth Street, trod the stairs at Eleventh, and walked the block and a half to his apartment on Bank Street, the sentences he would need for the report in the morning began to collect in his head.

When, after a fitful night of sleep, he was entitled to climb back onto the same train for an interminable ride to the Bronx and access at last to his computer, the words clicked out onto the screen with a beautiful sense of relief.

Homer was not usually much of a writer. His personal style was terse, the facts set out plainly as he could manage. But there was just so much to say today. He was still working when his partner arrived just after eight with a coffee and a cheese danish in a stained paper bag. Homer did not look over to the facing desk as this breakfast was arranged neatly on a napkin, as the danish was cubed with a plastic knife, and each bite chewed, one by one. Only when he had finished, and the completed pages had been spit out by the network printer, did Greeley look at his partner, passing the report over their desks.

"Looks like I left too early," was the response, expressed through mouthfuls of danish.

"You didn't miss much," Greeley said. "A gang killing in an alley."

"Now that's the Homer I'm accustomed to," his partner said. "Your report had me worried for a minute there."

"What do you mean?"

"Kind of sentimental, isn't it?"

*Sentimental?* That was a word of condemnation in Greeley's private vocabulary, conveying as it did a sense of everything he considered unprofessional behavior. Sentiment was the doubt that led a good cop to contradict the instructions in the manual; it was the sand in the works of a well-oiled organization, police or civilian. It was the first signal that an officer was losing his commitment to the force. Homer took back the report and reread his first few lines with as much detachment as he could squeeze into the inner voice in his mind. "You really think so?"

8

## A MINYAN FOR THE DEAD

"Don't worry about it," Jill Morganthal assured him with a squeak of new vinyl as she squirmed into the springs of her desk chair. "It just reads like something Shelly Lowenkopf might've written when he used to work here—wondering about the perp and what made him such a jerk. But it's complete, and factual, even if it gets a little . . . wordy now and then. No one's gonna *say* anything to you about it."

Homer sat, stunned, over his neatly typed report.

*Like something Shelly might've written?*

What more could anybody say?

9

# 2

"One good thing about olefin," Shelly Lowenkopf said to the Young Couple who had spent the last twenty minutes trying to decide between the tuxedo sofa bed in the flame-stitch print and a rust-colored tufted velvet job on the other side of the display floor. "There's hardly anything you can do to it. It doesn't stain, and it doesn't shred. I mean, you can light it on fire if you want, but otherwise it's damned hard to get rid of."

And he smiled a practiced sly grin.

There was the instant of silence that always followed, and then—the result. It was a moment Shelly really enjoyed, the moment of truth, when his efforts were either rewarded by a laugh or a grin or a half-smile, auspicious omens of a deal closer; or by a silence that hung in the air between him and his customers, letting all of them know that the beautiful moment of sale wasn't about to happen between them. Shelly looked at the Young Man in jeans and a sweatshirt, at the Young Girl in a pleated dress, and felt he had put in a performance as a shopper's advisor that was reasonably convincing—if not to the customers themselves, at least to the other salespeople who sold furniture on the topmost floor of Macy's department store in Parkchester, the Bronx.

The Young Couple looked at him; they looked at each other; and back at Shelly. And the success of his sales pitch was perfectly clear.

A poor reaction: He almost snickered, but she didn't let a twinge of humor disturb the pout with which she looked over the sofa bed as if it were a poor orphaned thing she was being asked to take in as her own. Shelly had sprung his best line about the couch —if it got no more of a reception, he was probably wasting his time. He turned his head as if to cough, casually surveying the traffic on the floor, and felt his spirits sink as the elderly woman he had steered to a Colonial bedroom set called over Stu Begelman to write up her order. Ten percent of fifteen hundred dollars was more than these two were going to spend on a sofa bed, if they ever did make up their minds.

"Tell me about the velvet again," the Young Girl murmured, wagging her finger at the rust.

Shelly was about to explain once more the difference between tufted and woven velvets, and why the latter was worth the few hundred dollars more it cost than the former, when a tap on his shoulder from Jimmy, a stock man, saved him the trouble. There was a call for him. Shelly apologized to his customers with an expression of deep regret on his face. If they liked, Stuart Begelman over there could help them think it over. And, with the unhappy smile of a funeral director, Shelly stepped behind an eight-piece leather sectional to the hidden buying office beyond, where he picked up the phone with jaunty relief and balanced it on his shoulder.

"Hiya, boss. What's up?"

The voice on the other end softly but firmly said,

"Shelly? I asked you not to call me that. We are partners, you and I—it's a business arrangement. You've got to learn to respect what you've negotiated."

Shelly appreciated the sentiment and nearly explained the pleasure he took in using the word *boss,* which stood in his mind for his entire transition from the public to private sector. But he remembered how Max had to strain to hear over the telephone, since he refused to wear his aid, and said only, "Okay, partner. What's cooking?"

"You're cooking," said Max. "I've got a check here, made out to you, from our client."

"A check? Already? But they've already sent a retainer . . . and we haven't found out anything yet."

"Not a check for our services, Shelly. Your commissions! And, I have to say, if you ever get tired of the P.I. business, it seems to me you could make a good living selling furniture."

"I've had a good week, Max."

"It's talent, my boy—didn't I tell you? I can always spot it in someone. A *kep* for business."

Shelly did not need Maxim Pfeiffer starting all over again to sell him on the advantages of private enterprise—he had taken the plunge already, hadn't he? There was no reason to tell Max that his departure from the force had less to do with the lure of lucre than—

"Just tell me one thing, Shelly," Max said, with a sudden drop in register that signaled a serious message. "Just promise me that you're not concentrating on selling to the exclusion of our business there."

No, he could honestly say he wasn't—on his first undercover assignment as a private investigator, Shelly had been especially careful to deliver the services his client was paying for, and had kept a close eye on store security at every opportunity. It was a peculiar job, to say the least, watching the store cops, whose involvement management suspected in the biggest shoplifting operation they had ever encountered, discovered in the recent inventory. Thirteen samples had been removed from the furniture floor over the last seven weeks, but only three of those had actually been purchased. The inventory record was confusing, but it came down to this: three pieces sold out of thirteen removed, and that spelled grand larceny. Someone was stealing samples right off the showroom floor and it was unimaginable to the sales manager that anyone could accomplish this without the help of Security. So a private firm had been brought in to investigate, and the contract had been given to Maxim B. Pfeiffer and Sons—largely, Max told Shelly, on the strength of the new undercover operative they had acquired from the police force.

But it had been Max's own generosity that had prompted him to insist that Shelly receive all the commissions he earned undercover—a gift for his new partner.

That had been, what—two months before? It seemed like years to Lowenkopf—a lifetime, at least. And, in a way, it was a lifetime ago.

Shelly had spent two months on disability after his release from the hospital following an accident on Long Island that had resulted in a myocardial contusion, a bruise he had not allowed to heal. Afterwards, in the throes of a heart attack, Shelly had experienced *something*—his death or a dream about it—that had a strange effect on his recovery. The more his body healed, the less his mind anticipated returning to his old job. As if his life had actually ended and a new one begun, Shelly found himself looking around for an occupation that seemed better suited to the new point of view he had brought back with him from the Beyond. His Vision, as he called it, included an out-of-body experience, the usual Bright Light reported in these things, and a visit to a cosmic museum, where groups of spirits assembled around family portraits whose faces he recognized from his current incarnation. Thom was there, of course, and Isabelle, and his mother—but so was Homer, and Mordred too. The last was the most disturbing: Mordred, the matriarch of his soul's family, who in his day-to-day life climbed into his bed each night and—

"Shell?" Max said. "Are you still there?"

"Sorry, Max," said Shelly. "What were you saying?"

"It still bothers you, doesn't it?"

"It's nothing, Max. I'm all right. Really. What were you saying just now?"

"I was reminding you that it's Friday. You promised to come with me tonight."

"Where are we going?"

"To the shul, Shelly. You promised me."

The shul? Why on earth had he promised that? Shelly knew that his religion had made him attractive to Max as a partner, whose biological sons had shown no interest in learning the old man's trade, despite their presence in the name of his firm. The older one, Allen, was an attorney in Los Angeles; the younger, David, a professor of linguistics somewhere in the Midwest. Both had taken off after their mother's death and communicated with their father principally by check, mailed to him in folding cards on his birthday and Father's Day. So Max was looking to adopt, and, like many prospective fathers, was hoping for an heir of his own faith, who might follow in his footsteps when he'd gone.

But Shelly had made it clear to Max when the job offer came, over a game of three-handed pinochle in the park, that Jewishness described his birth and not much more. His parents had had him bar-mitzvahed at the synagogue of his grandfather, at which point his Jewish education had ended. Max had shaken his head and said, "Don't worry—I'm not trying to convert you. The shul I belong to is only of interest to people over sixty, it seems. But we're getting fewer lately, all the congregants moving to the Island. And we still need a minyan, like anybody else."

The Island was Max's way of referring to the cemetery, where more and more of his friends were relocating recently, so that, in order to assemble a minyan, the ten men necessary to hold a Jewish religious service, they had to recruit from outside. That was when Shelly had promised to attend.

"As a favor to me," Max had said, sensing Shelly's agreement. "I understand."

So—it was Friday already? Shelly was supposed to pick up Thom the following morning. But Max really needed this favor, and Shelly remembered the gratitude he had felt when the old man had played the ace of trump and said, "All right, so you'll try me out. We'll be partners. I'll be the senior partner and show you the business, and when the time comes, you can buy out my share. How does that sound to you? Better than going to work in an old suit, eh?"

And Max had done him one better—had actually taken him to a tailor on the Lower East Side who had measured Shelly from ankle to crotch and sewn his first suit to order. He was wearing it as they spoke on the phone, a gray pinstripe, 100 percent wool—although he had left the vest in his closet again. Max had told him to wear it, but there was only so much a person could change all at once in his life.

Shelly realized he had drifted off again only when the phone line went silent, Max on the other end waiting for him to speak.

"Hullo?"

"Shelly . . ."

"All right, Max," he said. "Tonight, then. I'll pick you up at the office."

"You said that already, Shelly," Max replied. "And I said I'll drive. There's no reason we have to pull up in front in that cramped clunker of yours."

"Okay. You drive, then." Max was usually most comfortable in his Lincoln.

"If I didn't know better, I'd be worried about you. But everybody needs a little time to make an adjustment. Go back and sell some more furniture. Just keep half an eye out for the crooks too, please. The service starts around four, so I'll pick you up at three and we'll eat first."

"It starts at four?"

"We don't have enough men for *mincha*—the afternoon service. And we don't have enough men for *ma'ariv*—the evening service—either. So we hold a *mincha-ma'ariv* service a little after four o'clock and combine the two. You can't say the afternoon prayers after dark, you know."

"I didn't, Max."

"Now you do. See you at three."

Shelly promised and returned to the selling floor in time to see that his Young Couple had made a deal with Begelman for the olefin flame stitch—the floor sample. Shelly's detecting antennae went up, and he hurried over to the sales office to check the receipt. It was true: The computer showed no more pieces in the warehouse stock, and the receipt showed the couple had charged the floor sample to their store account. Begelman watched Shelly look over the record of the sale with undisguised suspicion and claimed the computer screen on the flimsiest pretense.

"If you don't mind," he said, nudging Shelly aside. "I need to check a back order."

"What stock number?" asked Lowenkopf.

"Never you mind," said Begelman.

Shelly went back to the selling floor with the sense that he had overlooked something somewhere. He went into the stockroom behind Desks. Jimmy waited with a sofa bed, wrapped in plastic, while the freight elevator clanged in its shaft. Shelly checked and caught a glimpse of flame-stitch olefin through the multiple folds of thick plastic in which the sofa bed was wrapped. It sat upright on a handcart, which Jimmy tilted back toward himself, balancing the heavy piece of furniture on its narrow end. When he had first arrived on the floor, Shelly had tried to lift one of the sofa beds and discovered that the mechanism inside weighed too much for Schwarzenegger to take alone. The missing pieces had to have been taken by handcart or by two men together—which made the stock crew, of course, suspects as well as the security force. Jimmy didn't seem to mind Shelly's company, but they were joined a minute later by Enrique Rousseau, the security guard on duty, who wandered in, whistling casually, and watched them both closely as the elevator opened and Jimmy wheeled the sofa bed off the furniture floor.

"Shouldn't you be out on the selling floor?" Rousseau asked.

Shelly did not like to be questioned by private cops—real cops never do. For an instant, he felt the lack of a badge in his jacket pocket and his old Beretta at his hip. But he had traded those in on a P.I.'s license and replied, "That's just where I'm going, as a matter of fact."

The security guard gave him a steely gaze, which Shelly didn't bother returning. He strolled over to Mattresses, found no one there, and ambled toward the elevators, where customers were likely to alight. Begelman was there, of course, standing back just far enough to comply with the sales manager's orders. He was talking to Sally Pinter, the most senior pen on the

17

floor, whose career from the cosmetics counter on the ground floor of the department store to the heights of furniture commissions represented an unofficial history of the place. Aware of her status as a store icon, Sally spoke slowly, steadying her voice before she would respond to a question—what she wanted on her bagel, for example. Management often held her up as a model for the rest of the labor force, though her income, like theirs, reflected only her sales.

Shelly couldn't help liking her anyway, especially when, as now, she clung to Stu Begelman's sleeve, preventing him from zooming in on the gentleman with a moustache who stepped off the escalator looking both ways down the aisle. The gentleman was picked up by Frank Dupatechek, after Shelly the next most junior salesperson, having worked for the store only fourteen years. From the way Frank was leaning in toward the gentleman, Shelly thought he might be pointing out the path to the men's room, but Stu kept looking at them hard and glancing at Sally's hand on his arm, as if blaming her for lost revenue.

"It wasn't me, I said," Begelman was telling her. "They had already decided on that olefin. Of course, they hadn't really decided to *buy* anything yet," he corrected himself loudly when he saw Shelly approaching, "but they had already dismissed the rust. The velvet, you know, was tufted—"

It took Shelly a moment to realize they were talking about the Young Couple—Begelman anxious, no doubt, to defend his claim on the commission against a challenge he expected from Lowenkopf. Shelly was in no mood to quarrel over forty dollars—Max's news of his commission check, together with the money he would be making from his share of their partnership, was more than he had taken home in any month of his life. Still, he couldn't resist a chance to make Stu sweat for his 10 percent.

"I was the one who pointed that out to them," Shelly said thoughtfully. "The difference between a tufted and woven velvet. I suppose that means I deserve a share in the sale—wouldn't you say, Sally?"

Sally stared at him a moment, raising a finger that trembled in the air. She opened her mouth, but before she could reply, Begelman said, "So it was you! They were your customers, weren't they? Those two by the flame stitch?"

This wasn't what Shelly expected from Begelman. "I didn't mean to claim the whole sale, Stuart. You did the actual closing, and I'd never try to take—"

"You can have 'em," said Begelman, who reconsidered quickly and said, "I'll just take fifty, off the top. But the numbers, for the end of the month—they're all yours."

And he walked off as if afraid Lowenkopf might slip them back to him. Shelly turned to Sally for an explanation, who had already closed her mouth, and, as he waited for her to open it again, Frank Dupatechek joined them.

"Did I hear Stu say those two were yours, Shelly?"

"To what unexpected generosity I owe that, Frank, I couldn't begin to tell you—"

"Don't bother to try," said Frank. "They were looking at the tufted velvet before they went for the olefin."

"That's right—I showed it to them. They were worried about price, and those two are the cheapest items on the floor right now. I didn't let them *buy* it . . ."

Frank laughed. "Of course you didn't! They weren't really interested in buying it, were they?"

"They took the olefin, in the end."

"We'll see that back in the warehouse before the week is up. My guess is, the charge has probably been canceled on their account already."

19

"What do you mean?"

Frank took him around the shoulders and walked him across the floor, to the spot where he had shown the Young Couple a tufted velvet loveseat and sofa bed combination. An armchair sat beside an end table with a bronze lamp and a leather book, open to the middle. It looked as if someone had put down the book for a moment to fix themselves a nice pot of tea. Shelly was often tempted to sit down in that place, pick up the book, and read for a while himself. Or to stretch out full-length on the sofa bed, with his head on one armrest and his feet on the other.

Except the sofa bed and loveseat were gone.

# 3

Max was mercilessly forgiving—hardly concerned at all, in fact, with Shelly's report of the latest sample missing from the showroom floor. It made Shelly feel that Max didn't understand the situation fully. And of course he felt he had no alternative but to explain it to him again.

"All right," said Max when he had listened to Shelly's tale for the third time. "So another piece of furniture was stolen. While you were on the phone, talking to me. So I shouldn't have called you, that's all."

Shelly shook his head. "That's not the worst of it, Max. I had just shown that piece to some customers, minutes before."

"So we know it was there, on the showroom floor, just before it wasn't. And know when it must've been stolen. Good work."

"No, you don't understand," Shelly insisted. "The couple I showed it to—they could've been the ones who stole it."

21

"They could've been—true. But they also could've not been. We'll have to see. In the meantime, all we really know is that another piece of furniture was stolen."

"Isn't that what we were hired to prevent?"

"We're not security guards," Max said. "Sure, it would've been nice if we could've prevented any more floor samples from disappearing. But we weren't hired to watch them. We were hired to find out how they're disappearing."

"We don't know that either."

"All right, but we will. Won't we?"

"I hope so."

"Is that what you did on the police force? Hoped?"

Of course not, thought Shelly. He would start talking to suspects, while Homer scanned the grounds, turning up clues from cigarette butts and burnt matchsticks and smudges of mud on the carpet. His suspects would have to talk to him when he held up his badge—most of his job was figuring out which ones were lying, and why. Now no one had to talk to him, and there was no Homer crawling around. He said, "On the force, you work on a case until you solve it, or until the captain decides you can't, and another one comes along. But these people are paying good money, Max, for our time and a result. We've got to deliver more than that."

"We'll deliver," said Max, taking him around the shoulders. "It's true, we're getting paid by the hour. But the hours don't pass any faster. Keep your eyes open and we'll figure it out. Tell me, how many man-hours would your captain commit to breaking this kind of thing—a shoplifting ring on the furniture floor of a department store?"

"Undercover detective hours? None."

"So—we're the only game in town. Us, or another agency, who'll charge just as much. So take your time,

Shelly—take it, but don't waste it. If we solve the case, no one will care how many hours we worked—they'll just thank us. And if we don't, they won't care either—they'll just fire us, and when the time comes to explain their P and L to their board of directors, they'll have someone else to blame for their inventory shortfall. Come on, no more business tonight! We have just enough time to stop at Nate's for some pastrami and chopped liver before heading down to services."

After so much understanding and forgiveness, how could Shelly refuse? Besides, he had not been to Nate's for a very long time—since his father's death, in fact. It had not been a deliberate decision to stay away, or even a conscious one, but the memory of square potato knishes, horizontally halved so that the middle could be filled with mustard and sauerkraut, still evoked a memory of childhood that stuck in Shelly's throat. His father would stop for those, handing the boy the hot delicacy on a sheet of wax paper, with a napkin stuffed in his shirt pocket. Shelly had shied away from that smell—of potato steam and pickle sauce and the thick salamis from the freezer case lying by the slicer—while a waitress in corrective shoes passed in and out among customers at the counter, carrying mushroom barley soup to a diner at one of the eight small tables crammed together on the floor. Now, with Max, he could become one of those diners, watching the customers at the take-out counter and munching a pastrami sandwich on seeded rye.

"They still make corned beef and cole slaw with Russian dressing?"

"What else?" said Max. "You'll see."

The dominant impression Shelly took away from their dinner at Nate's was one of size—how much smaller and narrower the delicatessen was than he remembered it with his father. The same frenzied pace of orders being taken, with the fat rolls of bologna and cooked breasts of turkey sliced and wrapped in white paper; half of a cow's tongue waiting to be sliced and weighed by the pound; and the orange-brown rings of kishke, stuffed derma, sitting on the counter, under which baked apples and strudel and cherry cheese danish gleamed, moist and fresh. But the scale of everything—the height of the counter and the tables and the waitresses—was all down below his shoulders. Shelly felt like a grown-up who had inadvertently stepped into a child's world, which proved itself too small for him, even if it was the world of his own childhood.

Max, on the other hand, was having a wonderful time. Like Virgil in the Inferno, he felt an obligation to point out to Shelly all of the elements of the cultural heritage Max felt his new partner had forsworn. Shelly did not feel he had abandoned, for example, any inclination toward cold borscht with sour cream—he had never liked beets to begin with, and didn't feel that any improvement had been made by converting them to purple soup. If Max thought ordering the stuff and smacking his lips as he ate it would tempt Shelly to a reevaluation of his cultural heritage, he was free to do so; Shelly, for his part, concentrated on his corned beef and tried to dodge the memories that clung to his fork with each mouthful of *kasha varnishkas.*

"CEL-RAY or DR.BROWN'S?" asked Max, while the waitress stood over them, pencil in hand, condescending to take their order. These were two kinds of drinks—celery and cream soda. Shelly chose the latter, and Max nodded. "Make it two," he said significantly. There were two kinds of people in this world—those who went for celery and those who went for the cream; he was evidently one of the latter, and was pleased to have Shelly confirm for him his guess about his new partner.

"The right choice, eh?"

The waitress, with forty years of experience in the business evident in the striation of her lips, had known them all—the seltzers, with a lemon or a lime; the glasses of tea with a spoon and a cube of sugar, held in the mouth; the egg creams, without egg and without cream; and the endless requests for glasses of water with and without ice, or with less ice, or with more. And she knew better than to side with any of them, or against any, either. CEL-RAY or DR.-BROWN'S—that was a contest in which she had long ago opted for neutrality, and no amount of charm or hinted tip would shake her from her philosophical ground.

"CEL-RAY, you said?"

"DR.BROWN'S."

Max was, by his own estimate at least, still a handsome man: at seventy-two he was still trim, white haired, with an angular face softened by moist brown eyes and a lower lip that he would purse like a rabbi in front of attractive women within two or three decades of his own age. The waitress gave him a look that said she noticed him, but for all his charm she wasn't buying anyway. Max made a face, but when she left, he turned a rueful grin on Shelly.

"Don't worry. She won't resist me for long."

Shelly never doubted it.

Max was, after all, a pleasure to watch in the deli. He knew, or at least tipped his hat to, more than half the customers who came through the door, and 80 percent of the ladies. He ate voluminously, following his borscht with a spring salad—that is, greens topped with sour cream; and he completed his meal with potato *pirogen*—boiled dumplings of mashed potato pinched into half-moons of dough, again topped with sour cream. By the end of their dinner, Max wore a trace of cream along the lower edge of his neat moustache, as if caught in the cat's whiskers. And with each wink at another lady, and each sip of his cream soda, he relished the response, the smile of a wrinkled, lipsticked mouth, and the sweet, sticky, carbonated flavor.

It was the same story at the synagogue. When they pulled up in Max's Lincoln, the faces of two elderly men standing on the sidewalk in front lit up to see them arrive. One of them had a pedestrian by the crook of the elbow and lost his grip on the young passer-by when he looked up to beam at Max. Inside, it was clear that they were counting every head; but it was more than a quorum they shared with Max. He was one of them, a member of their community, although Shelly knew Max now lived in Flushing, in a house with three empty bedrooms and a half-empty bed.

"So what do we have here?" said Sol Schneider, as Max showed Shelly the prayer books and gave him a yarmulke from the basket in the anteroom to the sanctuary. "A new recruit? Or just a one-night stand-in?"

Max gave Sol an ill-concealed frown.

"Just a stand-in, I'm afraid," said Shelly quickly, before Max could answer differently for him. "Max wanted me to see your beautiful synagogue. And I can see why he did."

"Beautiful?" said Schneider. "You call this beautiful? You should see the plans for the new wing."

"He's not making any donations to the building fund," Max said, "so forget it, Solly. This is my new junior partner, Shelly Lowenkopf. Recently recruited from the police department. The homicide squad."

Solly's brow wrinkled. "Homicide?"

Shelly had never actually served on the homicide squad, which was an interdivisional assignment out of headquarters; he had covered homicides for his precinct, however, and, to support Max's claim rather than undermine it on a technicality, nodded once, with humility.

Schneider squinted, eyeing him closely. "And Jewish?"

Max frowned. "You want he should drop his pants?"

Sol Schneider was a man in his late sixties who had come to America with his family when he was eight. His father had been a tailor in the town of Bratislava, in what is now Czechoslovakia; when the immigration officer at Ellis Island had asked his name, he had thought he was being asked his occupation and answered the question *schneider*—which was to say *tailor*. The official wrote "Schneider" on the first line, and their family name of Gronski was thereafter lost to history. Sol Schneider né Gronski now squinted at Shelly, smoothed the fringe of gray hair surrounding his bald dome, but said nothing further about his descent—which was a private matter among himself, his ancestors, and the civil servants who admitted them to the country.

Shelly felt the same scrutiny from the other six men who had assembled, waiting for the rabbi to join them. Schneider was the only one who actually asked, but each of them seemed to have the same question in mind: Just how Jewish was this homicide cop? It was a question for which Shelly had no good answer—and each of them in turn tried to read in his eyes just what he had to say about it. After Schneider, the next to venture near him was Dave Horowitz, who had been trained as a furrier by his uncle on the Concourse, but gave up the business in sixty-eight to open a head shop on Lydig Avenue, where he sold psychedelic posters

27

## Richard Fliegel

and incense burners and water pipes. Paraphernalia, the place was called, and it did so well he opened two more the following year, on Jerome Avenue and Fordham Road. Then came Altamont, and the deaths of Jimi, Janis, and Jim; the demand for black lights and lava lamps fell precipitously. His businesses nearly failed, meeting their rents only on the strength of poster sales, primarily of rock stars. As poster after poster of Morrison, Jagger, McCartney, and Garcia was rolled, rubber-banded, and registered, Horowitz began to experiment: he switched his stock to records, then to tapes, then to CDs. He tried his luck with a video club early in the game, and his three former head shops once again became gold mines. Paraphernalia I, II, and III became Diskus I, II, and III, and Horowitz became an enviably rich man. But he wore his affluence well, showing off in the nicest possible way—giving scholarships to underprivileged kids in the local high school, sponsoring a Little League team, underwriting fireworks on the Fourth of July. His donations to the synagogue kept the doors open, which all the other members knew, of course, though he refused any plaques on the doors or the backs of the seats. Still, his financial clout gave him a certain psychological edge over his fellows in the synagogue, and when he approached Shelly it was with a natural graciousness, as if he felt he could offer a personal welcome to the place.

"So you're Max's new partner," he said, as if he had already discussed the new arrangement with Pfeiffer, which he had not. "I'm Horowitz—perhaps you've heard of me? No? All right, well, Max can't talk about everybody at once. I'm president of this congregation. Have you met the others yet? The hazzan?"

Horowitz waved toward an incredibly old, incredibly spindly man at the front of the room who was busy getting things ready for the rabbi's arrival. He wore

28

the most voluminous prayer shawl Shelly had ever seen: Not only did it cover all of his back and shoulders, which weren't that broad, after all, but it also covered the back of his pants to the middle of his thighs, where the thick black fabric stood stiffly, starched away from whatever bones still animated his limbs. He turned his head as he heard Horowitz pronounce his title, his lower lip trembling at the shock; and as the deep brown pools of his eyes met Shelly's, some tremor of anxiety passed through them. Shelly approached cautiously and offered his hand, which was touched ever so gently by the tips of the hazzan's fingers.

"Tsinger," he said, barely audibly.

"You're a singer—I know," said Shelly.

The hazzan scowled and turned his back, resettling a dog-eared prayer book in the center of the lectern.

"That's his name," said Horowitz, smiling. "Itzak Tsinger. I don't know if that's why they hired him in the first place, but it's the reason he keeps his job."

The hazzan gave Horowitz exactly the same scowl he had just bestowed on Shelly.

Shelly concentrated on names as Horowitz filled him in on the other congregants. Max had told him stories about some of them, and Shelly had the distinct pleasure now of linking names of characters in Max's stories with actual human beings. Tsinger was easy, of course, and there was Schneider, no longer a tailor, and President Horowitz himself, long since no furrier. The two men who had been standing outside when he and Max pulled up, and who had followed them into the synagogue, were the Minsky brothers, who had given up the family Wiener wurst business in SoHo, Manhattan, when Joel had pointed out to Jonathan that the building in which they labored over hot ovens was worth more as a rental property than they had ever earned making veal sausages. They had argued about it for a while and placed a call to a real estate agent, wondering, just in case.

And that had been that—after thirty-two years of working side by side, they had put down their utensils, washed their hands, and closed their doors for the first time at two forty-seven on a Wednesday afternoon. They never opened again as a food business, but became the New Fontainebleau, a complex of lofts and unstructured apartments with an art gallery on the ground floor and a penthouse on the roof. The income that resulted for each of them was more than either brother had ever earned in his life—not a great deal more than their best year, but substantial enough, and for doing nothing at all.

And yet, after the first few months of financial freedom, there grew in each of their faces a certain lost look, especially when one of them still glanced over his shoulder for the other. It was a habit they had developed working together all those years, which did not disappear with the job to be done. Without the job, however, they never knew quite what to do with each other, so Joel began to gravitate toward his daughter's house in Yonkers, and Jonathan to wander through the park. He knew about birds, which their father used to watch, and spent hours in the library of the Bronx Botanical Gardens.

The two brothers saw each other less and less—a dinner here, a movie there—until the only time they could consistently expect to see one another was in front of the synagogue. Somehow, by mutual agreement, they had taken on responsibility for standing on the sidewalk outside, cornering Jewish passers-by to collect the ten-man minyan necessary for a service. It gave them a job to share, a joint obligation. And, on a cold night, when they would watch for nearly an hour on the darkening street, you could hear their old bantering resume, as one of them despaired of their night's success and the other enlivened the hopes of his brother in their enterprise.

There were two other men, already in the seats arranged in four rows of six, with an aisle between the three on the left and the three on the right. There was plenty of room for more rows in the back, and stacks of folding chairs in the rear corner, but a greater number of chairs would only have made the congregated assembly seem smaller. One man sat in the first row, on the last seat to the right, facing the altar, as if all five seats to his left had been claimed—but Shelly saw nothing on them. The other man sat in the third row—the third!—two seats in from the aisle whether you counted from the center or the edge. Both men seemed at first to be sleeping, until Shelly realized the man in front was in fact reading something in his lap. His name, Max murmured to Shelly, was Jacob Zweizig; Jake did not seem to be enjoying his reading. That was only to be expected, Max said: Jake was their Ritual Committee chairman, and after all the years of worship in this shul, not to mention the four thousand preceding, there was hardly a synagogue anywhere who could agree on how to celebrate the high holy days. Rosh Hashanah had just passed, and Yom Kippur, and Jake was undoubtedly reading the suggestions of congregants who had participated.

The dozing man in the third row was Stanley Blumberg, who was snoring softly now, about whom Max had nothing more to say. It might have been simply a lack of time, since the other men were now filing down the center aisle, moving to seats on both sides that seemed to be chosen for them.

Shelly could not understand the pattern: Schneider took a seat in the first row, on the opposite side from

Zweizig, while no one filled in the seats between them. The second row seemed popular—Horowitz sat on the aisle on the left side facing front, while Max led Shelly to a couple of seats in that same row, flush right. The Minsky brothers sat in the third row on the aisle behind Horowitz, mumbling to each other as they made sour faces at Blumberg. Hazzan Tsinger, in front, made nine, and it took Shelly a moment to realize that the rabbi made ten. Of course, you couldn't forget the rabbi. Max had said he was a tall man with a proud bearing whose shoulders had been slowly pulled toward the earth as an object lesson in humility, or gravity. His voice, Max had said, was his best quality, with a trick in it that made you think he was questioning you, or pointing out some underlying inconsistency in your personal opinion, even when he asked the day of the week. Shelly usually felt uncomfortable around rabbis, whose faith he could not share, but whose commitment to it awed him. But Max just shook his head as if to say, *Just wait till you see him. Just wait.*

So where was he?

Shelly felt an uneasy stirring in the room, a restlessness that seemed to imply: *All right already, let's get on with it!* The rabbi was entitled to make an entrance, but enough was enough, wasn't it? When was he planning to come down the stairs at the front of the sanctuary and join them? Shelly checked his watch: It was past four thirty, edging toward five. Max had told him they couldn't do the *mincha-ma'ariv* service after nightfall, and the day was plummeting rapidly.

The hazzan moved around the altar in front as if there was nothing at all to concern him—rearranging the items on the rostrum, resettling the tallith on his shoulders. But it seemed to Shelly his eyes never wandered out to the congregation, and when, for an instant, Tsinger's gaze flickered to the stairs that led to the rabbi's study above, Shelly saw in their rich brown indifference a break of continuity. A waver.

Something was wrong.

The assemblage sat assembled for five minutes more. Then there was a noise of prayer books closing, and without anyone actually breathing a word of complaint, Horowitz stood up, waving his hand at the others, and said, "All right! I'll go, I'll go. I'll go see what the matter is. Some people just can't wait in a chair."

They heard his thumps on the carpeted stairs, and then he was gone. For a minute . . . two . . . five. Six. The hazzan was looking up anxiously now at the staircase, as were the Minskys, and even Zweizig moved a seat closer to the center, when Horowitz's shoes appeared again coming down the purple stairs.

Alone.

"Alone?" asked Schneider. But when he saw the change in Horowitz's previously robust cheeks, which were now paler than his tallith, he said nothing more until their emissary to the study came all the way down the stairs and stood at the front of the sanctuary.

"The rabbi will not be coming tonight," was all he managed to articulate. His throat sounded as if a fish bone were caught in his Adam's apple.

"Is he ill?" asked Max, starting to rise.

Horowitz held out a hand, to reassure and reseat him. "No, not ill, thank God."

The others agreed with their nods that God was indeed to be thanked for the rabbi's health. They waited, but Horowitz couldn't quite say what had happened instead.

Zweizig looked from face to face in the rows behind his and threw a substantial arm around the back of the next chair. "He doesn't feel like it tonight?"

Horowitz looked down at the man in front of him,

who didn't seem to be joking. Zweizig blinked, a twitch of such innocence Horowitz could only shrug in reply. "I don't know what he feels like, Jacob. But he can't lead the service tonight. He's not sick, or—God forbid—anything worse. He's been arrested, that's all."

## 4

Rabbi Sholem Pirski had not, in fact, been arrested. He was in the process of being arrested, and a difficult process it was turning out to be, as Shelly at once surmised when he and his new senior partner arrived on the scene before the rabbi's cuffing. Max had dragged him by the sleeve of his pin-striped suit jacket up the single flight of wine-red stairs to the rabbi's hole of an office, where a uniformed officer was reading Miranda one word at a time from a crisp white card.

"One. You have the right to remain silent. Two. Anything you say can and will be used against you . . ."

A plainclothes cop with a gray felt hat and matching stubble listened closely, scowling, making sure his junior associate got the emphases right. The patrolman was a big kid with a thick neck, but his cheeks were smoother than it would ever be possible to shave them again, and when he blinked his eyes were positively dewy. Shelly recognized the detective: Eddie Riordan, a veteran of fifteen years, cursed by the captain's opinion of him as a good teacher of rookies. As a result, the greenest were often assigned to him for a stint of common sense before they drew a regular partner. He didn't like rookies particularly and made no secret about it, so they usually managed to learn what was necessary to prevent hearing why.

". . . in a court of law. Three. You have a right—"

"*The* right, Michaelson, damn you!"

"—the right to talk to a lawyer, and to have him or her present with you while you are being questioned. . . ."

By his response to Ed's constructive criticism, this rookie looked to be in his second week of tutelage; he had size going for him, since he was nearly as big as Ed himself, who was about six-four, two-twenty, without the hat. That would win him points with Ed, who liked a student who could take a punch. The two policemen loomed over the rabbi, who sat surprisingly composed, elbows on his desk with the tips of his fingers pressed together. He was not old by anybody's count—in the earlier half of his sixties—but the eyes beneath his wiry brows were clear if watery gray, and he held his lips pursed in an attitude of amusement—whether at the cops or at the universe he kept to himself. The police, however, were not amused by the uncertainty and seemed to expand in resentment, filling all the available space in the room with their presence.

"Four. If you cannot afford to hire a lawyer . . ."

Knowing Max, Shelly was only a little surprised to find himself squeezed between Ed and the patrol officer, while Max took up a position on the other side of the kid, so that the four men stood shoulder to shoulder, ringing the rabbi in a dim cave of books and scrolls its inhabitant called his study.

". . . one will be appointed to represent you before questioning, if you wish. . . ."

"Max," Pirski said, interrupting the recitation with a gentle hand on the patrolman's forearm. "Come in, my friend! You'll have to excuse the confusion of my study at the moment."

"Rabbi—are you all right?"

The rabbi shrugged. "We'll see."

"If there's anything we can do—me or my partner—"

The rabbi fixed Shelly with a piercing stare. "Your partner?"

"From Homicide."

"Homicide?"

Max nodded. The rabbi pursed his lips, impressed. "So, we'll see. . . ."

Michaelson had stopped at the rabbi's touch and was having some trouble starting again. He glanced shyly at Riordan, who glowered at him, and then turned to the rabbi, and cleared his throat.

Pirski nodded. "Please, go on."

Shelly was tempted to prompt the kid himself, before Riordan weighed in with an expletive. But the rookie found his place on the small white card and resumed. "Do you understand each of these rights I have explained to you?"

The rabbi considered a moment. "To tell you the truth," he said at last, "I'm afraid I allowed my concentration to wander. Would you mind repeating it?"

"What?"

"The four rights."

"All four?"

"If you don't mind."

Michaelson looked at Riordan, who evidently didn't care for the request, but wasn't sure of the legal consequences of refusing it, either. Shelly wasn't sure himself what a defense attorney could do with it. Riordan frowned, which the rookie interpreted as a sign of assent, and began reciting Miranda again from the top, more slowly.

"One. You have the right to remain silent. . . ."

Riordan rolled his eyes around the cramped office. Shelly would have called it a sanctum himself—a retreat—like the narrow holes gophers run into so that larger animals can't follow. It could not have been more than forty square feet between walls, six feet by six and a half, and the space was further diminished by uneven shelves overwhelmed with books in Hebrew and Yiddish—even a few in English, whose titles were unreadable under a thick layer of dust. The room was thick with cigarette smoke—there was an ashtray, overstuffed with unfiltered butts, in one corner of the desk. Three of the walls were stacked with shelves within inches of the ceiling, and the dust from their contents as well as the smoke had so obscured the panes of a window on the fourth that Shelly found no reflection of himself in the glass, only a gray glint of the sky. The light of one lamp on the desktop and a stained glass fixture overhead did not produce enough wattage for him to make out the title of the top sheet of a manuscript on the desk directly in front of him. Its pages had been wrapped in a rubber band that had snapped but lay open on top of it, dangling down one side, while the cover page beneath it curled and yellowed, waiting. It looked as if everything in the entire room had been waiting centuries for the rabbi's attention, while he had put them off again and again to turn his mind to the Infinite.

Except he did not seem to be contemplating the Eternal at the moment. The rabbi was listening very carefully, stroking his chin, which was bearded thinly above the jaw and more densely below it. Black and gray hairs uncurled under his fingers and curled again as he listened to each word, as Ed Riordan did, but with a different purpose: He seemed to consider the underlying meaning of each utterance, waiting for a slip of the tongue that might be used to exonerate him on a technicality in court. Or was that his purpose, really? Shelly caught himself in his old habit of suspicion, a cop's turn of mind. What made him think the rabbi was listening for a loophole? It might have been habitual, the instinctive reaction of a textual scholar to a text he had never before encountered. Yet the rabbi's concentration, and the suspicion it provoked on the part of the plainclothes detective, induced a silence no one was willing to break, lending a new significance to the words repetition had made meaningless for Shelly.

". . . before questioning, if you wish. Now—do you understand each of these rights as I have explained them to you?"

The rabbi tapped his lips.

"Do I understand them? Does anybody really understand them? My understanding is, the United States Supreme Court has been discussing the meaning of these rights for the last two hundred years, and the Justices still do not see eye to eye. Would it not be presumptuous of me to say I understood them, when such distinguished jurists have failed?"

Michaelson understood that a question was being directed at him, but he wasn't sure if he was supposed to answer it. Riordan made a sour face.

"Just the words, Reverend. He means, do you understand the words?"

"Just the words?" the rabbi replied with a sad shake of his head. "What could be more difficult? I have spent my life trying to understand the words in here"—and he tapped a scroll on a bookshelf overhead—"and could spend another just as easily! Do you imagine I can understand the meaning of the words on that card, hearing them just once?"

"Most of our prisoners manage to," said Riordan.

"Then your prison must be filled with wise men," the rabbi speculated. "Perhaps I will not mind it so much."

"I'm sure you'll have a grand old time," mumbled Riordan. He glared at Michaelson again and said, "Finish up, already, will you?"

Michaelson blinked at his card. "Having these rights in mind, do you wish to talk to us now?"

"Not for a minute," said the rabbi.

From the lines on Max's face, Shelly could see how painful his benefactor found this sight so common-place to him, and it reminded Shelly how his years on the force had inured him to the shock an arrest represented in the life of an ordinary citizen. That was himself, now—an ordinary citizen. Shelly waited for Michaelson to produce handcuffs; when he held them uncertainly in the general direction of the rabbi's pale hands, Shelly turned to the detective.

"Are those really necessary, Ed? I don't think he's gonna bolt on you or anything."

The rabbi, right on cue, shrunk into the folds of his black robe so that he appeared frail as a bird trapped in a tent whose flap has closed behind it.

Ed was a good man; he had gulped a Styrofoam cup of Scotch when Shelly had cleaned out his desk at the station house, and he took in the situation quickly. He looked at Shelly's new suit, at Max in the nearly matching one, at the hopeful expression on the faces of the two older men as they watched Shelly talk to the detective. He was conscious of the gaze of the rookie uniform, too, but that didn't seem to bother him. He may have thought of his own retirement someday or just the latitude allowed him by their captain, but he said, "Let's not bother with the bracelets, Michaelson. Just hold on to him till you get him into the car." The rookie looked at the four older men and then he did

40

what he was told, returning the handcuffs to a hook on his belt and taking the rabbi's arm.

"I won't need the cuffs?" asked the rabbi.

"No," said Michaelson.

"Thank you," the rabbi said to him. He nodded to Eddie and said, "Thank you as well," turned to Shelly, and then Max. An expression of such warmth and gratitude passed between the two of them, Shelly could not help feeling a certain degree of pride, having contributed to the gift.

"Rabbi!" said Max softly. "There's no need to—"

"Let me say it!"

"Of course."

"Thank you, Max. My good friend."

And so Max received the first dividend from his investment in Shelly, and he beamed at his junior partner so brightly it made Lowenkopf uncomfortable. The rabbi patted Max on the back, and then, with a deep breath, headed for the door of his study so abruptly Michaelson had to jump to stay with him. Max followed Michaelson, leaving Shelly alone with Ed, his former departmental colleague. Lowenkopf wouldn't have pushed it ordinarily, but the handcuff gesture had meant so much, he couldn't help asking, "What's the situation, here, Ed?"

Ed's lower lip curled over his upper, settling into his teeth, where it twitched a moment before he said, "It's a bad one, here, Shelly. I don't wanna speak outta court or anything. But we got him cold."

"The rabbi? On what? Tax evasion? Skimming the poor box?"

Riordan shook his head.

"Not drunk and disorderly?"

"Murder, Shell. Homicide. Believe it."

"The Reb?"

"You never can tell who's gonna pull the trigger, can

you? I don't hafta tell *you* that. But even so—after all I seen—you'd say the same thing here."

Shelly nodded, and meant it. If Riordan was convinced by the evidence he'd seen, it would probably have convinced Shelly, too. If he'd still been on the force. But there was no point in bringing up to Riordan now the change in Shelly's perspective. "Who'd he kill?"

"An old lady. Lillian Levinski. One o' the parishioners here—or, at least, one of their crowd."

Riordan tipped his head toward the staircase leading to the synagogue below, from which a murmur was now rising. Somebody was going to have to tell those men their rabbi was on his way to the precinct house jail. No service tonight. Shelly felt a jab of dread before he realized that job wouldn't necessarily fall to him, since Max would accept responsibility for it. His part of their partnership was here, with Eddie. Finding out what only he could. He knew that was what Max wanted more than anything else from him now: to protect the rabbi, as a client. It was the reason he had hired Shelly, the reason he had taken him in as a partner. Shelly felt a great debt to Max and realized he could repay all his kindness if he could just find a hole in the case against the rabbi, so that he wouldn't have to spend a night in jail. This was what he had trained for during all his years on the force. He just had to find a way to set the old man free. He leaned back and wondered aloud with professional indifference, "Strangulation?"

Riordan tapped his breast pocket. "Shot her—*kabloom*—right through the back. The left upper torso."

"With a revolver?"

"An automatic, nine millimeter. Business machine."

Shelly nodded. Nobody fired one of those as a

warning shot. If you aim and shoot, you mean to kill somebody. Premeditated. Only the simplicity of the case was less appealing to Shelly now than it ever had been to him in the past.

"When did it happen?"

"The shoot? Tonight. Just a coupla hours ago. Heard by a neighbor, who didn't get an answer when she knocked on the door and called the janitor."

"Stiff?"

"The deputy coroner estimates time of death around three. Any idea what the rabbi was doing then?"

Shelly shook his head.

"Reading, he says," went on Riordan. "Reading! By himself, in this room, alone. Nobody came in, or knocked, or anything. Some alibi, eh?"

Shelly tried to read the clock on the desk, but the dust on its face made that difficult from his angle. Riordan noticed his glance and raised his sleeve so Shelly could read his wristwatch. "It's five thirty now."

"And you've broken the case already?"

"Pretty good, huh?" Riordan grinned. "Even Homer Greeley don't work that fast—I mean, even you and him didn't, when you were a team."

That tripped a warning light for Shelly: Eddie might think he was jealous, of the case or its closing, if he allowed too much doubt in his voice. But Riordan sounded pretty confident in his conclusion. Which worried Shelly more. The only way to get him to talk was to provoke him, to get him to brag.

"It'll still take some time to gather evidence."

"We got it!" said Eddie. "In the bags."

"Recover the weapon?"

"It was sitting in the top drawer of the desk over there. We opened it up and *bingo!*"

"Just lying there?"

"Uh-huh."

Shelly leaned over the desk to the top drawer, but refrained from touching it. There was a lock in the middle of the drawer, which showed no signs of being forced. "The Crime Scene Unit had their shot at this place yet?"

"On their way."

Shelly nodded. "You just opened up this drawer here and found it sitting inside?"

Riordan shook his head, spotting the trap.

"We didn't open it. We couldn't've. It was locked. We asked the rabbi if there were any firearms around here. He said, 'Only my gun,' and took a little key from a ring in his pocket and fitted it into the lock. We've got the key now in an evidence bag. He slid it out, the drawer. And there was the piece, still warm, with powder on the barrel. Michaelson's got it in plastic too. You know what I think we're gonna find? I think that gun's gonna match our ballistics beautifully. I can hardly wait for the report. You see anything by the lock there our guys should be sure to check out?"

Shelly sat up, to reassure Eddie he wasn't planning to make trouble for the lab team that would go over the desk for prints and fibers and anything else they could find. He was sure they'd discover whatever was there—to condemn or exonerate the rabbi. But, while they were on the subject, he thought he'd try planting a seed of doubt in the detective's inquiring mind.

"Don't you think the rabbi would've moved it someplace if he had just used it on a congregant?"

"It's hard to guess what people'll do. Didn't you always find that true? When you kill somebody, it throws off your clear thinking. Maybe he didn't think we'd come looking for it here. In a—y'know—Jewish church."

"A synagogue."

"Right."

"So you've got—what? Means . . . you've got a weapon. And you've got opportunity . . . if nobody really saw the rabbi in here, reading his books and whatnot."

"He says no one did."

"Well, I'll take his word on that. He's a rabbi, after all. But you still need a motive, Ed. Why would a rabbi kill an old lady? One of his congregants, yet. From what I've seen already, they need all the people they can get around here."

That should have given Riordan pause. The plain-clothes cop stroked his grizzled chin, as if he were thinking it over. But his eyes were dancing.

"Maybe they don't need congregants as bad as you think."

"That's why I'm here, Eddie. To add one more to the number. Ask any of them downstairs."

"We don't hafta ask anybody."

"You've got a motive?"

"That's right."

"Already? Two hours after the murder? You've got a weapon, and a suspect in custody, and a motive established too?"

"What can I tell you?" Grinning broadly. "We're that good. Yeah . . . we got a motive."

Shelly couldn't believe it. He and Homer had been a hell of a team, but they'd never produced that fast.

"Let's hear it."

"Money," said Riordan. "The oldest one in the book."

The oldest one in the book, thought Shelly, was jealousy. Wasn't that why Cain slew Abel? But all he said was, "You think this pious rabbi, who's devoted his entire life to learning and prayer, killed an old lady for her money?"

"Disgusting, isn't it?"

"You'll never prove that."

"Piece a cake," said Riordan with a shrug. "I'm ashamed to tell you how easy that's gonna be."

"How easy?"

"In writing."

"She wrote you a note? 'He's stealing my purse'?"

"As a matter of fact, we did find a note, crumpled, in her trash. It just said, 'Dear Sholem' at the top under a date—yesterday's. But the other is better."

*"Better?"*

"Better," said Riordan. "After all, a note can be forged by the killer."

"So what've you got? Affidavits? Signed by witnesses?"

"You guessed it."

"I have? Tell me already," said Shelly.

Riordan took pity on him. "I told you—we've got him. His gun was still warm, I said. There's a neighbor who heard some people arguing in Jewish and peeked out through her peephole. And yeah, there's a motive in writing. Her death was worth big bucks to him. Big bucks."

"He's not a contract killer?"

"She left all her insurance to this place."

"The synagogue?"

"That's right. More than two hundred thousand dollars. Now you don't get a cleaner motive than that."

# 5

Because it was Friday, and he could not see Thom, Shelly thought he might as well give Max his money's worth and stop by the scene of the crime on his way home. Mordred would not be coming over tonight, allowing him some time alone with his son; but Ruth had phoned earlier in the day to say that Thom would be away for the weekend on a birthday sleep-over. Thom was eleven—you had to expect these things now. They had made plans for him to see his son during the week instead, an unusual pleasure he cherished anticipating. If the thought crossed his mind that he might have called Mordred, telling her about the change in plans, it did not stamp its feet loudly enough to make him wonder why he did no such thing. When Max had asked him to fill out the minyan, that settled the practical question. His reluctance to call Mordred when the opportunity presented itself he did not question aloud.

Whatever banged around the back quarters of his brain while Max drove him to the apartment of the murdered woman disappeared once he stepped out of the Lincoln into the cool of the evening. He couldn't help feeling it was good to be back at the scene of a crime as he slipped under the yellow tape ruling off the area to any but authorized police department personnel. He had ducked under the strip without thinking, as a function of habit, and realized only when McCormick gave him a peculiar look that there might be some question about his access. Patrolman McCormick, however, decided the matter privately by turning his back to chase away a kid who kept sticking his head through the doorframe; and in that moment, Shelly moved into the Levinski apartment, sparing the leathery old beat cop any further ethical debate. Inside the yellow tape, access was no longer the assigned responsibility of any single individual, so no one paid him any attention. Shelly could poke around as he liked, so long as he kept his flat feet out of the way of the Crime Scene Unit gathering evidence.

In addition to McCormick, whose job was basically shooing away the curious, three other law enforcement personnel were still present in the apartment. The photographer had finished most of her work, covering the general scene and then snapping three angles of any significant element therein; she sat on a brocaded easy chair, red spiked heels up on the ottoman, smoking a cigarette, the ashes of which she tapped into the palm of her hand. That meant the place had already been tested for fibers and hairs, and already been fingerprinted, although the print man was squatting beside her, trying to get an overlooked smudge from the edge of a lamp shade covered in plastic. Under the plastic, the shade was fringed and yellow—whether from age or design, Shelly could not determine. The print man's job was made more difficult by his refusal to take off his hat, which had fallen so low over his eyes its brim blocked most of the upper half of his view. The photographer sucked a long draw from her filterless cigarette and seemed to be considering whether to drop her ashes onto the print man's crown when he looked up and said, "Hold the other end of this damned thing for me, will ya, Lowenkopf?"

Shelly hadn't expected the print man to know his name, and couldn't reciprocate, but that was to be expected: On a crime scene, the detective was in charge, with the lab technicians at his or her disposal. Since the crime had been discovered by the rookie Michaelson with Ed Riordan in plainclothes, it was not unlikely that a homicide team would be assigned to investigate. Shelly did not know how much these technicians knew or cared about the hiring and firing of police officers. But, for the moment, the print man didn't seem to care whether Shelly knew his name, or even if he was still on the force. Shelly gripped the lamp shade by an upper loop while the print man applied his powder, and that was all he asked of him.

"Hey, there, Shell. Heard you got the boot," said a deep voice behind him. Lowenkopf turned and at once recognized Jerzy Kuklok, the ballistician, a balding man in his early forties who wore green suit pants without the jacket, a white shirt with its sleeves rolled, and a square woolen tie, always knotted below the top two buttons, which he wore open. Beneath the shirt was a sleeveless undershirt that showed his perspiration in a dark spot below his collarbone. This had evidently been no cakewalk, since the spot was deep gray and spread across the entire vee between his shirt buttons. Jerzy was a good man with a bullet remnant, and Shelly was glad to see him on the scene. If the markings on the shells indicted the rabbi, Jerzy would find them; but if there were anything that might throw doubt on the rabbi's guilt, Jerzy would find that too. Shelly had once asked him how he knew a bullet had been fired from a certain gun, and Jerzy had lit up at the question as if no one ever asked how he determined anything. That was probably true, since most cops were more interested in results than in how they were obtained, due process notwithstanding. Jerzy had never forgotten the question, and usually told Shelly more than he wanted to know about the art of ballistic investigation. But Shelly would always choose too much over not enough, and he greeted Kuklok with more than his usual good cheer.

"Heya, Kook. What you got there?"

Kuklok showed Lowenkopf a crushed bullet he had dug from the wooden bedstead. "Exhibit number two, that's all. With this and the one they're digging from the body, we're sure to get a good sample for comparison. You guys haven't found the piece yet, have you?"

Shelly winced at the sound of "you guys," which suggested a team of detectives.

"There's one on its way down to the station."

"Good work," said Jerzy. "If I can beg off from my in-laws tonight, I'll give you an answer by tomorrow."

Shelly nodded noncommittally in lieu of explanation. "Any idea yet what happened here?"

"The whole story's pretty much laid out in there," replied Kuklok, dropping the recovered item from his handkerchief into a plastic bag on which he then scribbled an identifying note and his initials. Judging by the tilt of his shining head, *there* was the master bedroom, one of two in the apartment, down a little hallway from the kitchen. Interpreting the tilt as a gesture of permission, Shelly walked back, glancing at the sink. A single plate and fork sat beside a drinking glass in which a teaspoon leaned jauntily from a ring of brown liquid at the bottom to a lipstick smudge at the top. One side of the hallway was covered with photographs: A few were ancient, faded brown; a few were color prints; but the biggest number were Polaroids, nieces and nephews or grandchildren, maybe, arranged in the oval windows of a wooden frame. Shelly used the back of his elbow to edge open the bedroom door and entered quietly, stepping over a roll of carpet where the wall-to-wall had been unstapled and pulled back so that something could be scraped from the floorboards.

As Shelly moved into the bedroom, he felt a sudden longing for his former partner. It had always been Homer, after all, whose nose would twitch at the prospect of inspecting a roomful of objects for the information that could be wrested from their mute witness. Lowenkopf would go looking for a human being, a landlady or janitor, who could tell him more in five minutes of questions than he could learn in an hour on his knees. Homer, however, loved to scrape and sniff and poke into corners, testing the springs of the furniture, measuring the height of a desk leg or the depth of a gash in a throw pillow on the bedspread. To Shelly, the room made a show of ignorance, as if the knickknacks on the bureau and linens on the bed had been preoccupied when their owner had been murdered. Homer might have cajoled their secrets from then with a tape measure and a file. But Homer was no longer his partner; Shelly sighed and squatted down on the worn green carpet for a Homer's-eye view of the bed, which began, of course, underneath it.

What did he see? Shoes, mostly, with low heels and no heels and a pair of crisscross sandals with high heels; with rounded toes and square toes and those sandals with none. Six, seven, eight, nine pairs all told—what would Homer have made of that? They were all in pretty good shape,—no particular wear at the rubber heels, which, Shelly noticed, are thin on women's shoes. She either had them repaired regularly or replaced them—this lady did not want for shoes, which meant she probably did not want for other

things either. What could he say about the style? The
sandals were silver lamé, and there were black leather
bows on the closed ones with the rounded toe and low
heel. A pair of slippers were pink, with a fluffy white
ball shedding in front—not fleecy, but not fuzzy
either—the kind of things Harlow might have worn
beneath a sleek robe that kept falling open on those
mile-long legs of hers. Shelly glanced toward the
closet, which was open, and spotted the feather-
topped robe he thought he might find among the
flannel nighties and zippered dresses and quilted
housecoats.

Beside the robe, he found a black negligee, lacy at
the top, over the shoulders, but lined discreetly in
satin below. The lining was not crisp but creased,
mussed, with a strand of black thread, or hair. And it
was still faintly warm. So the woman of the house had
not given up on her ability to interest a man; and she
must not have given up on her interest in them either.
Why else select it over the warmer, softer flannel? But
she was not wearing it when she was found. She had
changed—for whom? The bed was neatly made, with
the lumps of two pillows beneath a bedspread of green
and red vines interlaced around a jungle of exotic fruit
trees. It had no other lumps or depressions except
where an additional woolen blanket lay folded near
the foot of the bed, mostly black with a plaid pattern
and black woolen fringes.

At the top of the bed was a wooden headboard that
matched the tables at each side. There was just room
on the far side for the table and then the wall; the aisle
between window and bed on that side was just wider
than Shelly's hips. The nearer bed table was evidently
the one she had been using: it held a clock radio, with
an alarm set for six (What was it, he wondered, she
had to do before seven A.M.?) and a porcelain box

decorated with wild Canadian geese in which was stored a collection of bobby pins. These two permanent fixtures shared a cloth doily, which had been otherwise cleared except for an unwrapped cellophane wrapper still sticky with the residue of a candy ball. She had not lost her taste for sweets, it seemed—what other appetites remained? If there was a glass for her dentures, it was not in evidence. Shelly jotted a note in his pad to ask Jerzy about her teeth. If she wore dentures, she was not preparing to go to bed—not alone, at least. Riordan had said she had been killed around three—after a late lunch, or maybe an early supper, according to the dishes in the sink and the glass on the night table. If the brown liquid in the drinking glass was tea, it would have dried within—what?—two or three hours? Homer would have known how long it takes a ring of tea to dry in a glass; the best Shelly could do was jot down another note to find out the missing information.

Where the woman had been standing, at least, would not have been in doubt even without the bloodstains running down the front of her bureau. Assorted bottles of lotion and scent had smashed on top, and the mirror above was smudged—perhaps with her hand, since the bloodstains did not reach that high except in the fine, scattered pattern of a bullet bursting through the far side after traveling through a body. Shelly stood in the place in front of the bureau and looked into the mirror—where he saw Jerzy, in the doorway, watching him.

"What was she wearing, Kook?"

"Wearing? You mean the . . ."

"The victim, yeah. Was she in a dress?"

"A dress? No. She was in one of those, y'know, one-piece satin things old women wear under their clothes."

"A slip?"

"Sounds right," said Jerzy.

"What was she doing? Putting on lipstick?" Shelly mimed the possibility in the mirror.

"Lipstick? I dunno. Didn't notice anything special about the lips—maybe if the coat's uneven, they'll be able to tell. Could've been doing her hair."

"The brush is here," said Shelly, indicating without a touch the wooden implement with nylon bristles that lay neatly on its back, flush with the base of the mirror.

"It couldn't'a fallen like that," admitted Jerzy, wrinkling his nose at the scent still in the air. "So maybe perfume or something."

"Maybe," agreed Shelly, although the scene smelled more like ointment. "She knew him, anyway."

"What makes you think so?"

"It looks like she fell face forward," said Shelly.

"That's how we found her," said Jerzy.

"I can see you in the mirror here," Shelly told him. "She must've seen anyone come into the room. If she didn't know him, she would've turned around, don't you think?"

Jerzy was silent for a moment before asking, "So maybe she knew the assailant. What makes you say *him?*"

"Why are you wrinkling your nose?" asked Shelly. "By the dishes in the sink, she wasn't planning on going out to eat, was she? But she was sitting at her makeup table. So she had a guest—who she thought was out there when she came in here to fix herself. By the amount of musk still hanging in the air, I'd say her guest was a man."

It wasn't too bad an imitation of Homer, Shelly thought as Jerzy nodded, kneeling on the carpet three or four feet from the bureau. Homer might have spotted something he had missed, but for a fast reading of the scene—not bad. Jerzy tapped the pile with a long finger and said, "We found an empty shell on the floor about here. Now you figure a shell ejected automatically from most pistols travels over the right shoulder and to the rear of the shooter—which would place him somewhere in here, holding the pistol in front of him, like that. Let's say ten to fifteen inches away. We can check that with a Walker test, if you like. But I'll bet the smudging on the corpse is enough to confirm some distance in here."

Jerzy was asking him for a decision, Shelly knew. The Walker powder residue test is designed to detect the presence of nitrites from a fired gun on cloth or other objects in the line of fire. The rug, for example, might be placed on specially prepared photographic paper and subjected to heat, which should reveal orange-red spots corresponding to the position of nitrite particles around the bullet hole. However, since the gun was less than eighteen inches from the body when it was fired, burnt powder would doubtlessly turn up as a grimy residue around the entrance wound. Given the caliber of the bullet, the size of the smudge would also indicate the firing distance. Jerzy's point was that the smudging would make the Walker test unnecessary, and, had Shelly actually been the detective assigned to the case, he would have told him not to bother with the Walker test. But Shelly was not the detective in charge of this case, and, rather than leave himself vulnerable to any complaints about his conduct at the scene, said carefully, "If I were you, I'd do the Walker, Kook. Just to be sure. You never know what somebody's gonna ask for later on."

Jerzy nodded and began to take up that piece of the carpet, exactly as if Shelly had instructed him to do so. While he cut a rectangle into the rug, Shelly sat on the bed, putting it all together. The old lady had eaten her meal alone, and had been surprised by the arrival of an unexpected guest. She had excused herself and come into the bedroom here, to fix up her face and so on. While she was doing that, the shooter had followed her in. She had seen him come in, maybe said something, but returned to her work in the mirror. In that moment he had pulled out a gun and shot her in the back—while she was talking, maybe. So she had known him and trusted him—or at least wasn't afraid of him. After all, what sort of man would an elderly woman trust to be alone with her in her bedroom?

The thought flashed through his mind: She would trust her rabbi, wouldn't she? But he wasn't working that side of the street anymore.

"Do you know, Kook, what the neighbors heard?"

"The neighbors?"

"Ed Riordan said some of the neighbors heard some arguing in here. In Jewish."

"Oh, yeah," said Jerzy, rolling up a rectangle of carpet and tucking it under his arm. "The lady next door. Riordan talked to her already."

"Any idea what she told him?"

"Why don't you ask her?"

It wasn't exactly authorization from the police department, but Shelly counted it sufficient to ring the doorbell next door and wait for the peephole to be slid across. There was no answer from the other side, so he spoke to the light in the peephole, using the name hand lettered on cardboard and forced into the slot beneath the doorbell.

"Mrs. Mendelsohn?"

"Yes? Who is it? Who are you?"

"My name is Shelly Lowenkopf. I've been looking into what happened next door. I was hoping you could answer some questions for me."

"I already answered some questions. I don't hafta answer any more."

"No you don't," Shelly assured her, thinking, Certainly not for me. "But it might help catch the person who did this, if you would agree to."

She closed the peephole, and he thought for a moment he had lost her, until she opened the door—just a crack, with the chain on, allowing him to see a pale blue eye under a wrinkled face and a bun, clutching the top of her housecoat. "Yeah? What else do you want to know?"

"You were the one who heard the shot?"

"That's right. I called Mr. Huffelman right away."

"He's the janitor?"

"He likes to be called the custodian."

"But you didn't get a look at the man who did it?"

"I got a look at him earlier. When he went in. A coupla hours before."

"But not when he came out?"

"The only way I could've done that would be to come to the door. Which is the last place I want to be when something's going on next door."

"Does that happen often?"

"What?"

"Something going on next door?"

She made a fish face. "Look," she said. "I'm not one of these neighbors who can't keep her nose in her own business. Mrs. Levinski was a very nice lady. She always offered to help if she saw me coming in with the laundry basket from the market, or anywhere. But I don't think she would mind my saying she was a very sociable woman."

"She did a lot of entertaining?"

"How much is a lot? She wasn't Pearl Mesta. But she didn't go lonely, either."

"Men?"

57

"I don't know what went on in there. But she had visitors from time to time."

"Could you recognize their voices?"

"Whatever she did was her business. I didn't listen with my ear to the keyhole."

"But you told Officer Riordan you heard voices here earlier tonight—"

"These walls ain't made of steel, you know. When people talk loud, you can hear."

"They were loud enough for you to tell they were speaking in Hebrew?"

"Not Hebrew—Yiddish."

Shelly remembered his mother's distinction: Hebrew is the language of Israel, and the Torah. Yiddish is the language people speak in Europe—or, at least, spoke. Before the Nazis got to them.

"You can tell them apart? Through a wall?"

"It's not so hard. If I can understand what they're saying, it must be Yiddish."

"What were they saying?"

"She was trying to get rid of him. He said something almost loud enough for me to hear, but I wasn't listening yet. I heard what *she* said, though—clear and calm and ladylike. She said, 'Don't you have to be going? To the shul?' "

"She said that word? *Shul?*"

"Don't you think I'd recognize it if I heard it?"

"I just wanted to be sure about that—"

"So? Are you sure?"

"I am. I'm sorry for interrupting."

"Apology accepted. You're gonna want to be sure about this, too, so don't interrupt."

"I won't."

"Good." She paused.

"So what did he say?"

"I'm getting to it. Where was I? Oh, yeah. Lillian

said, 'Don't you have to be going? To the *shul?'* " Mrs. Mendelsohn paused again, to see if he would interrupt. When he didn't, she went on, "And the other voice—the man's voice—said to her, 'They'll wait for me. They'll wait. They can't do the service without me.' "

# 6

There was no one on earth Alfonso Barreras wanted
to be so desperately as his cousin Benito Durazo, in
the shadow of whose accomplishment he lived all of
his days. Not only was Benito actually related by
blood to Clemencia Garza, the forty-year-old grandmother who had taken both of them in, agreeing to
raise them for the sake of the payments made on their
behalf by the welfare agency. But he was tall and
slender, with heavy lids, and the girls all went crazy
for him. Benito was fourteen, of course, which meant
that the world of tits and asses was an open book for
him, available whenever he wished to read it. If he
allowed his lids to fall closed, and peered up at a girl
through the lashes, she was as good as naked before
him, while he tried to decide how and where he
wished to enter her.

At eleven, Alfonso had great respect for power of
this kind, which he learned about at night in his
cousin's reports of the day's selections and experi-
ments. There was one girl that Benito had enjoyed
repeatedly, from a stimulating variety of angles, with

*devices.* Alfonso was not sure what *devices* were; he
knew they cost money, and could be bought in dangerous stores downtown when you cut school and hopped
a train. But the girl who had allowed him to use
*devices* lived, Benito regretted, a subway ride away—
further than Clemencia would permit Alfonso to go
without her. So Alfonso never did get to see the
girl—Gabriela was her name, once, although on another occasion Benito had called her Christina. It was
too bad, really; Alfonso would have liked to see her
enormous breasts, and the green fires in her eyes that
smoked like the candles on the altar after Clemencia
had snuffed them out for the night. The only girl he
had in fact ever seen Benito with was Teresa Escobar,
who was skinny, and giggled, and would never be
worth the exercise of his cousin's powerful charm.
That was why, Benito explained carefully, he seemed
to stammer when he talked to her, and to shuffle his
feet, in imitation of those boys whose tastes and
experiences were far less adventurous than his own.

But those were not the only reasons Alfonso wished
he were his cousin. If it were merely a matter of
wisdom, of information and sophistication, Alfonso
accepted Benito's assurances that he could acquire
them one day for himself. But talent was another
story. You had to be born with it in your fingers, in the
wrist and the eye, and everyone knew that Benito had
been so blessed. Early on, when Alfonso had first
come to live with them, Benito had shown him the
drawer in which he saved his drawings of the Amazing
Spider Man, whose every muscle and spider sense had
been captured, line for line, on the back of a letter
from the power company. At four, Alfonso could not
hope to copy a picture as well as that; but Benito soon
went on to astonish his cousin all the more by drawing
another freehand, not quite as accurately as the cop-
ied picture but in an original pose. Imagine! To make

Spider Man do whatever you wished. It was Alfonso's first taste of Benito's power, the power of his pencil. When Clemencia found the drawings, she did not crumple them in her fist and toss them into the trash—on the contrary! She taped them carefully to the front of the refrigerator, and showed them to her visitors, when she had any.

That was better than power; that was love.

And at school, when they went, the same thing— Benito would sit in his classes drawing, and when a note came home from the teacher with the picture folded inside it, Clemencia never yelled at him, never scolded him, but smoothed out the drawing on her knee and taped it to the refrigerator. Her Benito was going to be an artist one day, she explained patiently to Alfonso. You had to understand these things in an artist, and forgive him for what he was not. And she would brush back the hair from Benito's forehead with her soft pink hand, and kiss him there, two or three times.

Alfonso, too, wished to be forgiven.

So he would follow Benito, and do what his cousin wished him to do in order to be permitted to follow. He had been standing beside his cousin one day when the train passed overhead with one beautiful name spray-painted down the length of a car: CARERRO. That was all it said. But from the moment they saw it rumble overhead, there was no other canvas Benito wished to honor with his paints.

Alfonso did not see much of his cousin the following week. When he did, Benito told him he had learned where the trains were kept when they slept. It was a yard, like any other, with a big fence around it, but a manageable one. One night he came home with a gash in his face from the coils of barbed wire at the top. It was a cost, Benito explained, a cost of his art, which he paid gladly as any artist would who loved his

62

work. It was the most romantic thing Alfonso had ever heard of. But Benito would not let him come along. Too much danger for a boy, he said. Which only made Alfonso yearn more desperately to accompany him. But Benito was strict and never varied in his refusal.

And then, one day, Alfonso saw, pulling into the station over his head, the most beautiful train car ever. In big, bold letters, blue like the green of the sea, was written the name: CLEMENCIA. It filled the entire car, from the front to the back, covering the doors and the windows. In the bottom curve of the first letter, the capital *C*, were written in cool white letters: BENITO. And, in the bottom curve of the final letter, the small letter *a*, was written another name: ALFONSO.

If his life had ended there, struck down by one of the cars that roared between steel supports holding up the tracks in the sky, Alfonso would have been lifted to heaven by the feelings in his heart. He knew that wherever it went on its travels through the city, the car would carry their three names together. And people from distant places, from Brooklyn or Staten Island, would be waiting for the train to pull in, and look up when it came, and see his name in the little *a*: ALFONSO. And they would wonder who it was that had earned this distinction, whose life it was this name so honored. And it was his, in the Bronx, living with Clemencia, who might never see it, but would know they were thinking of her someplace, too.

So it did not matter, in Alfonso's opinion, when they caught Benito and took him away for a while.

Benito did not tell Alfonso how he obtained the cans. There were some things it was better for Alfonso not to know—Alfonso heard and respected that, trusting his cousin in this as he had trusted him in all things—in the stories he told in their bed at night and the stories he was beginning to share only now. There was danger involved. One could not steal a sackful of spray cans without a certain risk. But no man was an artist who refused to risk himself for the sake of the works he hoped to produce as a result. And Benito had friends who knew how to do things, how to steal what he needed without getting caught.

Most of the time.

It was longer than the months sounded. Alfonso made his bed and then Benito's, and ran to the drugstore for Clemencia's cigarettes. The nights were very long, and it took Alfonso hours to fall asleep. But, just as he began to believe that Benito would never come back, Benito did.

He was not even changed, really. He had done very well at the Hall, Benito said, because he had gone up with his friends, who took care of him. That was what you needed in this world, he said—friends who can take care of one another. Benito had the friends he needed, and he took care of them, and they of him. One of the things they liked very much for him to do for them was to write their name on the walls of playgrounds; on the handball courts was best. FURIES! Benito would write in brilliant colors, and it made every member of their gang proud, whenever he would pass it on the street. Alfonso understood just how they felt after seeing his car on the subway tracks. Only Benito did not use his own name when he signed his works anymore. From the time he returned to Alfonso and Clemencia, he signed himself as EL TORO, with a special twist to each side of the cross-line of the *T* so that it resembled the head of a bull. He did not forget his cousin, however, whose name he similarly changed. No longer would Alfonso see his own name written large; instead, he saw the new one: POQUITO 6, the little one who had come to Clemencia's home when he was six years old. Privately, Alfonso would have preferred to see his real name on the wall; but, he knew in his heart it was his name too, POQUITO, and it comforted him. If life did not always give you what you preferred, it was also true that whatever life had given him in the way of kindness, and of love, it had come from his cousin Benito. EL TORO.

So be it.

One day, Raoul Lopez and his brother Miguel stopped by when Alfonso and Benito were sharing some fries at Burger King. Raoul was the bigger one, with a bolder heart, but Miguel was shrewder, so they made a good team together. Raoul leaned over their table and said to Benito, "Hey, man, you see what happened on the Foundation?"

It was the concrete base of a building that had never been erected—the money had given out, or something, and they never bothered to pull it down, either. So a great expanse of concrete wall had stared at them through the fence, until Benito climbed over one night, clipping the coils of barbed wire with a pair of cutters Raoul had given him. Alfonso thought they might have slipped over together, because next to the huge Furies name that was there on the following morning was also WA, which had disappeared in the curls of its own elaboration. Alfonso had laughed at the sight of it, the unsteady hand too anxious to let the letter stand with its own integrity—a contrast to the work of art beside it.

"What?" said Benito. He had fries on a piece of paper with ketchup on them, and was down to the last few, drenched in red. He was trying to using a fry only half smothered in ketchup to spear and pick up another wholly smothered. Raoul watched for a minute and then lost patience, reaching across Alfonso to grab the fry dripping ketchup with his fingers.

"They overwrote you, man." He said it casually, as if it were no skin off his nose what Los Diablos did.

It was the first time Alfonso had heard the word: *overwrote*. He knew instantly what it meant. And he turned to his cousin with real fear in his eyes.

"Don't worry!" said Benito, laughing at him, shoving a fry in his mouth. "It happens all the time, Poquito." But his voice was quieter, with a threat in it, when he returned to Raoul and said, "Who?"

Raoul chewed for a moment, nodding his head.

"Him?" asked Benito. "The same?"

"El Gato," Raoul said. *"Sí."*

Benito sat back thoughtfully against the molded plastic of the booth and bit the end of his straw.

When Alfonso looked in the cup, there was still some brown liquid under the ice. He offered it to his cousin, who shook his head. So he drank it himself.

But the next time the name El Gato appeared, it was not in such pleasant surroundings. It was in the yard, at school, on a day Alfonso attended but his cousin did not. When he got home, he hesitated before telling Benito about the giant *placa* that had been written on the concrete floor of the yard where the classes lined up. Benito seemed to take it well, his eyes bright. But he did not come in until very late that night. And the next day, when Alfonso went back to the school yard, he saw a new *placa,* even larger than the first, challenging the dignity of the name. The first had read: Los Diablos, and had taken up six squares of sidewalk; but the new one read: Furies, and it took up twelve. Not only that, but all of the Furies had come to school that day, while only a few Diablos were there.

That was why there were no *incidents* in the school yard that day, although Miguel Lopez danced on the name of Los Diablos right in front of them, with Raoul and a dozen other Furies to back him up. Alfonso thought him cruel—he laughed at them as he danced, showing his teeth, which were too yellow and

crooked for him to be so proud of them. Benito had
not said anything, just glared at the Diablos as if he
wanted a piece of one of them, right then and there.
There was one among them, a big guy Alfonso had
heard called Torquemada, who looked like he might
have gone for Miguel, outnumbered though his crew
were—but another kid, tall and skinny, put a hand on
his shoulder and said something, and Torquemada
laughed and was able to hold off for a better day.
Afterwards, when Alfonso heard Benito talking to
Raoul about it, he learned that the name of the tall
and skinny kid was Rocio Lucero.

El Gato.

He was a graffito writer, Raoul said. As soon as
Benito heard that, he was interested. Raoul always
knew how to strike Benito's interest—Alfonso had to
concede him that. But he did not seem to have
Benito's best interests always at heart. It was an
insight he once tried to share with his older cousin,
but Benito would not hear such things from him.

Alfonso's first chance to see what had been done to
Benito's work at the Foundation came about a week
after the desecration had actually taken place.
Clemencia had taken him along with her to see the
welfare agency, so they could see how well she was
caring for him, and the bus drove past the Foundation
on its way to Westchester Avenue. It was only a
minute, through the dirty bus window, but it was
enough for Alfonso to understand the full significance
of the act. The beautiful letters of the name: FURIES!
which had stood like sentinels guarding their home
had been effaced with an ugly wriggle of red paint that
circled through the center of the letters so that the
original design of blue and yellow blocks could not be
repaired by a touch-up. It was as if a headstone over a
grave had been smashed with a sledgehammer—only

this was the name of living men, whose individual identities, linked in a network of mutual care, had been assaulted and degraded.

Alfonso was not a Fury—none of them would have called him one, and once, when Benito heard him call himself by that name, he had smacked him on the back of the head and said, "You do not need to mark yourself as I have done." Alfonso thought he meant the tattoos of snakes that ran up each of Benito's arms, their open fangs flashing on his deltoids. Benito would not allow him to take a tattoo, either. But even though he was not a Fury, the sight of their name scribbled over on the Foundation wall filled Alfonso with a profound sense of personal injury and injustice. And a hunger to see it addressed.

There were no *incidents* in the school yard that day; but, on the following Saturday, Miguel Lopez went to score by the trestle in the park, and on his way back some Diablos caught him inside the wall. Some of them, he said, had been in the school yard that day—Torquemada had been there, who now had danced on his bones. Raoul was especially angry because Miguel was *on his way back*—he was trying to leave their territory, not to penetrate it. That was what he said, at least. But when Alfonso went with Benito to see Miguel in the hospital, the face behind the bandages made him feel like throwing up. So that might have contributed to the way Raoul reacted to the *incident*.

Alfonso would not believe that his cousin had anything to do with it. He had heard him counseling Raoul with sympathy and good sense, telling him to keep a cool head, not to jump the way the Diablos expected him to—they were the Furies, their own masters, who worked out their own justice in their own way and time. Alfonso had seen how Raoul's eyes teared, but did not hear what he whispered into

Benito's ear. *"Sí,"* Benito replied, "they have done this to us, to all of us, *sí."* And he shook his head, with regret but also restraint. Although Alfonso saw the emotion like a fire pit in the back of his eyes.

Alfonso did not enjoy speculating as to what happened next. Clemencia was worried about the welfare agency, of course, and said they might even take her boys away—both of them, she said. But Alfonso followed his cousin's lead, as he had always done, and said nothing to the police when they asked. No, they had not heard anything during the night. No, Alfonso had never met this boy, had never heard of him, either. Yes, it was too bad the way problems were handled by some people in this neighborhood. He had felt the same way himself. Oh, yes, if they heard anything, they would certainly call. Clemencia took the white card and put it carefully in the drawer under the telephone. She made sure that the officer at the door saw her put it there.

They went to bed early, he and Benito, who did not want to, but gave in to his cousin rather than listen to Clemencia any longer. Alfonso tried to talk, asking about girls, but Benito said he was too tired to make up stories. But he could not go to sleep either. He sat up, leaning against the wall, staring into the darkness.

The night they had found Rocio Lucero dead.

7

When Shelly awoke on Saturday, he saw two choices before him: He could call Mordred with the news of Thom's change in plans, which left the day open for the two of them to share; or he could use the unexpected free time to look into the matter of Mrs. Levinski's murder. If he hopped the downtown A train, he could surprise her, sleeping in; they could breakfast in the Village, meander up to Chelsea for that holographic exhibit she kept talking about, and slip back down to her place for nooky before lunch. He showered and dressed quickly, and didn't stop for breakfast, but when he stepped out into the daylight, he didn't head for the subway but for his own Volkswagen squareback. He passed the West Side Highway, crossing to the eastern side of the northern tip of Manhattan, spanned the concrete bridge, and bumped onto the Cross-Bronx Expressway.

It took him twenty minutes to cross the Bronx, and another ten to make his way up the Bronx River Parkway to the Allerton Avenue Precinct House. He chatted a minute with the sergeant at the desk and then ambled over to the mailroom, where he saw with a certain satisfaction that his name had not been removed yet from the detective boxes. The plastic sticker had been peeled, but someone had written his name in again, in black Magic Marker, under the box where the label had been. Thus emboldened by evidence that he was not forgotten, Shelly decided to visit the squad room on the second floor, which would probably be empty on a Saturday, unless someone was working on a case that could not be put off until Monday. He had checked Riordan's mailbox, and didn't see a lab report in it. If Jerzy had been as good as his word, as he always had been, the report should have reached the station house by now.

The squad room door was locked, and no light showed through the pane of glass above the handle, but Shelly decided to slip the lock, just in case Homer was prowling around somewhere. They had not had much chance to talk since Shelly had left the force. He had been away on disability, of course, and while his partner had come to see him a couple of times in the hospital, it would have been awkward once he went home. When he had telephoned his decision to Captain Madagascar, Homer had been out; Shelly had hoped to talk to him when he came in to clean out his desk, but the others had arranged a little surprise, and everyone wanted to wish him well, and in the confusion of the celebration there really wasn't time. Homer had shaken his hand and made a joke about breaking in a new one, but Jill Morganthal had interrupted them with a lead on a case Homer was working on. And, of course, there was nothing on earth that could keep Homer from a new lead.

But, as it turned out, Homer was not in the darkened, locked room. Shelly wandered over to his old desk, which looked as if an industrial vacuum had sucked away the piles of papers that had congregated there over many years. All there was on the desktop now were a blotter with a light blue cover, a photograph of two girls—"For Aunt Jill"—and a paper cup in which a few daisies lay wilting over the edge. He dumped the wilted daisies in the trash can, which was not under the desk but on the right side, away from the line of sight of the captain's window. His old Remington had been replaced by a sleek new typing computer —with memory, no doubt. He could hardly blame her for that. Shelly had meant to change over himself, one of these days. But those days were finished for him now. He put the paper cup back on the desk, and then picked it up again, resettling it in the dried ring of water it had left behind. The neatness of Morganthal's desktop made Homer's own—with its carefully arranged pencils and paper clips—look messy in comparison. Shelly smiled and wished them luck together.

While the straightest path to the door wouldn't have brought him past Ed Riordan's desk, the path to the water cooler did, and Shelly couldn't help noticing the lab report on top as he passed. He deliberated the ethical consequences and, while he did, opened the report cover for a brief glimpse at what was inside. Eight minutes later he let the cover drop again, having read more than he needed to know. No wonder Riordan had figured this case could wait until Monday. He had the rabbi under lock and key, and all the lab results were coming in his way. The bullet that killed Lillian Levinski had come from Pirski's handgun; and the paraffin test suggested the rabbi had fired one recently.

If he had still been a cop, and this case had fallen to him, Shelly would have taken the weekend off. But he had to proceed along a different line now. Having a client meant you couldn't let the chips fall where they might; you had to take an interest in one particular chip and give it every possible chance to fall right side up.

Shelly descended the green staircase to the basement, where Rabbi Sholem Pirski sat alone in a narrow holding cell with a book on the bench beside him. The rabbi seemed smaller than he had in his office, but the evident seriousness of purpose in his watery gray eyes gave him a dignity from which the ham-fisted loan collector in the next cell shied away. When Shelly entered, the policewoman on duty was Alice Drubman, a blond woman with the shoulders of a linebacker and the sensitivity of a ballerina. She had come to Shelly once or twice, as many others did, when the captain was displeased with her. After all, who had more experience than Shelly in dealing with Madagascar's displeasure? When the captain's bullet head sunk into his shoulders like a turtle's, or when he shifted his bulk on his wooden chair, resettling the pillow underneath him, it had been Shelly who knew how to back out of his glass-walled office with the least chance of a paperweight flying after him. Shelly did not want to trade on personal friendships, but, after a few minutes of catching up, asked if there wasn't someplace she needed to take the rabbi's neighbor. Alice was a good cop and a conscientious officer who couldn't help frowning at his request. But, rousting the collector in the next cell, she found some excuse in her paperwork to leave Shelly and the rabbi alone together—"For a few minutes," she said.

He gave her a wink and a nod.

The rabbi did not look up when Shelly first approached his cell, his eyes hidden by a black hat he had acquired somewhere between his office and the street. Once or twice the brim tilted back, and Shelly thought he saw the man's attention wander over, but it never seemed to focus on the space beyond the bars; and it wasn't until Shelly cleared his throat, twice, loudly, that the rabbi's gaze finally focused on him. When it did, an expression of genuine pleasure filled his face, smoothing the wrinkles in his cheeks, by his eyes and his mouth, as if even their brief acquaintance in the rabbi's office, under the most difficult of personal circumstances, had established a bond between them that the rabbi was eager to develop. Once having alighted on Shelly, the gray eyes fixed on him, without wavering, as if they expected to learn from him something of great significance in this world or the next.

"Max's friend," the rabbi said, pointing a long, unsteady finger at him. "Isn't it?"

Shelly nodded. "The name's Lowenkopf, Rabbi. Max didn't get a chance to introduce us."

"Call me Sholem," said Pirski.

Shelly didn't think he could do that, but said, "Shelly, then. I used to be a cop around here."

"Nice place," said Sholem, glancing around the gray walls and green steel bars.

"How are they treating you?"

"Treating me?" the rabbi said, his arms rising and falling in a gesture of acceptance. "Better than they treated Jews in the camps." He raised his eyes to heaven for an instant, mumbling a prayer of thanks to the Deity for that relative kindness.

"I hope so," said Shelly.

"Hope is a terrible thing to lose," said the rabbi. "They did not lose it in the camps, so there is no reason you and I should lose it now." "The camps" had to mean Auschwitz, Dachau, Buchenwald, Treblinka. Shelly saw the old man's fists grip the green steel bars, and a chill whistled down his spine.

"You're not in that kind of trouble," he said.

"Not in danger of my life?"

Shelly began to see the resemblance. "You mean, if they find you . . ."

"Guilty of murder. What is the penalty, please?"

"The penalty?"

"The punishment for my crime."

"You haven't even been arraigned yet. You're a long way from sentencing."

The rabbi ticked off the steps on his fingers. "The first step is arraignment, no? They should have enough evidence to hold me for trial, don't you think?"

Shelly never liked to predict the judicial process, but in this case it seemed a good enough bet. "I guess."

"Then the next step is the Grand Jury. Without a defense attorney to plead my case, isn't it?"

"Right."

"Well, then? What comfort there? I should think they have enough for an indictment against me."

Shelly had seen plenty of men indicted on less. "Maybe."

"The next step is the trial, no?"

"The trial. Yes."

"When it will fall to the judgment of twelve men and women to decide my guilt or innocence."

"The burden of proof is on the other side," said Shelly, glad of it for the first time. "Which means uncertainty is in your corner. They'll have to establish your culpability beyond a reasonable doubt."

"So what's reasonable?" said the rabbi. "Is it reasonable that a beautiful woman should be gunned down in the prime of her life? To tell the truth, if I were one of the jury, I wouldn't find that reasonable, myself."

It had not occurred to Shelly that Lillian Levinski might be considered "a beautiful woman in the prime of her life" by a man near her own age. Just how old had she been? The rabbi himself had a few years in his beard.

"How old are you?"

"Sixty-three," said Pirski. "From the way things look right now, I doubt I'll see sixty-four."

"Things don't look so bad to me," said Shelly.

The rabbi leaned back against the wall, miserably. "If I were where you are, and you were where I am, they wouldn't look so bad to me, either."

Shelly felt for the old man, in his fears. But he found his hopelessness troubling, too. Drawing close against the bars he said, "Where is your faith in God, Rabbi?"

The rabbi glanced over glumly. "My faith in God is fine," he said. "It's people I'm not so sure about."

"You'll have your turn on the witness stand—your chance to explain your side of the story. Don't you think your goodness will shine through?"

"Is that what I have to depend on? To keep me out of the electric chair?"

"They don't use the chair anymore."

"That's a relief. So what will it be? Hanging by my neck from a noose?"

"An injection."

"Good Lord! A shot! I hate needles."

"In this state, the death penalty is only available if you murder a police officer in the execution of his duties. You didn't do that, did you?"

"God forbid!"

"Then your life is not on the line."

"It isn't?"

"No."

"You're sure of it?"

"Absolutely."

"Thank God! Praise the Almighty."

The rabbi sat forward, pushed back his hat, and wiped the sweat from his brow with a handkerchief from his pants pocket. Then he craned his head forward and patted the back of his neck. Finally, he blew his nose in the handkerchief, folded it in half, and stuffed it back into his pocket.

"You know, Rabbi," said Shelly slowly, "you don't act like an innocent man, exactly."

"I don't? Does an innocent man act differently?"

"For one thing, you don't sound convinced that, in the end, your innocence will carry the day."

"I'm not convinced at all," said Pirski.

"But you are innocent?"

"Do you see that as the crucial question?"

"Don't you?"

"Not entirely," the rabbi replied. "There is a difference on earth between law and justice. Just men are punished in human courts, and evil men not only escape—they triumph. Haven't you paid any attention to the fortunes of good and evil these last fifty years?"

"I've been trying to do something about it, myself," said Shelly.

The rabbi's face darkened and his shoulders seemed to grow broader. "Then you must know how frequently good people suffer, while those without mercy enjoy the fruits of their labors! How often generous, gentle spirits are cheated by those without a shred of human decency!"

"I've seen my share of con men, I suppose. But they usually wrangle out of jury duty . . ."

The rabbi scowled at this distraction. "But the essential point is, there is no assured connection between innocence before God and innocence before one's fellow men and women. Like those on a jury. Is there?"

"No, there isn't," said Shelly. "But I don't agree."

"With what? You just conceded—"

"I don't agree that that's the essential point."

"What, then?"

"The essential point is: Where were you yesterday between two o'clock and the time the police arrived at your office?"

It felt good to be asking his own kind of question, and the rabbi had to think before he answered it.

"I was in my study, reading," he said finally. "From three o'clock, on."

"And where were you before three?"

"Before? Isn't that when they said Lil died?"

"The estimated time of death is not an exact moment—an hour one way or the other is a normal range."

"I see."

"So answer the question, please."

"The question?"

"The one I just asked. Where were you before three o'clock yesterday afternoon?"

"Before three? How much before three?"

"Where were you between two and three? And between one and two, for good measure."

"Between two and three I was in my study. Reading a very interesting midrash on Genesis. It concerned the line, 'Cain rose up against Abel his brother, and slew him.' The author of the commentary believed that Cain could only 'rise up' if he was smaller than Abel, so Abel must have been larger than—"

Shelly said, "Rabbi, if you don't answer my question, it is going to be very difficult to establish that you did not murder Mrs. Levinski."

Pirski stopped in the middle of his recitation. "What question was that?"

"I asked," repeated Shelly, "where you were yesterday from one to two o'clock."

The rabbi tried to remember. "Do you think the police will be very insistent on that point?"

"I should think they would be. Haven't they asked you about it already?"

Pirski shrugged as if to say, "It can't be helped." "People ask all kinds of questions. Like casting a fishing line into the middle of a green lake. *Kerplunk!* and the little ball bobs on the surface until a tug and what-have-we-got-here? Isn't this a lovely shiny thing?"

"You mean when they don't know exactly what they're looking for. We call that a fishing expedition."

"All of life is a fishing expedition, isn't it? What do we really know before we know it? A man marries a woman, whom he promises to love for an eternity—and only then gets to know who she really is. Are you still married, Mr. Lowenkopf?"

"Did I say I ever was?"

"Your face did, just now. Are you?"

"No."

"You see? The most important decision of your life, and you made it blindly. Children?"

"A son."

"So! Is there any more important choice? You selected the mother of your child on a fishing expedition."

Shelly hesitated. What had he actually known about Ruth when he'd made her his wife? She was slender, with white arms, and she laughed at his jokes. He remembered the rustle of her skirt, the dip of her collarbone, the coolness of her palm on his cheek as she looked up into his face, her blue eyes taunting and daunting, promising a sweet surrender—a lioness who became a lamb. He had to admit, he wasn't really thinking about her likely capability as a mother then.

Shelly's mouth was dry. He licked his lips. "You haven't really answered my question," he said.

"Your question?"

"About yesterday afternoon. Your whereabouts between one and two o'clock . . . ?"

"Oh, yes, that question," said the rabbi slowly. "Let

me answer a different one first. Or, rather, pose one—a purely hypothetical question. Let us suppose that a certain man knew who had murdered a woman —really knew it."

"A witness?"

"Let's not imagine a witness, no. Instead, let's imagine a man who knew both people involved in a horrible crime. And he knew what had happened to one, and what the other was capable of, given certain circumstances. Let us even imagine further that this knowledgeable man possessed certain information that the police did not, very incriminating information that he cannot in good conscience reveal."

"Concealing evidence germane to a criminal investigation is itself against the law."

"Yes, well—there are other Laws. But back to my question. Do you suppose it possible for this good, caring, knowledgeable person to disclose evidence of his personal innocence without compromising spiritual responsibility for the trust in which the information was given to him?"

"Are you saying somebody confessed to you something about the death of Lillian Levinski?"

"Me? Who said anything about me?"

"Somebody confessed to *somebody*, then, something that would clear you of suspicion?"

"We do not take confession," said Pirski.

"All right," said Shelly. "Did somebody *admit* something to someone that would exonerate you?"

"Not exactly," said the rabbi.

"Do you know who committed this crime?"

"They would believe me if I told them, wouldn't they?"

"Probably," said Shelly.

"Well, I can't," said Pirski. "But I know for a fact that *I* didn't commit the crime. Doesn't that count for anything?"

"Not really."

"But I'm just as reliable a person as I would have been, incriminating another man. Why doesn't my testimony concerning my own innocence, which I ought to know better than any other man, carry as much conviction as my testimony about the guilt of another, which I can, in the end, only surmise?"

How could Shelly reply to that? The answer had to do with the role of self-interest, which would have been glaringly apparent to anyone else, but seemed to be invisible to the rabbi. Shelly said, "The courts don't work that way. I'll give you two pieces of advice—not that you asked for either. Get yourself a good lawyer. And, if you're innocent, cooperate with the police. It's going to be awfully difficult to clear you if you're not giving them straighter answers than you're giving me."

The rabbi smiled. "The difficult tasks are usually the ones most worth undertaking."

"I guess—but that doesn't make them any easier."

The rabbi nodded sympathetically. "I thank you sincerely for your unsolicited advice," he said, returning to his bench and his book.

Shelly started out of the basement, but caught himself at the stairs. He turned back to the rabbi, who was tapping his chin with his fingers, already deep in thought.

"You're not going to give me an answer, are you?"

"To what question?"

"The same one I've been asking for ten minutes now."

"Which is?"

Shelly sighed. "Where were you yesterday between one and two o'clock?"

"Oh, that," said Pirski absently, running his thumb down two columns of finely wrought letters.

Shelly waited.

Pirski read for a moment, glanced up, and seemed surprised to find Shelly still there. The rabbi blinked at him, twice, as if trying to remember what he intended to say. He looked down at his book again, back at Shelly, and finally closed the tome with a resigned thump.

"Are you really off this case?"

"I wash my hands of it completely."

"You will not be reporting to the others the results of our little talk together?"

"I'm not a policeman anymore," Shelly said. "Max asked me to look into it, and now I've looked."

"So you're finished?"

"Absolutely."

"But you still would like to know . . . ? Just as a matter of personal curiosity?"

There was a trace of professional pride in it, too, and a sense of obligation to Max. Shelly said, "Just to have touched all the bases."

They heard footsteps on the stairs—the police-woman and her charge returning to his cell. Before they actually entered the basement, Pirski wagged a finger.

Shelly leaned in closer to the bars.

"The truth is," said the rabbi, "a little bit embarrassing for me. Yesterday afternoon, between one and two o'clock, I was a visitor in the home of Lily Levinski."

**8**

When Shelly returned to his apartment in Washington Heights that evening, the upper lock was unlatched when he fit his key in the door. His first thought was Ruth, who would on occasion use Thom's key to let them into the apartment when he arrived home late; but he was sure she would have called him if Thom's weekend plans had changed. Isabelle had a key, too, and would stop by on her way down from the Bronx to the coffee shop she managed in mid-Manhattan. But his sister never locked the bottom lock again after she had opened both of them; she expected it to lock itself, when it slammed behind her. The only other key to his apartment was the one he had given most recently—and it lay on the ring with a big red plastic heart on the marble-topped table inside the door. If he had any further doubts about the identity of its owner, they dissolved in the cloud of steam that wafted from the kitchen, accompanied by the aroma of burnt tomato paste and the single syllable repeated: "Shit! Shit!"

The noise of the oven door creaking open and

closed covered the squeaks of the front door opening, which he never let slam behind him. So it was as if on cat's feet that he crept to the kitchen doorway, beyond which the lithe figure of Mordred turned from the oven to the countertop, wearing nothing but an apron and a pair of oven mitts. She dropped a blackened chafing dish on the counter with a thud, which was followed immediately after by a clang as the oven door closed itself, relieved of the weight of her casserole. If that's what it was. There was cheese on it—brown mozzarella—and the burned carbon of tomatoes stuck on the sides and in the corners. There was an appealing stink of garlic and the pungent scent of aluminum about to warp over a flame. He reached in to turn off the burner under a pot in which water might once have boiled in anticipation of some sort of pasta. But there was no spaghetti in the pot, and no water, either. He turned the dial, cutting the flames that licked the bottom of the pot. Mordred must have sensed the difference in heat behind her, because she turned at once, saw the rumpled sleeve of his corduroy jacket, and cried out, "Shelly! I had it all timed perfectly—and then the eggplant—"

So that was what it was—eggplant. She glowered at the sizzling heap in the gloomy aluminum pan, where strips of purple peeped out from under a brown and orange topsoil. She couldn't quite describe what it had done to her; but there was no need, really, since the incriminating vegetable lay before him in seedy recalcitrance. She had struggled with it—from her previous efforts, he could imagine how bravely—but the day had been lost once again. And yet it was no easy thing telling victor from victim. True, the eggplant was not about to resurrect itself to make any stirring ratatouille; but Mordred herself showed signs of the battle, with red scars of tomato sauce over her left brow and on her chin. Her clothes were strewn about the floor—her black denim skirt, streaked with white flour, lay heaped on top of one red Converse hightop, with her fishnet panty hose, likewise powdered, stuffed in the ankle of the other. Her blouse, a stretch of gold nylon, soaked in the sink, with faint orange stains along its broadly scooped neck. Each piece of attire had evidently come off as it succumbed to the parmigiana, leaving her finally no defense but the white cotton apron, under which her breasts rose and fell with effort. Her eyes, when she looked at him again, carried all the despair of a novice pilot forced to bail out on a virgin flight—only this was not her first assault on Italian cooking, and that fact seemed to burn her gray eyes more intensely than the smoke.

But the swelling of a tear in one was more than Shelly could bear. "What did it do?"

"It's what it didn't do!" she said, pulling off the oven mitts with her teeth, indicting the guilty food-stuff with a twisted spatula. "That eggplant refuses to be cooked. Look! Look at my fingers!" And it was true—her smooth white fingers, which so gracefully curved around the lens of her formidable Nikon, were now marred with tiny cuts where the knife had slipped repeatedly, until she had given up peeling, and marked with white burns, where the oil had spattered in frying. Shelly took hers tenderly in his own rough hands and pitied them their scars. He raised them to kiss them, but she pulled her hands from his, when a bubble of oil lying low in the frying pan suddenly leaped for freedom. She grabbed the pan just above the plastic handle, to remove it from the burner, and burned her fingers once more, as Shelly shut the flame completely off, which had—alas!—merely been low-ered. It was the wound that really stung her pride, and she lifted the pan from the sneaky burner and dropped it into the sink, where it sank into the soapy water with a tremendous hiss of defiance.

She stared at it for a moment as a huge gray cloud rose from the sink, and the heavy pan dragged her soaking blouse to the stained porcelain bottom, where it landed with a muffled thump. "That can't be good for the frying pan, can it?"

"I suspect not," said Shelly.

"Or the blouse."

"Not *good* for it," agreed Shelly.

Another woman might have lost control as her golden spandex wrapped itself around the cruel aluminum. And for a moment she wobbled, a moment in which Shelly thought she might collapse into his arms with a shudder and a sob. But Mordred merely took her lower lip between her teeth, wiping the last bits of flour from her hands. She untied her apron, letting it fall to her ankles, stepping out of it. She looked at him ruefully.

"So where are we going for dinner tonight?"

Shelly thought Italian might not be the way to go at that point, so he suggested the Japanese place by the Washington Bridge where they served Don Buri over starchy rice in painted bowls, and miso soup with bean curds, and tangy salad, and cool, green tea ice cream.

Mordred surveyed the scene in the kitchen and decided not to disturb her earlier outfit. She left it lying where it fell, on the kitchen floor, while she went to choose another from the small but growing assortment in the corner of his closet. It had started as a single hanger—a dress for a party she had changed out of, returning afterwards to his apartment. Then it had been joined by a second hanger—a sweatshirt she decided to keep there to sleep in. And then a sweater to wear out. He couldn't quite remember at what point he stopped opening the closet on that side in order to reach for his clothes.

While she dressed, Shelly picked his way through

the debris in the kitchen, retrieving first whatever clothing could be relegated to the basket in his bathroom. He could understand her need to abandon the reminders of her recent engagement, but the sight of worn clothing discarded where it had fallen made him inexplicably uneasy. Skirt and panty hose went into the laundry basket; the sneakers he stood ankle to ankle outside the kitchen doorway. Pushing up his sleeve, he reached into the sink for the spandex blouse, wrung it out, and stuck it on the curved top of his tiny refrigerator to dry. By the time she emerged from the bedroom in a man-tailored shirt—his tailored shirt—and tight black toreador pants, he had dumped the eggplant into the trash, washed out the pan, and buried it in the cabinet under the sink, where it could no longer remind her.

For the first time, he thought he understood what his former partner had felt, during all their time together. Shelly was by no means fastidious—Homer would certainly have testified to that. But there was a limit, he supposed, to what even a rather sloppy cop could put up with—especially in his own apartment. It wasn't that he minded having her around. It was just that she did not seem to be bothered by chaos, which was the only word he could use for the trail of dirty laundry she seemed to forget about as quickly as she stepped out of each piece.

He had usually enjoyed her stepping out of them— but that, too, was a problem lately he didn't quite understand. For some reason, whenever they began to make love, he would start to think about the vision that had come to him when his heart had given out—Ruth called it a dream, and Isabelle, a life-after-death experience. Mordred had never really expressed an opinion, one way or the other. True, he had been reluctant to talk much about it with her, although she had asked him more than once about it. But he didn't understand the connection. Love and death? Sex and sin? He couldn't quite articulate it, but the link was sure taking its toll on their lovemaking.

"Japanese food?" she said.

"I thought you liked that Mount Fuji thing. The deep-fried ice cream."

She made a wry face as she passed the kitchen. "I like eggplant parmigiana, too. But we've all got our limitations, I suppose. Come on, Shell. Japanese." And with a fetching shrug, she took his arm comfortably into hers.

There were few things on earth Shelly loved more dearly than strolling down the sidewalk with Mordred on his arm. She knew it, too—and when he parked his car, locking his own door and then coming around to lock the passenger door of the squareback from the outside, she waited for his elbow. It wasn't that he liked showing her off: He always felt a little ridiculous in front of other people, as if he could hear them wondering what a girl of her age and obvious sexual appeal was doing with an old—let's say, middle-aged—man like him. Whenever he mentioned the difference to her, she always replied that middle age began at twenty-two; they could grow old together. It was her physical presence beside him, the tickle of her fingers in the crook of his elbow, the warmth of her sweater when her upper arm collided with his, that sent a thrill of contentment and desire through his limbs. Their time together over the small plastic table in the Japanese restaurant, scooping Don Buri out of porcelain bowls with chopsticks, then their fingers, gave an emotional resonance to his yearning that heightened it; the delay, as they licked their way through deep-fried green tea ice cream, only made the promise of what lay ahead that much sharper to anticipate. It had been a long time since Shelly had had a girl who seemed genuinely to want him, not just in solving her problems, or even in her bed, but in her life, so that dinner together was as inviting as climbing in under his quilt. Mordred did not laugh at his jokes to please him, but because she found them funny; she did not smile to make herself becoming, but the tenderness of her smile, revealing a trace of bright red lipstick on the tips of her polished teeth, touched him profoundly. She was no good with chopsticks, but never let that incapacity prevent her exploration of the pleasures of the Asian palate. Nor, for that matter, did she allow his occasional incapacity to interfere with any other exploration—which had never really been a problem.

Until now.

It wasn't physical—he had assured her of that until, when he began to doubt it himself, she started reassuring him. Shelly never claimed to have mastered any particularly soul-stirring technique, but the generosity of his sexual impulse, which found giving pleasure wonderfully exciting, had always made him a reliable lover; and a certain deliberate gentleness of his touch, acquired rather than learned as the intensity of his youthful need mellowed, made him often better than that. After their first encounter, on a staircase, Mordred had commented how pleasantly surprised she had been by his performance; whether the lovemaking was really that good, or her expectations really that low, he never got around to asking. For his part, he considered himself lucky in her, for she urged him on when encouragement was most useful and admired his handiwork in the afterglow; she gave him credit for their successes and did not blame him when their passion was less than totally exhausted. In truth, she had not had many opportunities for complaints with Shelly. That is, she had never had many.

Never until now.

It was not a deficiency of desire. After dinner, as he

watched her slide her legs onto the squeaky seat of his car, and then watched her slide them out again in front of his apartment on Bennett Avenue, Shelly felt the stirring in his trousers that promised a full head of steam for the evening's journey. And later in his bedroom, as he lay on his back underneath the covers and watched her step out of her panty hose, he felt no sudden laxity of interest. She raised the hem before slipping in beside him, and he saw the glint in her gray eyes when she found his confidence rising. When she drew alongside him, holding his face between her hands as her breath warmed him, her limbs beginning to move across his own, so that the bones of her knees crossed his thighs—that was no problem either. Her skin was very white, almost clear, with two little freckles under her left eye; she had slowly begun to ease up on the eyeliner, as faith in the draw of her irises grew, although her lipsticking had become, if anything, heavier. Still, the lips beneath the cherry red were full and pressed against his own with convincing abandon; her thick lashes, when they fluttered, conveyed an authenticity of appeal that only stiffened his resolve. Whether she hoisted herself onto his hips or snuggled in between him and the stiff cotton sheet made no difference at all. And when he found her, with only an occasional touch of guidance, their individual rhythms mated like the rods and springs of a well-oiled machine, rising and falling with a synchrony that took no calculation or attention or effort.

It was the fact that they fit together with such gratifying efficiency that allowed for Shelly's trouble. As his fingers slipped from hip to thigh, his mind slipped from the muscles that arced against his own to the spirit within that propelled them. She was a dear, sweet girl, fully a woman, with her own agenda of fear and desire that had somehow aligned with his own. For a few minutes he would allow his imagination to wander, to conceive of an alliance between them that might endure beyond the moment of convenience. And then the differences between them would occur to him, one by one, like mosquitoes. She was a traveling woman by profession—a photographer. During her last trip, to the Persian Gulf, he had missed her more than he should probably have allowed himself to miss anyone ever again. She had a tin ear for jazz—he had tried to introduce her, to help her hear it more than once, but she had managed to find the licks of a sad, sad sax very nice—"nice." But how important was music, really? The question alone was telling, since, before meeting Mordred, he would have said "enormously." Now it did not seem an impossible problem. Only age was that, the difference of a dozen years or so between them.

"Lower," she murmured into his ear. "Mmmnh! That's it . . . right there—"

She was twenty-six ("almost twenty-seven") and he was into his forties. Not far—just over the line. But into his forties, regardless. Even if he allowed himself to believe, as she would repeat whenever called upon to do so, that the difference made no difference to her, there was still the inevitable reckoning of the future. When she was forty, he would be almost fifty-five; when she was sixty, forget it. He imagined her, a trim retiree of fifty-nine, strolling down the sidewalk to the Japanese place with a wobbly old fool on her arm. Or, later, he pictured her in a black leather miniskirt and veil, weeping over an open grave. He would have to die before her, sooner or later—how fair would it be if he didn't? After all, he had died already once, from a heart attack. How long did he have before the next one?

"Alley—oop!"

Her arms closed suddenly around his ears, and his head was pressed down between her breasts. There

91

was a chunk of black rock on a silver chain that dangled in the hollow there and now swung perilously close to his jaw. Slippery as a fish, she wriggled out from under him, still holding him close as she threw one thigh over the ledge of his hip and rotated after it.

"Ungh! Unn-nnghhh . . ."

For a moment he doubted his purpose, having let his thoughts wander—but no, there they still were, intact, interlocked. He slid down a bit for a little extra maneuvering room and a snugger fit until Mordred, having settled herself more securely on top, started counting the beats aloud.

"Oh, Shel-ly! I love you, you know . . . I do . . . I really do . . . ungggh!"

"I believe you," he said, and kept to himself the follow-up, *for the moment.* He couldn't help wondering how long it could last. He found himself thinking about death more often lately. It was why he had quit the police force. Having experienced it, he could not shake the certainty he would face it again soon. He found the memory replaying itself whenever he failed to suppress it. He saw the crash site in the parking lot spinning out of control as he tumbled over the side of the car; felt the grip of steel on his chest as pain streaked down his left arm; and saw the blue-white glow in the blackness as he lifted out of himself. The flames from the gas tank crackled below as he drifted free as a cloud, rising to greet so many old friends, who waited, happy to see him. Once again he entered the great bright station, its enormity estimable by the muffled roar of echoes, where hordes of souls passed briskly by him, moving hither and yon. Once again he passed into the silence of the hall he thought of as a museum, in which family portraits hung on wires suspended from the sky. He felt himself elbowed again from group to group, drawn by some prescience to the crowd around the portrait of his spirit's own family, where he saw once again the faces of his son and sister, of his partner Homer, and, seated in the center as the matriarch, the ancient, affectionate, thoughtful face of . . . Mordred.

Just as she groaned.

At that point Shelly always lost his erection.

# 9

Felipe Montoya liked to play basketball on Saturdays, and could usually pick up a game in the Housing Authority playground in the Parkside Projects, where his family had lived until they had moved to Kew Gardens, in Queens. It made him feel good to be there, among the pink brick buildings separated by green lawns, where he had first felt his adolescent muscles lengthen and grow hard, on the basketball court by day and in the grass between the bushes and the back door of a building by night. He had sat with his buddies on the green wooden benches at night, sharing a cigarette or looking through the paper for a movie. Now that he was a cop, it made him feel good to go back there, where younger guys, who would look up in silence as he passed, now held the benches. Felipe understood that silence—whether it was intended to convey fear or hostility, there was always respect in it too. And the games were wonderful, a pure physical relief that helped him stay connected to the neighborhood, though he no longer lived within its borders.

94

He lived now in a nice house on Country Club Road, from the back of which he could look out over the Sound. He had come to check out the area on the advice of a pal on the force, and when he went to look at a house, there were swans on the beach—swans! That had made the decision easy. In the morning every Saturday he cooked himself a breakfast of three scrambled eggs with bacon and coffee and ate it on his back porch overlooking the grasses in which the mother swans raised their babies in the spring. He would move the plates from the table, clean them in the sink, and then run for five or six miles down the shoreline. After eleven he would shower and dress, run a few errands, and zip down to the playground by one. Then the game and a late lunch: Resnik was good for a pizza, and Schorske and Pitallano would come, if they didn't have to go over to Burke for Resnik's favorite calzone. Another week he might have suggested a couple of rounds of pool. But this week he shook his head when Schorske said they might try a few frames of bowling. Felipe bought the weekend paper instead, and read it on the parkway, since he had only an hour to kill before his first appointment at the community center, where he had volunteered to teach reading.

He had never thought of himself as a teacher, or even much of a reader, really. He would never have volunteered for any of these each-one-teach-one schemes had he not been talked into it by "Speedball" Stevens, one of his all-time heroes. And a lefty. Speedball had pitched for Fordham once, and the Mets after them; his E.R.A. wasn't the greatest in the league, but it wasn't the worst, either. And he had come from this neighborhood—that was the wonderful thing. It made every one of them, every kid who grew up in that part of the Bronx, feel he had a chance, too, to be whatever he wanted to be. If that was an illusion, Felipe didn't mind. It was a spur, and a comfort, too, whenever there was reason to doubt. And there were plenty of reasons to doubt, he knew, growing up in the Bronx.

Which is probably why Speedball was able to reach the kids who joined the boxing club he set up in the projects. He did it right there in the community center, in the middle of the place. He used his name and famous face to get some equipment donated—businessmen love nothing more than writing checks for an athlete. Speedball would say, "If it makes them feel good, giving us cash, that's all right with me. I want everyone to feel good—you, me, the kids, and their parents. Why shouldn't our benefactors enjoy their involvement, too?"

He was right, he was always right—that was the thing about Speedball. He talked to everyone as if they were reasonable, and the first thing you knew, the most volatile gangbangers became reasonable too. The deal was, if they wanted to box in his ring, they had to be clean while they did it: no drugs, no drinking, no weapons, no fights—not even foul language. They had to sign up and bring in the name of the family they lived with—whoever that was. And they bought it. They went along with all of the terms he set down. Because they knew he had been one of them, had come from these streets. They believed him and respected him. And they liked the equipment a lot. A real ring, with ropes that gave when you hit them. And gloves, with laces that no one stole. You could use them for free, while you were in the gym, so long as you followed the rules. If you left them there, you could always have them. But if you stole them, you were stealing them from your friends.

When Montoya came in on Saturday, Speedball was in the ring, sparring with a big guy who kept letting his left down. Each time he did, Speedball slipped another one through. "Keep it up, there, I said. Isn't that what your girlfriend tells you? Keep it up, Oralio! Keep it up!"

Oralio got mad and swung a haymaker, which Speedball ducked. As the punch sailed by, he reached under it, landing a soft jab on the jaw. The kid had lost his balance with his own wild swing and went down backwards. Speedball stood over him, extending a glove to help him back to his feet.

"That's the way to take it on the chin, Oralio. Don't let them rile you so easy."

Oralio did not accept the offered hand. "I slipped. And the name's Torquemada, man."

"Hey," said Speedball, who at sixteen had been a member of the toughest black gang in the Bronx. "No war names in this gym, remember? You want to be Torquemada, that's okay with me—just do it on the street. In here you are who you've signed up as, with a Christian name and a family name. I don't care what your family is, but I want to know who they are. And you've got to know it, too."

"I know who my family is," said Oralio, looking around at some of the other kids in the gym.

Speedball didn't press him. He never really pressed anyone, Felipe thought, which is one reason all of them love him. He takes them as they are.

Speedball looked over and said, "Hey there, Felipe! Our man on the beat! You come to show me how?" And he mimicked a boxer throwing a punch.

"I came to teach reading," Montoya said.

"Aha!" said Speedball. "Got you! You bleeding-heart cops are such an easy touch."

"I figured I had nothing to do anyway, and—"

"Guilt! That's what it is. You feel maybe you're missing out on something, between your pistol and billy club."

"I don't have to do this, you know."

97

"Don't let me talk you out of it, just when I talked you into it! You'll see, it's a good thing. You teach a little girl to read, it feels better than shooting her head off."

"Fuck you."

"I'll give you a chance later. Now get your butt up the stairs."

It was a narrow staircase, made of wood, so all the steps creaked when he trod on them, as if they were testing his weight. At the top was a small room, large enough maybe for a desk and a water cooler, into which three desks, four chairs, and a couch had been forced—with a crowbar, Montoya assumed. At one desk on the left, a young woman sat under a lamp, reading side by side with a fifteen-year-old gang-banger, whose arms and shoulders under his T-shirt were covered in tattoos. By a quick glance, Felipe was able to see enough to identify him as a Diablo—but the kid sensed his attention, crossed his arms, and then stood.

"I think that's enough for today," he said, and started out the door.

"Ernesto!" said the young woman sitting beside him. "We're right in the middle of the chapter."

"Finish it yourself," he said from the stairs. He must have felt some regret, too, because he nodded toward Felipe and said, "Can't read under these lights without a rubber hose. See you next time, Maria."

She sighed. Ernesto disappeared, and Montoya leaned against a desk. "Not an easy task, eh?"

"It would be easier," said Maria, closing her book with a bang, "if you people would come in here with a little respect for the ones who live here."

Montoya liked the way her eyes grew big when she reprimanded him—the way her curls shook, and the skirts of her dress. *"You people?* What kind of people do you think I am?"

"A cop," said Maria.

"What makes you think so?"

"Anyone could see that. The way you stand, so sure of your footing, even here in this place. The way you looked over his shoulder just now."

"You mean that gangbanger's?"

"Ernesto's. He was just a student here."

"I wasn't reading *over* his shoulder—it was the shoulder I was reading. Are all the students like him?"

"A lot of them have been in and out of prison—in and out of gangs. And their sisters and brothers, who haven't decided yet whether to join one or not. And their parents—they come in too, if they believe this is a place they can learn to read without being made to feel like a fool."

Her eyes were lovely, and Felipe wanted to make sure he did not blow his chance of ever gazing into them more deeply. "So this is a literacy program for the Diablos and their families," he said. "Is that what you're telling me?"

"Listen," said Maria, "would you rather be teaching them how to read? Or reading them their rights?"

It was a point, Montoya conceded. And he got lucky, because when his two o'clock appointment arrived, trooping up the steep staircase, she turned out to be in her forties, the mother of one of the boys downstairs waiting for the ring. She looked at him, and then at Maria, and said, "This is the new teacher?"

Maria also turned to Montoya. "I don't know. Is it?"

Felipe sized up the woman, and she matched his expectations perfectly—the age, height, and attitude he had intended to teach reading. He bent at the waist slightly and offered his hand to the woman. "My name is Felipe Montoya, Señora."

"Imella Sánchez," she said.

"You can use the desk by the couch," Maria said, handing him the book she had been reading with Ernesto.

"No instructions?" he said. "You could sit on the couch and be critical."

She gave him a wry face. "I'll be downstairs if you need me," she said to Imella. "Try to be easy with him. You're his first."

Imella winked at her.

Forty-five minutes later Imella got up from her chair, gave him a sweet smile, and tramped down the stairs. Montoya stood up and stretched his legs. He hadn't expected her to read at all, so her competence was a surprise—she knew all of the letters in uppercase and most of them in lowercase as well. What she did not know was how they fit together to make words. The book Maria had given him wasn't the best choice, either—how could a woman who had raised seven children (plus two of her sister's, she had told him) be interested in, or challenged by, a picture book about dolphins? But he had done his best, circling the words *or, the, and, he,* and *she* when he first found them, and pausing for her to read them when they came up again. She was able to do so, most of the time, which made her feel she could read a little—not much of a start, he thought, but something.

Maria was much more effusive when he went downstairs and she joined him in the yard for a cigarette. "For your first time," she said, "you did wonderfully." He believed her, every word of praise she delivered in puffs of smoke. He liked the red marks her mouth left on the filterless tip, and the way her lips pursed when she drew in the smoke. "This is bad for us both," she said, as she tipped her head toward his for a light, and he wasn't sure whether she meant the tobacco or something else sparking between them.

He said, "Do you live around here?"

She nodded. "Around the corner."

"I grew up in this neighborhood myself," he told her.

"It's beautiful here at night."

He had never thought of it as *beautiful,* but when she turned and her dress swirled around her, he saw it in a different light. The sky was a deep blue-gray, turning to black, and the seesaw and swings, the silver slide, and the monkey bars were all empty of children. The city around them was also blue, with pedestrians moving beyond the links of the fence and cars moving behind them. Pink bricks faded to gray overhead, as the street lamps lit, illuminating a halo of leaves in the sycamores, orange and brown. It seemed to Felipe that the jarring traffic noises, the blares of horns and the screeches of brakes too suddenly applied, had for some reason surrendered their individual expressions and issued forth only as a soothing symphony, heralding the evening. Maria stood in front of him, blocking his view of the fence, framing herself in the sycamore branches. She touched her finger to her mouth to take out a speck of tobacco that had stuck to her red tongue. When she said, "I'm sure you're going to make a terrific teacher," he was convinced of it, in every muscle, valve, and chamber of his heart.

"You're an inspiration," he said.

Maria looked at him, and suddenly seemed to notice what was taking place between them in his mind. Either to break his mood, or to change the topic—or to draw him further into the charm of her world—she said, "Have you seen the paintings yet?"

"Paintings?"

"I'll show you."

She took his hand to lead him, and he didn't care where they went. There was a painting on the wall of the community center that had been sprayed onto the side next to the water fountain. It showed a family—a man, a woman, a boy, and a girl—who stood together as in a portrait, with the parents behind the children. It was crudely accomplished, but it had a simplicity that seemed to say, "This is the way a family should be." And wasn't, at least for the artist.

"One of the kids did this?"

"Yes," she said. "There's another one started on the other side." She took him around the back, behind the white concrete building, where a more ambitious scene had been laid out in black spray paint. It showed a playground scene, where mothers pushed children on the swings while their fathers played cards on the benches. It took up the entire rear wall, the long wall of the building, and was filled with activity: on the basketball court, in the sandbox, on the handball courts, and in the trees. There were birds with big beaks and long feathers, which had never seen the Bronx except in the imagination of a child who grew up here. And there was food, served on picnic blankets and the benches by mothers whose baskets were full of sandwiches, and bananas, and chocolate chip cookies. It was as if the New Deal architects who designed the playgrounds of the Bronx had seen their vision of a public area fulfilled, and then stuffed with flowers and all good things imaginable. Except in outline, in black paint, waiting for the colors that would make it rich.

Montoya whistled softly. "I'd like to see this when it's finished."

"The boy didn't come in today," said Maria sadly. "Perhaps he'll be back tomorrow."

A chill ran down Felipe's spine.

"What is his name? Do you know?"

"Mr. Stevens knows him better than I do," Maria said, "but I think his name may be . . . Rocio."

# 10

The following morning Shelly saw his grandfather crouched on the edge of his double bed, bending forward in grief or prayer—Shelly always had trouble distinguishing between them. Shelly sat up, and the old man looked over, scratching under his beard, with a casual glance of suspicion at his godless godson. That was when Shelly rolled over—except he had never in fact sat up, so the momentum threw his sleeping form over the edge of the mattress. He landed hard on the ground, his head ringing, until he realized the pain in his head was throbbing at a different rate from the noise, and reached for the telephone.

"Hullo, Shelly?"

*Max?* Perhaps they had caught the thief on the furniture floor. The thought produced a rush of relief in Shelly, but also an undeniable disappointment. If he could have just kept those commissions coming in for another week or so, he would really have socked away a few bucks. He said, "Yeah. Max. What's up?"

"You spoke to Sholem?"

Shelly rubbed his face and felt on the night table for his glasses. "Forget it, Max. It's hopeless."

"Hopeless? Nothing is hopeless. What did he say?"

"Nothing. He wouldn't talk to me."

"All right, we'll talk about it later. Now is not the time—in the middle of a tragedy."

A tragedy? What could be . . . Shelly remembered the Reb in his cell, under the scrutiny of the mug in the next cage. "Did something happen to Pirski?"

"The rabbi? No, this is about his victim."

*"His* victim?"

"No, of course not *his*. You see what this business has done to me? Now I'm indicting my friends. I mean *the* victim—the woman who died. Lily Levinski."

It was the first time Shelly had heard Max pronounce the name of the deceased, and he was surprised to hear a note of personal intimacy in his voice.

"Feel like telling me about her?"

"When you're here," said Max.

"Where?"

"At the mortuary. A funeral service for Lillian. All of her friends are here." Which meant, of course, all of his suspects.

When Shelly arrived at the mortuary on the Concourse, he was surprised to see a large crowd gathering in front—nearly double the number of the evening before. The difference, he realized, was in women, who stood in a group apart from their husbands, talking to one another in low voices, shaking their heads, some of which were wrapped in fringed shawls. They looked at first like a crowd of aging immigrants until Shelly noticed that the fabrics were wrong: Instead of cotton, these shawls were woven, finely embroidered of expensive wool.

Inside, Shelly found Max, who moved away from Schneider when he saw Lowenkopf enter.

"Nice turnout," Shelly said.

"This is it—the whole community. Everyone came."

"You didn't really need me for a minyan, then."

"We don't need a minyan for a funeral, Shelly. But how many men do you see? Still nine, including the hazzan and the mortuary's own rabbi."

"But all the women—"

"Don't count in a minyan. You see?"

Not for the Orthodox, Shelly saw.

Schneider passed them, moving to a seat in the front part of the mortuary's sanctuary, wiping his red eyes on a handkerchief. Max patted him on his shoulder as he passed and sighed deeply.

"She was a lovely lady, Shell."

"You knew her?"

"We all knew her," Max said with feeling, and then hesitated before going on. "Lily was a member of the congregation in her own right. Women don't come to *mincha-ma'ariv* services, you know. They're usually home, preparing the Sabbath meal, waiting for their husbands to come home. They'll come on Shabbas morning, or on high holy days. Or they'll come for a wedding, or a special occasion. But Lillian would come on Friday afternoons, sitting alone behind the *mechitzah*. Among all those empty chairs."

He glanced toward the back of the room, where a section of chairs was closed off from the front section by a sheer lace curtain on a rod.

"She sat all alone? Behind the curtain?"

There was a long pause before Max said, "You weren't brought up *frum*, were you?"

"You mean Orthodox?"

"Observant. In our tradition, the men and the women are separated during services. To prevent distractions. The men sit in their regular seats, in front. And the women sit in the back, behind the curtain."

It wasn't hard for Shelly to understand why more of them didn't make it to services, then—it was a wonder that Lily did. And he began to wonder whether it wasn't a wonder to the other men as well. They were either an unusually emotional crowd, or Lillian had meant a great deal to each of the men, because there were many red eyes among the congregants seating themselves in front. The hazzan was at the *bima*, the area around the altar, busying himself as he had the night before with a prayer book. As each man came in, he adjusted the yarmulke on his head and tucked a black prayer book under his arm, heading for a seat with a heavy step and a solemn air, nodding in silence to the others as he passed down the aisle.

The women came in from the street more casually, filing into the seats behind the *mechitzah* with babies in their arms, pulling older children into chairs alongside them. The atmosphere behind the curtain was less grave, as the women murmured to one another, preparing to listen rather than participate. Shelly noticed that they had no prayer books with them.

By the time Max led Shelly to a seat in the first row, all of the others had assembled. Schneider's red eyes had welled over, and he was making a quiet sobbing sound in the back of his throat. On the far side of Schneider, Jacob Zweizig stared ahead blankly, not seeing Hazzan Tsinger as he passed back and forth before his eyes. In the row behind them, David Horowitz sat all alone, one arm over each of the chairs to his left and his right, holding himself deliberately erect. By the grip of his fingers on the chair backs, Shelly saw a great deal of restrained emotion in the man, whose public composure just barely concealed a great private inner turmoil. Even Stanley Blumberg managed to be awake for the occasion, sitting across from the Minsky brothers in the third row of chairs. The Minskys sat silently, side by side, neither of them apparently able or willing to look his brother in the face.

"What's going on here, Max?"

"Grieving, Shelly. We're at a funeral service."

"Are they all like this?"

"You mean so—"

"Emotional? It looks like they've each lost their dearest friend." Shelly turned to Max, and only then noticed the tear in the corner of his partner's eye.

"Max?" he said. "You all right?"

Max waved away his sympathy. "It was a long time ago. If you want to feel sorry for someone, feel for Schneider."

Shelly glanced at the man across the aisle, who was now weeping silently.

"Her latest?"

Max shook his head, placing a finger to his lips, as a young rabbi descended the stairs and took a seat in the first row. "Not her latest," he whispered. "Her husband."

*Schneider?* Shelly stared at the back of the Czech's bald head, from which his yarmulke kept slipping. He held it on with one hand as he stood, the worn prayer book gripped in his other. Shelly followed the congregation in standing also, as the hazzan sang out a clear, sad note. From the deep chests of the aging men came a hoarse sound, like wind through empty rain barrels, which suggested a rough melodic line only when they rose together to emphasize a phrase of special significance. When the psalm ended, and the hazzan began to read from his prayer book, the men accompanied him, each of them reading at a slightly different pace, rocking forward and back in their places, *davening*. During prayer, it is said, the soul floats a little in front of the body, so the men leaned into it and sank back, closing their eyes and reciting the lines of Hebrew they had pronounced so many times before. Next to Shelly,

Max stood relatively still, his head bent over the prayer book in his hands. But his eyes were closed, too. As if by common agreement, they all seemed to pause at once. And then David Horowitz, their president, advanced to the lectern.

He said, "We have come today to honor the memory of a beautiful woman. Lillian Levinski was beautiful at the end of her life, which was long and full of kindness. But I will always remember her as a young woman, with a voice like the sigh of a baby nestled into her mother's arms—full of peace, giving peace even as she stirred something deep inside our hearts. Each of us has his special memory of her, his own Lillian. As for me . . . that I shall never hear her voice again, never hear her pronounce my name—"

And he choked for a moment before controlling himself.

"Lillian Levinski—wherever you are—may you rest in peace with God," he said, and seemed surprised when the hazzan burst into the first wails of a song. Horowitz looked at Tsinger as if they had agreed to do something else next, but the congregants were untroubled by it, and Shelly found himself moved by the rhythms of a prayer whose words were a mystery to him. He had taken a prayer book at Max's instruction when they entered into the sanctuary, but whatever deciphering of the Hebrew letters he had been forced to learn to perform his own bar mitzvah nearly thirty years before had slipped away from disuse over the years since then. His grandfather had been a religious man, in his shul on the Grand Concourse, but Shelly's father had already let their family's spiritual connection slide as he made his way in the new country, and by the time their tradition had fallen to Shelly to learn, it was an obstacle to be overcome for the sake of his lingering grandfather. He could have made out the letters one by one, if there was all the time in the world; but the pace at which these old men recited their prayers was much too fast for him to follow. Here and there as the service progressed, he could recognize a word as it disappeared among those succeeding it. Shelly finally gave up trying to read along and listened to the sounds of the men around him murmuring their ancient tongue, exactly as he might have listened to American Indian medicine men or the priest of an African tribe. Max reached over and turned the page of Shelly's prayer book for him.

Shelly felt ignorant of the culture of these people. That it was his own heritage did not make him enjoy it any better. But there was nothing he could do until the service ended, when he could turn his attention to a professional interest, by eavesdropping. He hoped to learn how each of them felt about Lillian. But the talk was not limited to grieving over the deceased. In fact, as Shelly walked around he heard very little discussion of Lillian—at least, in English. Of course, it was the women who did most of the talking, and the men who did most of the grieving. But it seemed to him odd until he had a chance to catch Max by the collar and ask him just what he had meant by "her husband."

"I meant her husband," said Max. "More or less."

"Well, which was it?" asked Shelly. "More or less?"

Max shrugged. "Depends who you ask."

"I'm asking you."

"I'm not the right person to be asking."

Shelly looked around the room, at the women, starting to gather up their children, and the men, who stood silently in twos and threes, lost in their memories.

"There's no one else I can ask, Max. How complicated could it be? Were they married or weren't they?"

"They were married," explained Max, "a few years

· ago. Then something happened—who knows what? She wanted a *get*—you know what that is? A writ of divorce. In our tradition only the husband can draft one. He has to give it to his wife to set her free."

"What if he doesn't want to?"

"Ah . . . what if he doesn't? Jewish law says that a woman can go to the *Beit Din*, the religious court, who can order a man to give his wife a *get*. In the old days, if he refused, they could force him to do it—they could lock him up if he didn't."

"But now?"

"What can they do now? They have no real power anymore. Lillian went to the *Beit Din* for a decree, complaining of three things: that he clicked his teeth in his sleep, that he bored her with stories about his first wife, and that they didn't have sex often enough."

"Are those acceptable grounds?"

"Any grounds can be acceptable if the court is sympathetic. There is a story that a woman once went to a *Beit Din* because her husband didn't like her soup. The rabbis decided that there must have been something more wrong, or she never would have brought the case to them. So they granted it, and commanded the husband to issue a *get.*"

"Is that what happened to Lillian?"

"Not quite. The *Beit Din* heard her case for a *get* and they commanded Sol to issue one. But he snubbed his nose at them."

"He refused?"

"He said that the grounds were insufficient. He told them he would put his teeth in the glass at night, and stop telling stories about his first wife."

"And the sex?"

"He said a man has to draw the line somewhere."

"Did that satisfy her?"

Max fell silent for a moment, remembering. "She was a truly remarkable woman, Shell."

"I take it she didn't go for the compromise, then."

"She did not. But that was as far as Solly was prepared to accommodate her."

"He refused to give her the *get?*"

"Absolutely."

"Couldn't the court issue one for her?"

"Only the husband can."

"So what did she do? Make him regret it?"

"She was too fine a person for anything like that. She went to a civil court and applied for an American divorce on the grounds of irreconcilable differences. Schneider sat sullenly throughout the hearing, refusing to cooperate, which, of course, only convinced the judge to give it to her."

"Do they recognize that?"

"Who?"

"I don't know . . . the congregation. Those women over there. The Orthodox community."

"That's three separate answers," Max said. "Those women, I suspect, do recognize it. The congregation, of course, is made up of individuals, some of whom are sympathetic to Sol, others of whom sided with Lily. The situation in our community, if by that you mean the *official* Orthodox community, is more complicated. They are, of course, divorced under American law. Orthodox Jews in America live by the laws of the land, Shelly—as a rule, we tend to be a particularly patriotic group."

"So the divorce is recognized."

"Of course it's recognized—how could anybody miss it? Just not for every purpose under heaven, that's all."

"For example?"

"Have you ever heard of an *ag-u-nah?* In the old days, if a man was lost at sea, but there weren't two witnesses who could swear to it, his wife became an *agunah*—a chained woman. She had no husband, of course, but couldn't be married, either. Lillian was in something of the same position."

"Chained . . . to Sol?"

"In a manner of speaking. You see, they were divorced. No one doubted that. Only, without a *get*, no Orthodox rabbi would agree to marry her to anyone else—even if she found an Orthodox man willing to take her. Which wouldn't be too easy, since their marriage might be viewed as adulterous and their children as illegitimate."

Shelly whistled. "So that left her—where?"

"Nowhere," Max replied. "Neither married, nor available. A woman on her own."

"An *AH-gu-nah*," said Shelly.

"The accent falls on the last syllable," Max corrected him.

But Shelly's attention had shifted. Like a grief-seeking missile, his gaze sought out and located the still-half-a-husband Sol Schneider, who slouched in a chair in the first row of the sanctuary, weeping uncontrollably into his hands.

# 11

Max spared Shelly the graveside service, since the edge of the grave always brought out the most powerful emotions; Max was not sure how his new partner felt about those he had witnessed at the shul. It was a cool, crisp day at the cemetery on Long Island. A wind blew, a melancholy whistle sweeping across the headstones that helped the mourners restrain their individual expressions of grief. Afterwards, those who wished to do so could retreat to the Schneider apartment on Waring Avenue by the park, where Sol would be sitting *shiva,* keeping the week-long vigil of mourning in remembrance of his wife.

Max was not entirely surprised to see Shelly Lowenkopf knock at the door half an hour after the graveside mourners arrived. He was more surprised to see the box of prune danish Shelly bore with him, its pink cardboard sealed with a red and white string. There were some Jewish traditions that transcended the difference between modern, liberal, and traditional observance, and prune danish seemed to be one of them. Shelly handed the box to one of the women who had taken charge of Sol's kitchen, who rinsed off a platter from the cabinet, lined it with an unfolded napkin, and arranged the danish for display on the kitchen table.

The apartment had been prepared ahead of time, presumably by some of the other women who passed up the graveside service in order to arrange a meal to be served to the mourners who came to the house. Near the platter of danish was a variety of pastry—twisted dough wrapped with honey and nuts just big enough to pop in your mouth. There was honey cake, of course, and strudel, with cheese filling and with grape. The other end of the table was set with fish—herring and smoked whitefish and sturgeon and lox—with rye bread and bagels and hexagonal crackers made of matzoh. There was cream cheese and farmer cheese and a sliced yellow cheese like Muenster, only sweeter, and plenty of hard-boiled eggs. A salad plate was put into Shelly's hands by the woman who placed his danish on the table, and he was commanded to eat.

He took a little salad with sour cream, and then tasted one of the herrings—*matjes,* he thought it was, in a purplish sauce. The flavor brought him back suddenly to his grandmother's kitchen table, where his grandfather would sit on Sunday mornings, with the *Forward* in one hand, scowling at the editorials, and a piece of seeded corn bread in the other, scooping gobs of onion and herring in creamy white sauce, which he shot between his whiskers into his mouth.

The thought of his grandfather helped Shelly see Max and his crowd with some perspective. His grandfather had been a truly religious man: His preference would have been to study the Torah whenever he was free to do so. For Max and his colleagues, the shul was less of a link to God than to their own cultural history as members of a community that was rapidly aging. They had been reared in this tradition and kept it as a token of faith to their parents and the generations who had been left behind to confront the Nazis in Eastern Europe and Russia. Their families had died in the Jewish Pale, a territory that crossed national borders in the Ukraine, Poland, Czechoslovakia, and surrounding areas in which Jews had been permitted to reside. Some had crossed Poland from Warsaw to Gdansk, where they took ship, acquiring new names from the German shipping agents who managed that trade. In this Shelly was one of them, connected by birth and family heritage, although the religious tradition they practiced and cherished had never been his own. What would his grandfather have thought of these people? Shelly couldn't help wondering. And what would he have thought of his grandson?

Max had disappeared momentarily, but he soon came out of the bedroom, closing the door quietly behind him. In a fast glimpse before it shut completely, Shelly saw some of the men huddled around in an effort to solace Sol. The grieving half-husband sat on the edge of a neatly made bed, queen size or bigger, gripping the spread in his bloodless fists, fighting off a crying jag. One of them—maybe Horowitz—bent over him, whispering urgently in his ear, but Schneider shook his head violently, unwilling or unable to forgive and forget. Max glanced back, shook his head, and then turned to Shelly with a cheerful expression.

"So? Gloomy enough for you?"

The apartment had been prepared for sitting *shiva* with an array of special symbolism. The mirror over the table by the entrance door had been covered with a white pillowcase, which had been tucked in at the corners. Half a dozen wooden boxes served as seats for the family mourners, who seemed to be limited to Sol himself. Music was not permitted, nor any sort of distraction such as cards or business talk. An air of solemnity was supposed to reign, although the women

115

in the kitchen seemed to be enjoying one another's company, and, when the door to Sol's bedroom was closed, you could even hear an occasional laugh from that quarter.

As usual, Max was drawn to the sound of women's laughter. "Let me introduce you," he said to Shelly, who considered himself a vehicle for Max to mix with the ladies.

"Why not?"

He shrugged and felt uneasy, recognizing the gesture as one of Max's. Max seemed to recognize it too—he clapped Shelly on the back and led him into the kitchen, where three women had been enjoying a joke but abandoned it at once. By the way that she blushed on their entrance, Shelly guessed that the joke had been at the expense of the tallest of the three, who was younger than the others by thirty to fifty years. She couldn't have been more than nineteen, though the dress and apron, and kerchief in her hair, made her look several years older.

"I didn't know there was anyone here like you," he said without thinking, and only then realized the declaration he had made. The two older women examined him closely, and Max grinned even more broadly.

"Ladies," he said, "I would like to present my new *partner,*" lingering on the last word. "Shelly Lowenkopf is new to my firm, a recent recruit from the police department—from the Homicide Division."

The youngest one glanced over, her eyes wide, but looked down quickly, blushing. They were brown, unlined and unshadowed, but still strikingly large against her pale complexion.

"Homicide?" said one of the others suspiciously. She was shorter than her companion but also twenty pounds heavier, with a definite resemblance. She seemed to address her question not to Shelly or even to Max, but to the white-haired woman at the sink, who was skinny but wiry, scrubbing a pot as if she intended to scrape off a few layers of aluminum.

The old woman mumbled something in reply.

"That's just what I was thinking, Mama," said the short one fiercely, as she handed a plate to her own daughter for drying. "That's a dangerous job, isn't it?"

It came as an accusation: How dare he take the risk? Didn't he care about the women in his life? Did he realize how they would suffer if anything happened to him? Or didn't he have any women in his life?

Shelly wasn't sure how to answer a question that hadn't been asked aloud. The young one seemed more than casually interested in his reply.

"For some men, maybe," said Max. "Not for Shelly, here. One of the shrewdest *keps* in the outfit." And he tapped his own temple for emphasis.

*"Nu?"* said the girl's mother. "You planning to introduce us or not?"

Max did, and Shelly learned that the pot scrubber was Sol's mother, Helen, with her daughter Irene—the one Shelly suspected Max had his eye on. The slender girl was Irene's daughter Julia, who risked a glance at Shelly when her name was pronounced. In that fleeting contact of their eyes, Shelly felt an entire life of modesty and self-containment, as one might see in the face of a girl raised in a convent who steps out into the larger world for the very first time. The question behind Julia's bright eyes was, *Might you be the one?* And it pained Shelly's heart to have to acknowledge that no, he wasn't *him.*

Julia's eyes dimmed, and Shelly knew they would never glow so brightly for him again.

Irene watched this silent exchange, and relaxed her guard a bit. If Julia knew he wasn't the one, she could handle him herself. Irene's comforting arm settled around her daughter's slender shoulders and she asked in politeness and idle curiosity, "So what brings you to a house of mourning, Mr. Lowenkopf?"

"Max," replied Shelly.

Irene gave Max a disapproving scowl, which he returned as a smile, and Shelly realized they were flirting.

"I asked him to the synagogue, to make a minyan," Max said.

"Then you're here to replace my husband," said Irene.

Shelly wasn't sure how she meant that, and he wasn't sure if the glint in her eye was for him now or for Max.

"He was the tenth man," Irene explained, "my Abie was! The last one to make a minyan. But he went to the doctor with a little gas, and they brought him home dead."

"A heart attack. Eight months ago," Max murmured.

"Such a young man!" went on Irene. "Can you believe it? Our hazzan, old Tsinger, had an aneurysm at the same time. He comes home fit as a fiddle and my Abie comes home in a box."

"Itzak Tsinger's not what he once was," Helen reminded her daughter.

"You should see Abie!" said Irene. Then she seemed to remember Shelly and turned to Max. "This is a fine conversation to be having with a guest."

"I invited him just to the shul," Max replied, with a shrug. "He decided to pay a *shiva* call on his own."

Irene didn't believe him; which meant, if true, it would resound to Max's credit.

"I wanted to come," Shelly said.

"If you don't mind my asking," Irene asked, "why?"

Shelly hesitated. "There's always a lot to be learned about a case right after the funeral. It's a time when people think about their own mortality, and everyone wants to get something or other off their chest. You'd be amazed at what you hear, if you listen."

"Are we a case?" asked Irene.

Another stumper; and again Max came to his rescue.

"I've asked Shelly to look into this business about Lillian. To try to do something for Rabbi Pirski."

Max was playing a big card—but Irene wrinkled her nose as if she had smelled something rotten. "That *farbissener*—it's about time they got him."

"Irene!" said Helen.

"It's true, and you know it, Mama," insisted Irene. "A man ought to get what's coming to him."

"The police seem to agree with you," Shelly said. "They're holding him in a precinct cell. But the ballistics report has come in, and it doesn't look good to me."

Max was not happy to hear it. "You think the tests will show . . . ?"

"I *know* that the tests will show that Lillian Levinski was killed by a bullet from the rabbi's own pistol. The one he kept in his desk drawer."

"But how can they prove it was the same gun? The same size, maybe. But the identical pistol?"

"They can do it—take it from me. Inside the barrel of a rifle or a handgun are a series of grooves etched in the metal. These produce what are called lands, which cut grooves into a bullet as it passes through, so that it rotates in the air along its axis instead of rolling head-over-heels toward the target. The caliber of a firearm is the distance from one land to another on the opposite side of the barrel."

Max shook his head, not about to accept it so easily. "So? Let's say they measure the same. There are different guns of the same caliber."

"Yes, but the number and direction of the grooves

119

they carve into bullets is different from manufacturer to manufacturer, and from gun to gun. They'll take the bullet out of Lillian and any others they find in the room. Then they'll shoot a fresh bullet from Pirski's gun into wadding, or into water. They match up the test bullet against the ones they recovered from the scene under a special comparison microscope. If they match, the bullets came from the same gun. Any judge and jury will accept it."

Julia seemed to follow his explanation rather well, but her mother's eyes were crossing.

"All right," said Max, "so let's say they can prove it's the same gun. That doesn't mean he used it, does it?"

"Not by itself. But the rabbi said he always kept it in his desk drawer, and always kept the key in his pocket. Did you see the lock on the drawer? It wasn't picked or forced. Now how do you suppose someone got into his pants, took out the key, got the gun, used the gun, and returned the key, without tipping off the rabbi that something was going on?"

"Sometimes, when a man is reading," Max said slowly, "when a true scholar is deeply engaged with his material—anything could happen and he might not notice."

"They also took a G.S.R.—a gunshot residue test," Shelly said. "They apply a coat of melted paraffin to the hands and wrists, which opens up the pores, flushing out traces of nitrites left behind when a gun is fired. Any bets on how that turns out for Pirski?"

Max thought for a minute. "Is gunpowder the only thing that leaves a residue on the hands in that test?"

"No—sometimes tobacco, for example, might be picked up instead . . ."

"Ah!" said Max. "There you have it."

"What?" asked Shelly. "Does the rabbi smoke cigars?"

"Not cigars—cigarettes! He chain-smokes them, in private. Didn't you notice the ashtray in his office?"

Shelly remembered it, overflowing with filterless butts. But before he could reply in the affirmative, he felt a tugging at his jacket sleeve.

"Excuse me," Irene said hesitantly, "but are you saying that someone believes the rabbi shot Lillian?"

"That's exactly what I'm saying the police believe," Shelly repeated.

"Impossible," said Helen.

He turned to Irene. "Isn't that what you were suggesting a moment ago yourself?"

Irene placed her hand to her mouth, in shock at the idea. "That he murdered her? With a gun? Bang, bang—just like that? Like a criminal?"

"But you just called him a . . ."

*"Farbissener?* That's a sourpuss—a mean-spirited individual. Not a murderer! How do they imagine he could do such a thing? As a rabbi?"

She took Max's arm, to comfort herself. And he patted her hand with his own.

Shelly shrugged. "You never know. Any kind of person can be a killer."

But the others were not inclined to wonder at that strange fact. For the first time, Helen, Irene, and Max were together, shaking their heads in agreement.

"Shelly," said Max, "he couldn't. Not Sholem."

Irene was content to let Max speak for both of them, but she nodded her acquiescence.

Helen snorted.

Even Julia was looking at him again, with sympathy in her eyes. He was mistaken, her expression said. She felt sorry for his error, deeply and sincerely. But how long would he persist in refusing to see it himself?

"Somebody shot her," Shelly said. "A neighbor overheard a conversation Friday night between Lillian and a man. Lillian told him it was time for him to go, or he'd be late for services. The man is reported to have said, 'They can't begin without me.' That sounds like a rabbi to me."

"It all depends how you interpret it," Max demurred.

"How else could you interpret it?"

"You and I are in the business of defending people, Shelly. Not prosecuting them. That turns the whole thing around."

"How?"

"Well . . . a rabbi is certainly the obvious one whose absence would hold up a service. But if you assume the speaker could not have been the rabbi—based on what you know about his character—then it must have been somebody else."

"All right," said Shelly, "then who? You could pray without the hazzan, couldn't you?"

"Since his surgery, we often do."

"Well, then," Shelly said in exasperation, "is there anybody else essential to a service?"

"Don't forget who we are, Shell," Max reminded him gently. "A regular congregation could conduct a service without a hazzan, or any particular worshiper. But we are a special case. In order to make a minyan, it takes every one of us. Until all ten assemble, the service cannot begin."

"That would mean—"

Max's spotted hand dropped heavily onto Shelly's shoulder, and he shuddered with a sigh of remorse. It was the only way he could stop Shelly from saying aloud what he felt he should say aloud himself.

"I'm afraid it must be true," he said, apparently to Helen. "The murderer is one of our minyan."

# 12

The telephone rang on Homer's desk, and, as she was starting to do all the time now in the hope that it would become expected of her, Jill Morganthal reached across the double expanse of their facing desks and lifted his receiver from its cradle. As she nestled it under her chin she almost said "Hello," and would have said something a moment later, but didn't get it settled in right, before the voice on the other end was talking to her.

"Felipe Montoya here. I think I got something."

Again, she almost explained that she was not Homer Greeley but his newly assigned partner, Officer Morganthal; but the name Felipe Montoya rang no bells for her, and if he was an informant who really did have something, it would have been a shame to lose it just because Homer had gone to the bathroom. So she said nothing and Felipe continued.

"About that kid the other night. Lucero. Remember? With the spray can, by the fence?"

He was evidently expecting an answer now; Jill felt

to go on any longer without identifying herself would constitute a clear dishonesty, which was not a luxury she allowed herself, no matter how helpful the tip might eventually prove.

"I read the report, Officer Montoya," she said. "I'm afraid Sergeant Greeley can't come to the phone at the moment. But I can take whatever you've got for us."

"Who the hell are you?" said Montoya.

Jill sighed. It was always like this: Not only did she have to prove herself each day as tough as a man, but, having secured the desirable placement as Homer Greeley's partner, she had to demonstrate on a continual basis that she could be trusted as an equal partner with him. It was a trial, but she was accustomed to facing trials. She would do whatever she had to do to prove herself again; she was tough and she was smart—if she hadn't been, would Homer have requested her as a temporary partner? It was true, he had expected his old partner back after a brief medical leave. But was it her fault that Lowenkopf had decided to resign from the force rather than come back? And hadn't the captain specifically asked Homer how their pairing was working out? She would rather he had responded with something more than "Well enough, I suppose," but that was a small thing, really—he had made no sustained objection when Madagascar had partnered them more or less permanently. That "more or less" had been a concession to Homer, she conceded, but they had been working out fantastically —far better, it seemed to her, than Homer had ever really worked out with Shelly Lowenkopf.

In fact, Jill could not understand why the officers they encountered, and technicians and support staff, did not stand up and give her a round of applause, welcoming her with open arms after struggling with Shelly Lowenkopf. In almost every area of police work she considered herself superior to Homer's previous partner: Her annual arrest record for her first two years was far better than his; her skills of observation, detecting details at the scene of a crime, made his an embarrassment. Oh, she had read his notes, as well as Homer's, on many of their cases together, and it seemed to Jill only fair to admit that Homer had carried their team for years—you could see it in the notes! Lowenkopf's were all about the people he encountered, what they seemed to be feeling, or not feeling, about the case. Greeley's were filled with real information: the height and weight of each person, and the color of their eyes and hair. When she read Homer's notes, she could picture each suspect standing in front of her; when she read Lowenkopf's, she found herself lost in a confusing whirl of possible motives and doubts. So she could not understand—for the life of her—why, whenever they were out together, and Homer looked her way, there crossed his face first a look of surprise, and then one of wonder, followed inevitably by a blankness that could not hide a certain disappointment from her. Jill was much more like him than Shelly had ever been; why did he continue to miss his old partner so much?

"Hey!" Montoya said. "You still there?"

"Still here," said Morganthal. Was this Montoya—Felipe—one of their friends together? Or was his connection to Homer personal and individual? Was she dealing with someone who knew Lowenkopf too? And, if so, did he like him or see him for what he was?

"Where is Homer, exactly?"

"He's not available," said Jill, who preferred not to go into details with a strange man over the telephone. "My name is Jill Morganthal. I'm a detective working with Sergeant Greeley now. I can take your information, or take a message for him. Or you can hold on until he returns to his desk."

"In the can, eh?" said Montoya. "All right. Just tell

him I found somebody who's willing to admit he knew Rocio—says he was a really nice kid. With a sense of humor."

"You think he may be able to provide a lead to the killing?" Jill said while she jotted down the note.

"That's your job to find out, isn't it?" She didn't know quite how to respond before Montoya hung up.

Jill realized she had not taken any numbers from him, either the informant's or his own. If they were going to follow up on this lead, Homer would have to call him. She hoped—and knew in the pit of her stomach—that Homer would have gotten his number the first time they had talked.

She sighed again, and consoled herself with the thought that she and Homer really shared what was essential to a police team: a common vision of the importance of their work, a desire to make the city safe for decent women and children to live in without fear. There was all sorts of evil on the streets out there, but they would face it together, secure in the knowledge that each of them knew the good guys from the bad guys.

If the thought crossed her mind that a certain amount of ambivalence might be an appropriate response to the complexity of human aspiration and suffering, she brushed it away as she did the one curl of brown hair that insisted on slipping down over her brown eyes whenever she bent her head to write. Her message was short and sweet: MONTOYA CALLED WITH A LEAD. J. It would have been easier just to tell him about it, if he ever returned from the john. What was keeping him? His visits there seemed to be growing longer and more frequent with each week they worked together as a team.

Homer Greeley was not, in fact, in the john anymore; he had stopped in just to comb his hair—to check it, really, since it didn't really need to be combed again, which he saw when he looked at it again in the mirror. What he had really wanted was the walk, a chance to stretch his legs in the hallway back and forth again. Except that he did not feel like walking back yet—at least, not with the long strides that had carried him away from the squad room. He stood in front of a window at the end of the hall, gazing through the crosshatched wire mesh, past the black-and-whites parked on the curb in front of the precinct house to the prewar apartment buildings that bordered on the Allerton Avenue station house. This neighborhood had once been the country, he knew. Shelly had told him how his parents had moved to the Bronx for his mother's health; they had come for the air. And Shelly himself remembered a farm on his walk to school. Where had they gone, those stalks of corn? All Homer saw now were storefronts on the street level, with dwellings overhead, where generations of immigrants had come to their first America. Lots of Jews once, like Shelly's family, and Italians, too—the two groups lived together in neighborhoods all over the city. Now blacks and Latinos were the groups moving in, but the streets retained markings of its earlier inhabitants. Not just the stores—the kosher butcher, bagel shop, and corner delicatessen—but also the enterprises that failed long ago.

At the very end of the avenue, where it entered Bronx Park, were two square blocks of brown brick buildings that had been built in the thirties as a cooperative, one of the earliest in the city and maybe the country. It had been funded and organized by idealistic people who had wanted to raise their kids together in socially conscious groups. There was a clubhouse for the eight-year-olds, and another one for the age group a year or two ahead. The co-op had eventually failed, and been sold. But the brown brick buildings remained apartments with beautifully land-

scaped courtyards, and the neighborhood still called
the place The Coops in common parlance. So the
aspirations of one generation created the scene for
another, as cultural groups replaced each other in the
alleys and on the roofs. What was going on right now,
in the alleys around the precinct house? On a rooftop
nearby, two kids were balled together. Good for you,
Homer thought. Go to it. If Rocio Lucero had been
doing more of that on Friday, he wouldn't be stretched
out on a slab in the city morgue.

He felt a sudden jab on his shoulder and spun
around. It was Jill, hanging on to her leather bag strap.

"You got a call," she said. "From Montoya. He
thinks he's got someone willing to talk about Lucero."

"Who?"

"He wouldn't say," Jill told him demurely. "Why
don't you call him and ask?"

She was always making those remarks, implying
complaints about how she was treated because she
was a woman. Well, Homer thought, she had come
pretty far pretty fast. There were plenty of men who
would have liked to be his partner after Shelly. And
several of them, Homer felt, deserved the assignment
at least as much as she. Hadn't he taken her on, in the
first place, on a voluntary though temporary basis?
And hadn't he then allowed the assignment to drag on
indefinitely? He didn't see what she had to complain
about, all things considered.

"What's his number?" he asked.

"I thought you had it," replied Jill.

When he dug it out of the directory and called
Montoya at his home, Greeley was pleased to learn
that the person who might talk to them was Speedball
Stevens. He had heard about Stevens's project in the
community center, and though he had dismissed it at
the time as a waste of high-profile energy, Shelly had
raised some good points about finding some other

avenue for the energy on the street. Homer had thought about it since then.

Jill, however, scowled at the place when they pulled up in their Reliant. There was a basketball game in progress on the court outside, and they arrived just in time to see a big guy go up for a rebound, miss, and dig his elbow into the belly of the kid who brought it down.

The big guy said, "That's the way it goes, José," as he dribbled off with the ball.

José sat on the floor, rubbing his belly. "I'm glad you're on my side, Torquemada," he said.

Jill snorted. "There you have it—the battle of the streets is won on the playing fields of the projects."

"Let's go find Speedball," Homer said.

They found him inside the center, applying a gauze bandage to the forearm of a teenager, who flexed his fist, watched his muscles tighten under the gauze, and trotted off with a wave of thanks to Speedball.

"Wonder how he got that," Jill mused.

"I never ask them," replied Speedball. "If you do, they won't bring 'em to you—they'll just bleed all over instead. Can't have anybody slipping on these nice waxed floors."

Homer introduced himself and mumbled something about Jill. He explained they didn't want to interfere with the fine work of the center—he said whatever he thought Shelly might have in such a situation. And when Stevens heard why they had come, he was immediately forthcoming.

"Rocio Lucero never stood a chance," he said quietly, first to Jill. When she did not respond with much sympathy in her eyes, he directed himself to Homer.

"He was a gangbanger?"

"He was a writer—a graffito artist."

"And a gangbanger?"

"He was a Diablo," Stevens conceded, "like many others here. And his life, up to the point of his death, was like many of theirs as well."

"All we want to know is—" Jill began.

"I'll tell you what you *need* to know," said Stevens, "if you allow me."

"Go ahead," said Homer. "Tell it your way."

Speedball glanced at Jill, to see if she would say anything. Then he said, "His mother was a strawberry —one of those women who will do anything for crack. She must have been very beautiful once, but by the time I saw her, when he dragged her in here to sign him up for the center, she looked like a scarecrow in a fright wig. About six months ago she was arrested. For prostitution. In one of those houses."

"A whorehouse?" asked Jill.

"A crack house," replied Speedball. "She would blow anybody for a hit, right there on the couches, in front of the other customers. I think Rocio saw her once. Somebody dropped a dime on that place and I keep hoping it was him."

Homer had taken calls like that—he never wanted to know who made them.

"So the social services came and took him away," Jill said. "To a foster home?"

"No, they didn't," said Speedball, with a grudging respect in his voice. "I don't know how he avoided it, but Rocio managed to stay on his own, waiting for her. I don't think he ate much at first, other than what he ate here, which was by no means a diet. We're not licensed to dispense food, but the teachers here will sometimes share their lunch with a kid who looks like he needs it badly enough. Rocio used to look that way a lot of the time."

"Didn't he have any relatives?" Homer asked. "Even friends, who were willing to take him in?"

"He made friends," Speedball said. "They were

called Los Diablos. They fed him and they made him feel good about himself. They liked him, as a person, and that was probably the first time anybody had ever let him feel that way."

Jill snorted. "And all they asked in exchange was—"

"That he be one of them," Speedball answered. "And he was one of them—he became an important man, in their reckoning. He was smart, for one thing, and they recognized it. One of their leaders, Oralio, always used to call him a 'funny fellow'—I have no idea where he learned that phrase."

"From TV," said Jill.

"Probably, in Oralio's case," Stevens agreed. "But Rocio was an unusual kid. He had a lot of time to kill, living alone, waiting for his mother's release. He used to fill it reading. That's why he stopped by this place—not to box, but for books. He read all that we have here, which aren't so many, and then one of the teachers showed him how to get a library card."

"It was found on his body," Homer said.

"Very sad," Speedball continued. "But, you know, you could see it coming."

"How?"

"About six weeks ago, his mother came out," Stevens said. "Rocio had done that first painting— did you see it on the wall by the water fountain? It was meant as a gift for her, something for him to show her on her release. He brought her down here, and we all told her how much we thought of Rocio, and I could see he was judging every single thing he had done since her arrest as it was reflected in her smile. And she did smile at him—she smiled a lot. Whatever happened next, I can vouch for the fact that she did love him on that day."

Stevens fell silent for a moment, remembering, until Homer prodded him. "What did happen next?"

131

"I don't know, for sure," said Stevens. "You could see the change in Rocio. He was alarmed, but determined not to allow things to return to what they had been. Then he was angry, full of rage. And then he just seemed to surrender, and his spirit collapsed inside him."

"And you have no idea why?"

"A couple of weeks ago, his mother took in a new boyfriend. Rocio didn't like it, but, you know, those things happen—a woman takes a new lover and her kids have to adjust to it. Everybody needs love, after all."

He looked at Jill as if he expected her to nod, but she held her attitude stiffly.

"He complained to you?"

"No, he didn't complain. He struggled against him, for the soul of his mother. And then, I think what happened was this man decided to pimp her again, and Rocio objected, and he was thrown out of the house. He went nuts."

"What kind of nuts?"

"I saw him on the street with some of the others, and his whole demeanor was different. He was fearless—not brave, but indifferent to the consequences of his actions. This is a very political community they live in; you've got to know who's going to feel how about what you do. And with Rocio, it was like he didn't care anymore."

Homer knew what he meant. "As if he didn't care if he lived or died."

"I think he didn't anymore. He didn't care about anything. You know, he used to tell me about a graffito work on the side of an abandoned construction job, not far from here. They call it the Foundation. Rocio thought it was beautiful—he used to tell me about it. It was an inspiration to the work he was laying out on the back of this building. He wanted me to go see it, to show it to me. Then I heard he had written it over—in a squiggle of red spray paint."

"Gangs overwrite each other all the time," said Jill.

"Rocio didn't," said Speedball. "And then, one day, he did. There was an incident in the schoolyard, with some Furies, last week. And a couple of days ago, a boy was beaten pretty badly in the park. I think he was a Fury too. So then, when I heard that Rocio had been on the edge of their territory, overwriting their *placas* at five o'clock at night—"

He shrugged.

Homer said, "It sounds like a terrible waste."

Speedball looked around, avoiding their eyes. "I'd better be getting back to the others," he said with a vague wave of his arm. "Before they overrun the place."

Homer caught his hand and shook it. "Thanks."

"All right."

Jill said nothing, but glared at the paintings on the walls until Homer drove her away in their car.

## 13

On his way in to the furniture floor on Monday, Shelly stopped off at the office, where Max gave him both the check for his commissions on furniture sales and his monthly salary check—his "partner's dividend," Max called it. Shelly opened the latter envelope first, and was amazed to discover the check was made out for $7,643.21.

"We had a good month," Max explained with a shrug. "They won't all be like this. So you'd better put away a few dollars for a drier month."

Shelly nodded, dumbstruck. His monthly sergeant's take-home had been a thousand dollars less than half of that. He had to pause momentarily to steady his fingers as they opened the second envelope. He lifted the check out slowly, until the tops of the letters showed: EIGHT THOUSAND THREE HUNDRED SIXTEEN AND 00/xx dollars.

"Eight thousand three hundred . . . ?" Shelly said aloud, the rest of it sticking in his throat.

Max grinned. "Sounds like the furniture business is even better than private investigations this month."

The numbers swam in Shelly's head. "Max—that's more than fifteen thousand dollars, for this month alone!"

"Not bad," said Max, pursing his lips. "Still having any regrets about leaving the city payroll?"

Shelly sank into the chair behind his desk—a new leather one with an adjustable headrest. The desktop was blond wood with a lovely grain, which swirled now in knots before his eyes. It was the most money ever in his name at one time that wasn't already committed to a car or a home. And it wasn't a loan—it was his own, earned income, his salary plus commission for mid-August to mid-September. He understood that this case presented a special chance, an unusual opportunity for double income. He understood that his monthly income would not always reach these exalted levels. But fifteen thousand dollars! What was he going to do with all that money? It was a problem that required some sustained attention. A voice in the back of his skull hoped they didn't catch the thieves on Macy's furniture floor for another six months at least.

When he arrived at his undercover assignment, it looked as if his luck might have broken. Stu Begelman was watching with a predatory eye as each person stepped off the elevator; and the floor did seem unusually dead, even for a Monday morning. In the sofa bed section, Shelly saw Sally Pinter leafing through a wilted copy of *Home Furnishings* that had been planted on a coffee table to accessorize a Haitian cotton loveseat. Frank Dupatechek stood with a phone in his ear, his newspaper opened to the racing page. Under the scrutiny of the security guard, Enrique Rousseau, the stock man, Jimmy Hollings, was transporting a leather-and-chrome chair from the Modern area to the far end of the showroom floor, where Harold Leming, the designer assigned to the furniture division, waited impatiently in one of the decorated "rooms," with an angular steel end table upside down in his hands.

Shelly had always rather liked that chair, a knock-off of a famous design by Mies van der Rohe, and it occurred to him that a fifteen-thousand-dollar monthly income ought to be able to buy him something really comfortable. When Jimmy dumped the chair off his dolly directly in front of Leming, the decorator put his boot on the lower rung of steel tubing and shoved it back flush against the half-wall, dropping the end table with a clang beside it. Then he crossed the display grouping and fiddled with the straps on a black and white sofa he had placed opposite the chair. Shelly took advantage of the moment to lower himself into the leather strops and panels that made up the seat—which, he found, were too low for his back and too sharply sloped backwards for anything approaching comfort. It was an ordeal to sit in it, and the leather was sticky, so that the sleeve of his suit jacket stuck to the armrest when he tried to stand. He had to edge his hands awkwardly toward his body and use the leverage of both elbows to raise himself from the seat, like a heavy load calling for two cranes.

"What do you think you're doing?" Leming asked from behind him, as Shelly managed to hoist himself upright. The decorator's foot was tapping out each second of his valuable time wasted by Shelly's shenanigans.

"I was trying out the chair," Shelly said.

"This chair was not designed for 'trying out,'" Leming sneered in reply. "It was hardly designed for sitting." He pronounced the last word with a vague grimace, as if the image of a rear end descending on the object was visually offensive to him.

"What do you do with it, then?"

"It is a work of contemporary industrial art—you look at it, Mr. Lowenkopf."

Shelly looked at it; and it did look sharp, sloping black leather reflected in chrome. But he wasn't about to sink twelve hundred dollars into a conversation piece that hurt your tailbone when you tried to sink into it after a long day of surveillance. "Do you sell it with a painting to sit on?"

But Leming was not amused. "Why don't you check out one of the other rooms, in the back, where the more *traditional* chairs are displayed? You ought to be able to find something in a plaid wing, say, or a rocker?"

Shelly understood the suggestion was intended as a slap, but he did enjoy sitting in a roomy chair with a tall back and arms, and didn't mind at all, in fact, some gentle stimulation while he sat. He was not particularly fond of Early American furniture— plaids with lots of dark woods—but rather liked the curve of a rolled arm and a soft, plump, overstuffed cushion. There was one such grouping in the corner of the floor, in tender blue-gray leather, that always made him go boneless, flopping back his head and closing his eyes while his jaw dropped open. The pieces had been designed on a massive scale, a really big chair and matching sofa with no ottomans or loveseats or modular pieces attached or stuck between them. It was the first place that came to mind when Leming suggested he lose himself in the backwaters of furniture design, and, despite his opinion of the decorator, Shelly decided to follow his advice.

It was absolutely the best place on the showroom floor to lose yourself, to wipe away the immediate circumstances and allow yourself to succumb to the draw of your daydreams, or memories, or your thoughts. It was thinking Shelly wanted to do now:

about his newfound fortune, about the reticent rabbi in his precinct cell, and about Sol Schneider. He realized that the hours of his day had been purchased by the department store, but the missing floor samples did not seem to deserve his attention more than the minyan of Max's shul.

This was private enterprise, he knew, the flip side of the two checks keeping each other warm, folded back-to-back in his wallet. He was happy to join the ranks of the privately employed, but couldn't force his mental process to follow the hierarchy of priorities that would most please his accountant. If he had one. He wondered if he needed one now—and found that very pleasant to worry about.

Whichever way he turned the question in his mind, it pointed at Sol Schneider. Of course, it was logically possible for the rabbi to have murdered Lily Levinski, as Riordan seemed to think: He could have unlocked his desk drawer, removed his gun, brought it to her apartment—hadn't he told Shelly he had been there? —and shot her in the back. For the sake of her insurance policy. But it didn't *feel* like any of the people he had met since Max dragged him down to the shul. In the first place, Pirski would have known the insurance policy would make him a suspect; if he had killed her, he would never have returned his gun to his desk drawer and locked it again with his key. That made absolutely no sense to Shelly—not on the level of human emotions, which was where he earned his bread. So the rabbi couldn't have murdered Lillian —that, Max had said, was their starting presumption, as members of the private sector. Their client was innocent. So, then, where did that lead him?

Together with the neighbor's eavesdropping, it led to the conclusion that the killer had to be one of the men in the minyan at Max's shul—which narrowed the range of suspects to seven men, once the rabbi was ruled out, since Max and Shelly provided each other with alibis at three. If he had still been a detective, Shelly would have questioned each of the seven, maybe had some of them tailed, and run down each of their alibis until one of them started to stink. If he had one who looked good for it, he could even have tapped his phone. But, as a private investigator, he had no other men to disposition on the case—just the two of them, him and Max. Except he didn't really have the two of them, since they had no paying client on that case, and his own time, during the day at least, belonged to a department store that had hired them to recover furniture.

But if he did—if he had had even his own time to dispose of on the Levinski case—he would start with Sol Schneider. It was hard enough dealing with a woman who was, or wasn't, your wife—Shelly had experienced both with Ruth and couldn't decide which was worse. But dealing with a woman who was still *almost* your wife, an *agunah* unable to find another husband to replace you—that couldn't be easy on Sol either, Shelly was convinced. And when he remembered the negligee in her closet, that clinched it for him. Who was she wearing that to please—Sol himself? If so, he had been there just before her death. If not, could Sol be harboring jealousy about her? Was faithfulness a problem for an almost-ex-wife and -husband? From the way Max talked about her, Shelly thought of Lillian as a woman of appetites—hadn't he found a candy wrapper alongside her bed? There were plenty of questions he would like to put to old Sol, if he ever got the chance to leave the furniture showroom—and if Sol had any reason to answer to him.

"Shell?"

It was a very familiar voice. Until he heard it, Shelly had not realized that his eyes had closed. He opened them and saw in front of him Homer Greeley, in a tailored gray flannel suit. Behind Homer, regarding Shelly with a scowl usually reserved for people who put their feet up on anything other than an ottoman, was the sales manager, a balding man with a watch chain that ran to a real pocket watch. Shelly had seen the watch, had seen it flip open at a touch of the manager's thumb whenever a stock man lingered in the loading bay too long or a salesman returned late from lunch. Beside him was Leming, the decorator, who murmured something into the sales manager's ear with a sympathetic shaking of his head.

Shelly didn't much care what the furniture men were talking about, and, pleased as he was, he didn't jump up and hug his former partner. The first thought that crossed his mind in fact was, Is it time for flannel already? And then he recognized it as a Homeric question, one that Greeley might have wondered. It made all of the years they had worked together rush back into his memory, and, sustaining the self-restraint that had always been the hallmark of their relationship, Shelly stood, placed one hand briefly on Homer's sleeve, and mumbled, "Hey, there. So how are you doing these days?"

Homer was only slightly more effusive, but it amounted to a reversal of roles for them. "It's good to see you," he said, with a twinge at the edge of his mouth that, on a lesser man, might have broken into a smile.

What the hell was he doing there on the furniture floor of Macy's? That's what Shelly meant to ask him next. But Homer was acting oddly uncomfortable, clasping his hands in front of him and then tapping his forefingers together, and Shelly sensed that more would be forthcoming if he held his question. He said, "Do you shop for furniture here?"

"Not often," Homer confessed.

"They have some deals on velvets right now," Shelly said. He hadn't meant it as a sales pitch, exactly, but it must have satisfied the sales manager, because he walked off, leaving Leming to his displays. The decorator watched them a minute or two longer, and Shelly was just beginning to wonder whether he ought to introduce them, when Leming, too, went stomping off after an occasional chair he had espied in a rattan arrangement in the Modern section.

"Do you get a discount while you're, uh . . ."

"You wouldn't believe it, Homer. Discount? Hell, they're paying me commissions, undercover. Can you imagine the city allowing that? I'm taking in whatever I earn on the floor here, plus my salary from the agency—which, as a partner, is more than you and I ever earned for any week of our life, no matter how many lives we saved! I mean, public service is a rewarding choice—no one knows that better than me—but I can't tell you what I'm bringing home this month!"

Homer hadn't gone into police work for the financial reward, and it seemed crass of Shelly to suggest that it might be a reason to select one line of investigative work over another. But he couldn't help asking. "A lot, huh?"

Shelly nodded.

What was a lot, really? Homer said, "More than five grand for last month?"

"Three times that, Homer."

*Three times?* For nothing riskier than selling furniture? With no kids crumpled at the foot of a fence with cans of paint in their hands? What he said was, "I've got a case right now you don't see every day."

Shelly wasn't sure if Homer meant to remind him what he had given up or if Homer was having some problem with it. It was difficult for Shelly to believe either possibility, so instead of responding with a question, as he felt he was expected to do, he said, "You always did."

"What?"

"Have cases no one had ever seen before."

Homer gave him a peculiar stare, which Shelly thought he understood. It read: *That was you, wasn't it, turning every case into a once-in-a-lifetime affair?*

"Well, this is different," Homer said. "A gang war in the offing, looks like. One gang overwrites another; they retaliate and get hit back for retaliating." He wanted to say the whole business was maddening to witness—killing after useless killing, all of the victims so young, with no role for the police except to keep track of the bodies. But that would have been out of the characters they had settled on when they first started working as a team. And yet he couldn't say nothing at all, having come so far. He said, "The whole thing gives me a pain."

Shelly considered him a moment, and his old role came right back to him. "Frustrating, huh?"

"You said it."

"Doesn't take long before everyone thinks they're reacting to the other guy. How many so far?"

"One."

"Just one?"

"One dead. Another in the hospital."

"And you want to—"

"Figure out where the next one's going to be before it's a number in the monthly statistics."

"Have you carded the kid in the hospital?"

"A Fury."

"And the dead one?"

"A Diablo."

"So you've got both sides identified, as groups. Anything on the kids themselves?"

"The dead one overwrote the other side's graffiti."

"And the one in the hospital's also a writer?"

142

Homer hesitated, trying to remember if he had heard anything like that. He hadn't—but what surprised him more was that it hadn't occurred to him. "No."

"So who did the dead kid overwrite?"

Homer flipped through the pages of his pad. "I have some names from the fence . . . here we go. Poquito 6. And El Toro. The usual sort of names."

"It just seems to me," said Shelly, "that if someone is killed for overwriting, then the killers must know the writer. And the pals of the kid who was killed must realize that, too. So if anybody is likely to be shot next with a drive-by shotgun, you could do worse than start with the writer."

Homer stared at him.

Shelly blinked.

"That was amazing," Homer said. "I've never heard you do that before—read the writing on the wall. Or any sign from the scene! You're starting to sound like me."

It was intended, at least, as a compliment. Shelly said, "Thank you."

Homer sighed. "Now all I've got to do is drive back there and face those kids again."

He passed a hand through his blond hair, and Shelly slapped his shoulder. "Go to it," he said aloud. But, if he had given words to the sentiment tingling his scalp, he might have replied, "And you're starting to sound like me."

# 14

At three o'clock on Monday afternoon, Rabbi Sholem Pirski was arraigned on a charge of premeditated murder at the Bronx Superior Courthouse. Max and Dave Horowitz were on hand with a bondsman to make bail and to drive the shaken spiritual leader home. The rabbi had held up respectably under his weekend in the slammer. His beard, of course, concealed the usual signs of unshaven neglect, and he carried himself with the air of a man who had undertaken a self-imposed retreat, like a Hindu holy man in the Himalayas who shuts himself away to contemplate God undistracted by the demands of the world of relativity. Pirski had been allowed his books, and in their pages he had reconciled himself to whatever befell his earthly frame. Only his eyes, which were lined with red all around, showed the strain—but whether it was from reading under dim cell lights or any other reason was impossible to tell.

By four o'clock, however, Shelly received a call from Max, beseeching him to do something—to uncover some sort of lead that would release the rabbi from his current trial. Shelly was in the middle of closing a sale on an eight-hundred-dollar recliner and promised Max, yes, he would look into it further, just as soon as his hours on the furniture floor expired. When five o'clock came and he punched out, bidding good-night to Sally Pinter, nodding at Frank Dupatechek and grunting at Stu Begelman, Shelly's reasoning ran only two steps long: If the best-looking candidate was his client, who looked second best for the murder? And an answer to that question came quickly: Who would want to murder a woman more than her half-ex-husband, who no longer enjoyed the pleasures of connubial bliss but was still linked to her by ties of custom and religion? Sol Schneider had refused to give Lily her *get,* and his refusal to divorce her had made her an *agunah.* If there was still passion on one side, at least, there might be a motive for murder.

And Shelly knew just where to find him. After the death of his wife, Schneider would be sitting *shiva* for a week and could be found in his apartment, where visitors were welcome. True, it was a time of grief, which should not be interrupted on a whim. But if Sol was the killer, he had forfeited whatever rights he might have had to grieve in peace; and if he was not the killer, he would certainly want to assist in clearing the rabbi's name and bringing his ex-wife's murderer to justice. Shelly never had much trouble explaining to himself why the demands of his case justified intruding into the intimacy of people's most personal moments. If it had caused him no regrets as a policeman, when his purpose was to punish the guilty, he felt even less remorse now, when his purpose was to exonerate the innocent. In leaving the force and signing on with Max, he had crossed an invisible line, and found himself in territory far better suited to his own temperament and inclination.

Richard Fliegel

Sol Schneider's door was open, as was usual during the period of mourning. Inside, Irene seemed to be alone with her brother, their mother and Irene's daughter having been dispatched to the routine of their ordinary lives. The apartment was far quieter than it had been on Sunday, although the remains of prune danish from the day before were still in evidence on two paper plates on the table behind her. As soon as she saw who it was, Irene seemed to look past him, as if wondering who might be lurking in the shadows beyond.

"Mr. Lowenkopf, isn't it? Max's junior partner?"

Max had never called him that—but yes, he was Max's partner and *junior* by several decades. Shelly nodded, and said, "I hope you don't mind my stopping by again."

"What is there to mind?" asked Irene, cocking an eyebrow, which might have been a shrug or an inquiry.

Shelly wasn't sure whether or not the question was rhetorical: Did she mean there was nothing to mind? Or was she asking him if he had come for a reason she might well mind?

"I didn't get a chance to talk to Sol last time."

She considered that, weighing its implications. Shelly knew the more information he supplied to the sister, the poorer his chances of seeing her brother. If she assumed he wanted to tell Sol how sorry he was over his loss, he hadn't actually lied to her, had he?

"What do you want to talk to him about?"

Shelly shrugged. "Lillian."

He could see she would have liked to press him further; but how could she question that? She said, "Just a minute," and started toward the bedroom, pausing in the hall to wave vaguely in the direction of the kitchen. "There's some coffee on the machine, if you want some."

146

"Thanks."

"And there should be some danish in the fridge."

"I don't want to spoil my dinner."

Irene glanced toward the kitchen as if she regretted leaving it undefended. "That's why most people come after dinner."

From the kitchen came the appetizing aroma of turkey gravy, which was warming in a pot on the stove. Shelly had no intention of imposing on their meal, but he had not eaten since lunchtime and the drama of making furniture sales worked up an appetite in him. He strolled into the kitchen—not to eat, he told himself, but to check out what he might want to order at Nate's later on. It was the smell he found so arresting—he thought it reminded him of Ruth's kitchen, when his ex-wife had still cooked meals. But it was a different aroma than Ruth had produced, and it took him a moment to reach further back in his olfactory memory and recognize the combination of onions and celery and sliced carrots reheating in a little oil and plenty of salt as the scent of his own mother's kitchen. He wandered in, as if he were crossing the threshold to another time.

He did not find a home-cooked meal. There was a large basket on the counter, its red cellophane unwrapped, its separate cardboard containers emptied of potatoes, vegetables, and gravy, each of which now simmered on the stove. A small turkey sat in a broiling pan on the open oven door, waiting for its moment to be reheated. There was a card, from Dave Horowitz, with his signature and no other comment. None was necessary, of course—the gift was meant to feed Sol and his family during this time when even cooking might prove too much for them. And the thought suddenly occurred to Shelly, Could store-made turkeys have been the secret behind his mother's home cooking as well?

At that moment Sol Schneider came out from his bedroom in a crumpled pair of suit pants, a short-sleeved white shirt, and black socks with a green stripe across the toes. His lack of shoes was a part of his uniform as mourner, and the jagged rent in his shirt, about a hand's length deep from his collar to his heart, was more than a symbol of tearing his clothes in grief.

"Mister Lowenkopf," said Schneider, offering his hand. "So good of you to have come again."

"So soon," said Irene, following her brother from his bedroom.

Schneider held on to Shelly's hand to lead him away from the kitchen, into a living room furnished in overstuffed fabrics with lots of exposed wood trim. It was a man's room now, strewn with newspapers folded to articles continued from earlier pages and abandoned where they fell; but a woman had recently been through the place, so that the knickknacks stood in a neat line on the shelves of a wall unit and there was no dust on the table next to the armchair or its match in front of the couch. All of the wood was dark, stained to a high gloss, and the velvet on the set of matching sofa and armchair had been pricey, woven stuff when the purchase had been made fifteen years before. It would soon be time to replace it. But Shelly chased all furniture thoughts from his mind as he settled down to learn what he could about the death of Lily Levinski.

Sol fell heavily into the armchair with a sigh that might have come from either one of them. Shelly sat more carefully on the forward edge of the couch— polite, attentive, watchful.

"I'm terribly sorry for your loss," he said.

Sol inhaled deeply and then let it out as if the passage of air through his lungs reminded him that he was himself still alive. "It's not that she was so young," he said, "but that she was so full of life. Do you know what I mean when I say 'full of life'?"

"That's what everybody tells me," said Shelly.

"Who?"

"Who . . . what?"

"Who's been telling you about Lily?"

"Well, I just mean . . . Max and all. Everyone who knew her and misses her."

Schneider wrinkled his face as if the mention of other mourners didn't please him at all. "Don't believe everything you hear," he said.

"I'm not sure what to believe," Shelly replied.

"What have they told you, already?"

"They said that you were divorced."

"We weren't *divorced,*" said Schneider, as if his emphasis gave a special meaning to the word. "In an American court, okay. But in the true sense, before God—never. In the *olam haba,* the world to come, Lillian will be received as my wife. That's what's important now, isn't it?"

"I understand she couldn't remarry," Shelly said carefully. "Does that mean you can't remarry now, either?"

"Me? Of course I can get married, if I find someone I like—my wife is dead. A widower is allowed to marry, Mr. Lowenkopf. Just as soon as the mourning period ends."

"Do you have . . . someone in mind?"

Schneider stared at him for a moment. "You know, it's not considered especially polite to come to a man's house while he's sitting *shiva* and inquire after his marriage plans."

"I'm sorry. I've been a cop too long."

Irene, who must have been listening at the entrance, asked, "Is that why you're here? As a detective?"

"It's not the only reason," Shelly lied, "but I

thought you would want to help us find whoever killed Lillian."

"Who've you got on your list?" asked Schneider.

"Well," said Shelly, uncomfortable under their joint gaze, "the first people we usually question are the ones closest to the deceased—"

"The family," concluded Irene.

"Yes," Shelly said. "They're the ones who know the most about the victim—who she knew, who she feared, who she might've had some sort of quarrel with—"

"And nine out of ten times," Irene said, "they murdered her themselves."

"It takes a lot of strong feelings to kill somebody," Sol observed philosophically. "And who feels more strongly about you than your family?"

"That's the idea," said Shelly, "more or less. So we were wondering . . ."

"Who?" said Irene, with the same inflection her brother had used a few minutes earlier.

"Who what?" Shelly repeated.

"Who has been wondering about what we might say? Just you? Or your partner, Max, too?"

Shelly knew his phrase "we were wondering" didn't refer to any particular *we*—it was a residue of his days on the force, when all references to investigating personnel were usually couched in impersonal plurals. But her question also suggested a particular interest in Max, whom Shelly was anxious to protect.

"Not Max," he said. "He doesn't suspect you of anything. But he is very anxious for me to make some headway on this case. So I'm starting with you, as sources of information. I'll ask you about Lillian, and who knows where it'll lead?"

They liked the sound of that better. Schneider said, "What do you want to know?"

What did he want to know? *Did you kill her? Did*

*you take the gun from the rabbi's desk and blow your ex-wife away?* Those were the questions on the tip of his tongue—the ones he always felt like asking. But you never learned anything, no matter what the answer, so instead he asked, "How well have you been getting along with your wife since the divorce?"

"He didn't kill her," Irene answered promptly.

"Who didn't?"

"Sol."

"That's not what I asked."

"Wasn't it? And I didn't kill her either. Next question."

"When was the last time you saw her?"

"Yesterday," said Sol. "At the funeral."

"I meant alive."

He thought a minute. "Last Saturday. She came to services. Sitting behind the *mechitzah*—the curtain, you know?"

Shelly nodded. "Did you speak to her?"

Sol was aghast. "During services?"

"Afterwards."

"I don't remember. Maybe I said a few words—how good she was looking or something like that."

"Did she look good to you?"

"I told you," said Irene, "he didn't kill her—and don't you look at me that way!"

"Do you mind if I ask my own questions?"

"Yes, I do mind. If they're stupid ones."

"I'll try to ask smarter questions in the future," Shelly promised her. "Do you have any smarter ones you'd like to suggest?"

"Don't you want to know who killed Lillian?"

"That's exactly what I'm trying to discover. Yes."

"Then why don't you just ask?"

"Who killed her?"

"That's right."

"Do you know?"

"Why don't you ask and find out?"

Shelly drew a deep breath. "All right—do you happen to know who killed Lily Levinski?"

"Not personally," said Irene, shaking her head.

Shelly waited. "Impersonally?"

"Not from firsthand experience. I didn't see it happen, or anything like that."

"But—"

"If you're asking me for an opinion—"

"I am—"

"Have you had a chance to talk with the Minsky brothers?"

"Irene!" said Sol sharply.

"It's just an opinion," replied his sister defensively. "I didn't offer it on my own. But when I'm asked by an investigator looking into a murder . . . I can hardly keep it to myself."

"What about the Minsky brothers?"

"It's nothing," Schneider assured him.

"Nothing!" snorted Irene. "Only enough to kill somebody—that's all! It was nothing like theirs that started the trouble in Borislav, remember—"

"Like what?" asked Shelly. "What trouble?"

"It was nothing," Sol explained.

"Jealousy," said Irene. "This was years ago—before Sol and that woman found each other. Sol was living at home with Mama and me—no, I was married. Sol was living with Mama, and we had just found a place by the station on Lydig Avenue—"

"And Lily?" asked Shelly.

"She was living by the park, on Mace," said Sol.

Irene glared at him. "She was seeing Jonathan Minsky," she told Shelly, "for a couple of weeks. They had gone out dancing maybe two or three times already. And then one night Joel had to reach his brother—about their business, I think it was. They were in Wiener wursts together at one time."

"I heard."

"About the fight?"

"What fight? I heard about their business in SoHo—"

"Who cares about their business? This is about Lillian! Where was I? Oh, yes . . . Joel had to reach his brother one night, and he thought he might be at Lillian's. So he went there, to find him. But he wasn't there. Lily was there alone. And they say Joel didn't leave while he couldn't find his way—do you understand that?"

"Couldn't find his way . . . where?"

"Home. Through the dark."

"He stayed until dawn?"

"How should I know? That's what they say . . ."

Sol made a sour face. "We don't know that for sure."

"No," agreed Irene, "but we do know that Jonathan almost killed Joel the next day."

"We don't know that either," insisted Sol, taking over the story so that Shelly would hear it right. "All we really know is that they had a terrific fight the week after. It lasted for a month and nearly ended their partnership. The rabbi sat them down together, finally, and they decided that neither one of them would see Lillian again. It was the only way to continue as brothers. And each of them loved his brother more than he loved anyone else."

"That's the official story," said Irene significantly. "But it didn't end there."

"Gossip," said Sol.

"So? That doesn't mean it wasn't true."

"What wasn't true?" asked Shelly.

Sol looked very unhappy. Irene gave her brother a glance that might have been asking approval, but when he said nothing in reply, she shrugged and went on.

"He's asking, Sol, he's asking! The official investigator. We've got to tell him everything we've heard—who knows where the crucial clue will come from?"

"Exactly," said Shelly.

"I know the business," Irene told him. "I wish I knew the rest of the story as well! Mrs. Stoehler—God rest her soul—is the one who knew it best. She used to live next door to Lily on Mace Avenue and kept her windows open all the time—for her cats—she always insisted they had asthma. But did you ever see a cat allergic to dust?"

Shelly shook his head. "And she said—"

"She said Joel stayed away for two or three months, and then couldn't stay away. He snuck back when Jonathan thought it was all over between them. He saw her two or three nights a week. You should've heard the sounds that came out of there—according to Edna Stoehler! And then, somehow, Jonathan found out. And he swore something."

"What?"

Irene shrugged. "Who knows?"

"None of this is true, according to Joel," said Sol.

"What would he tell you, then? That he's cheating on his bargain with his brother?" said Irene.

"He'd tell me the truth," said Sol.

"Not once you started to see Lillian," Irene pointed out.

"I wouldn't've seen her otherwise," said Sol.

"You see how men are," observed Irene to Shelly, as if he were some other species. "He listened for what he needed to hear and then didn't listen any further."

"Irene," said Shelly, "I'm the investigator. I'm asking. What do you think Jonathan swore when—or if—he discovered Joel had been seeing Lily again?"

Irene looked at Sol, who scowled and turned his head. She shrugged. "How should I know? All I can tell you is what the other women say."

"What do they say?" asked Shelly.

"Different things. This one says he might have said, 'You have betrayed me.' Another one says he might have said, 'You are no longer my brother.' Most people say he swore, 'Put an end to this, or you'll never be my brother again.'"

"But that's not what you believe Jonathan said?"

She looked at Shelly with a new respect in her eyes. "Does a man blame his brother when there's a woman around who could be blamed instead?"

"If he loves her," Shelly said.

"But Jonathan never loved Lily—only Joel did that. And it was Jonathan, remember, who swore the oath."

"What do you think he said?"

"He was not talking to Joel—that's the key to it! He was talking to Lillian when he swore, 'I'll put an end to this—from one end or the other.' And that's what I believe happened."

155

# 15

The first thing you should understand," said Jonathan Minsky, as he and Shelly sat on a red-checkered tablecloth under a flowering dogwood tree, "is just how many years ago we're talking. Old people tend to talk about twenty or thirty years ago as if it were yesterday. If you're asking me about Lillian, you need to understand that you're talking about things that happened more than ten or twelve—wait, more than fifteen years ago. Lillian was forty-seven."

It was after six, and the light was failing. But it was still light enough for Minsky to read the doubt in Shelly's face as he spoke.

"That's not the way she made it sound, is it?"

"Who?"

"Irene."

"What makes you think it was she who told me?"

"Please, Mr. Lowenkopf. Irene."

The name was said with so much satisfaction, Shelly began to wonder about her interest in the affair. Which is just what Minksy planned to tell him.

"My brother Joel, you have to understand, is a great

156

admirer of the ladies. Not an exploiter—an admirer. An exploiter only wants to climb into their pants. My brother's fascination lies deeper, in a woman's mysterious heart. The turn of an ankle, the suggestion of a sense of humor in a glance—these things thrill Joel, not just in his shorts, but in here."

Minsky tapped his own chest to indicate where his brother felt the principal resonance.

Shelly nodded, following his cardinal principle on personal interrogations: Always allow a talker to talk.

"When he was young, there were one or two girls who swore he had promised to marry them. But— take it from me, who knows my brother as no one else has ever known him—he never promised to marry anybody. Not Lillian and not Irene."

"Not the marrying kind, eh?"

"He would have married them all if he could! You see, he really loves women—loves them in a tender and intimate way. If he could split himself into a thousand pieces, and each one takes a wife—that would have satisfied him, I think, Mr. Lowenkopf. But he couldn't do that, and the allure of the one in the corner of his eye always kept him from making promises to the one in his lap."

"Lillian?"

"He couldn't help himself. I found her, and saw her a few times, and then he met her, looking for me. And for a short while he forgot himself, and saw her behind my back. And then we had it out, face to face, as two brothers should. The rabbi helped us do it. And then we both swore not to see her again—and neither of us ever did."

There was an uncomfortable silence before Shelly asked, "Are you absolutely certain of that?"

Minsky laughed. "Poor Irene!" he said. He picked up a pair of binoculars and watched a bird in a tulip tree.

Shelly waited.

Minsky put down his binoculars with a sigh. "Do you know why they call those tulip trees, Mr. Lowenkopf?"

Shelly didn't.

"Most people think it is just because of the flowers, which look like tulips, growing in its branches. And for all I know, maybe that is the reason. But if you ever pick up a leaf and examine the tip, you'll find a remarkable thing: The leaf splits at its end, curving away into two points—just like the flower! It's wonderful, a single leaf divided into two tips. And Joel and I were like that, two brothers from the same stem, joined for our lifetime, one to the other."

He paused, and Shelly squinted at the tall trees lining the curved entrance to the Botanical Gardens museum. He took off his glasses, wiped them, and pressed them to his eyes. He couldn't see the leaves any more clearly, a hundred yards away, but Minsky appreciated the effort.

"And you ask me if I'm absolutely sure! I'll tell you this: I never saw her again. If Joel had been able to help himself, he wouldn't've, either."

"Then he did see her again?"

"I suppose. That doesn't matter. He was willing to promise me he wouldn't. And if he can make a sacrifice like that, for the sake of our brotherhood, the least I can do is never to ask if he lived up to his word."

"But if he didn't—"

"He would have broken his word. That's true. But how many of us manage to lead the lives we know in our hearts we should? Have you always kept your word, Mr. Lowenkopf—even to yourself? I haven't. And I'm sure Joel hasn't either. But what can you do? He's your brother and you love him—is there any choice but to forgive him his human frailty?"

"That's very understanding of you," said Shelly.

"Not understanding," said Minsky, shaking his head. It was apparently important to him that Shelly get it right—enough so that he tried again. "Look—if he went back to her, that would have been a betrayal. There's no other way to consider it. And, knowing Joel as I do, if I ask, Did he go back? there's only one answer I'm likely to discover. So what are my choices, really? Only to ask or not to ask. If I ask, I damage our brotherhood, which is precious to me. So the only thing I can do is never to ask, and to assure you—as I assure myself—that neither one of us ever went to see Lillian again."

"So it's foresight," said Shelly. "And knowledge, of who your brother is. A little compassion—you can hardly deny it!—mixed in. And a good dose of appreciation, for what Joel means to you, and what you stand to lose by asking a question you don't really want answered."

"Precisely! You're a good listener, Mr. Lowenkopf. Max told me you would be."

Max had told Shelly where to find Minsky, but Shelly had no idea he had called ahead with a warning. And yet, for all the patience Minsky showed toward his brother, he couldn't help wondering just how fully the old man had forgiven Joel's partner in betrayal.

"Tell me about Lily."

"Lillian?" asked Minsky quickly. For all the years since he had pursued her, there was still a certain possessiveness in the way her name was pronounced. "You mean then, or now?"

"However you remember her best."

"I'll tell you how I remember her," Minsky said with some pleasure. "Do you see that little bird over there? With the spotted brown breast?"

In the gathering darkness Shelly could hardly see

past the padded shoulder of Minsky's coat. But he said, "Uh-huh."

"That was Lillian. A coquette! I know that young people have a great deal of trouble seeing the sexual power of their seniors. But even to her last day she exerted a powerful draw. Lillian enjoyed sex, you see—she reveled in it—and there was something about her that let you know in advance."

"She was . . . easy?"

"Not at all! What a pursuit she led you on . . . dancing and flowers and more flowers. She might let you think you were close, and then—"

He shook his head. But he grinned.

"It was just that she let you know once you had won her . . . it was worth doing! Look—look on the branch! Do you see how she does it?"

The spotted bird jumped up and down, and the other followed suit. Shelly did not see much resemblance to human courtship there. But then, his host evidently did.

"There you have it—the dance of life! Lillian was a nimble partner, a wonderful dancer. Now I ask you, Mr. Lowenkopf, if you seriously believe that a man such as myself—as old as I am, with all the spite drained out of me so that only this, the love of the living, remains to move me—do you really think I could have killed my own Lillian?"

The old man stared at him with clear blue eyes darkened by the falling evening. For a moment it seemed as if the leaves around them rustled in support of him, and the birds added their chorus as well. A gust of wind blew Shelly's curly hair away from his forehead, tearing his eyes. If the Gardens had a vote, they cast it for the innocence of the man who spent his days contemplating their complex beauty.

Shelly said, "It's possible that you did. When it comes to murder, anything is possible."

160

Night was about to fall, and Shelly was wondering just how safe they were in the park. But the old man seemed to have no such concerns. He settled back on his tablecloth, propped on his elbows, enjoying the breeze.

"I'll tell you something more possible, then," said Minsky, switching strategies without losing a beat. "For all his easy charm, Joel would never have stood a chance with Lillian—not a matchstick's in a windstorm—if he hadn't been lucky enough to catch her on the rebound."

"From you?"

"No—I mean both of us! You see, I had noticed Lillian for quite some time. And I worked up the courage to ask her out on more than one occasion. But she always turned me down—gently, God bless her! —until that one special day. That was really the thing I showed Joel—that Lillian had become obtainable for one reason or another."

"What do you mean?"

"She never went out on a date before that. She was single, but never accepted an invitation. Now what does that tell you about her?"

"That she was waiting for Mr. Right?"

"No—that she had found Mr. Wrong. You see, a woman does not like to be alone. There are too many things she cannot do by herself. When she has a husband, she takes her place among the wives as one of them, with responsibilities, and complaints, and a role in life. I realize some of the younger women claim this is no longer true. Some want to be alone; others want another woman. I wish them luck. For the women I know—they want a man. And they want others to know it."

Shelly nodded—whether in comprehension or agreement he chose not to clarify.

"Now, at that time Lillian did not seem to have a

man—and yet she refused all offers. We know from what followed that her tastes didn't run to her own sex. So why would she turn down an offer? I'll tell you why. Because she loved someone else! And the only reason she kept it a secret was—"

"Because she valued her privacy?"

"Because she couldn't claim him! He was married to somebody else. Who knows what happened between them? Perhaps he couldn't be unfaithful. But suddenly Lillian was available."

"This is speculation," Shelly said.

"No, it is not. I was there, in her apartment, when a call came in once. From the way she looked at me, I could see—it was Him. I left her alone in her bedroom to take the call. But it stimulated my curiosity, and while she was busy on the telephone, I wandered over to the wall in her kitchen, where she scratched numbers on a pad. In a box at the top was neatly lettered a name she did not want to forget. It had been blackened out and then written again, as if she couldn't bear to lose it. And below it was a number I knew by heart myself."

He paused, for dramatic effect. But instead of continuing, he waited for Shelly to ask.

"What was the name?"

"David. Instead of a dot over the *i* was a little circle, and I couldn't be sure, but it looked like it had been made into a heart."

"Who's David?" Shelly persisted.

"Who's David?" asked Minsky. "There's only one David I knew she knew also. Horowitz—the president of our shul! He wasn't the president in those days, of course. He couldn't've been more than fifty or so himself. But he was a married man."

"And you're implying—what? That something came up fifteen years later that opened an old wound? That she tried to force him to marry her? Or blackmailed him for money? And instead of paying her off, or to prevent a scandal, the president of your temple blew a hole in her back?"

Minsky shrugged. "It's a theory, isn't it? Better than an old man watching birds."

And then his interest in the conversation vanished with the daylight, which gave them a deep blue wink and faded to black. Minsky stood with an energetic sigh; he slung the binoculars over his shoulder, folded up his tablecloth, and headed for the exit from the Bronx Botanical Gardens. The car gates had already closed, and the last pedestrians were massing at the iron gate as stars began to appear in the clear night sky.

Shelly followed Minsky out, and as the old man headed for a bus stop, asked, "Can I give you a lift someplace?"

"Aren't you going to see Horowitz?"

"As soon as I can find out where he lives."

"All right," said Minksy, as if Shelly had asked. "I'll show you."

He led them on a circuitous route, up Mosholu Parkway and north on Jerome to the cemetery where the city buses ended. Shelly realized Minsky would have changed buses here, heading north to Yonkers and points beyond. They followed the bus route all the way to Scarsdale, where Minsky led the way through the winding streets.

"My niece lives in Yonkers. She's had me to dinner twice. And Horowitz had us all up once, to say the blessing over the doorframe when he hung the *mezuzah* there. But I think it's here on the left—now a right—and another one, there! The big house, at the end of the lane."

It was a big house—six or seven bedrooms, Shelly guessed from the driveway. There should have been a dog barking at the evening, or at least a row of lights

illuminating the grounds. The lawn was not mani-
cured, but not wild either, attended by a gardener who
was due back any day. The house was not neglected—
no broken windows, or gates, or cracks in the doors—
but there was an indescribable air of absence, as if
everyone had simply stepped out for the night. Shelly
knew what created the mood a moment later, when
they rang and no one came to the door. There were
hardly any lights in the windows. Of the twenty or so
that overlooked the front yard, only one showed light
behind it—on the first floor, a dozen yards to their
left. Shelly rang again, and when they still received no
answer, wandered over to the illuminated window.

"Maybe we should wait in the car," Minsky suggested, glancing around the dark grounds.

Shelly didn't answer, since there was nothing he
wanted to be repeatable after the fact. He just ambled
over to the window from which a light escaped,
shaded his eyes from the glare of the glass, and peered
into the room.

"Is this legal?" asked Minsky. "Peeping in?"

"We're just looking around."

"Well, then . . . don't we need a warrant or something?"

"We're not the police."

"What if they suddenly showed up?"

Shelly wasn't particularly worried about a private
security firm. For one thing, people who used them
usually posted signs announcing their hire—the signs
themselves providing the best defense. For another, if
a private security firm were on watch and found them
on the grounds, Shelly felt sure they could skip back to
their car without incident. Private cops didn't earn
enough to risk serious injury.

But there was something about the place that made
Shelly's antennae tingle. A normal house in a comfortable neighborhood that brooded more than it should

—as if the walls were waiting to tell a secret. Shelly had not believed in the Horowitz scenario, the one-time lover who kills his former beloved. He had followed Minsky's lead out of a sense of completeness, and because the old man had come along to see that he did. But he had too recently quit the force to have forgotten all that he learned, and every nerve in his policeman's skull was firing at him—trying to tell him something. But, because he was no longer a public servant, he decided to do what he had never been able to do before—to go in without a warrant and poke around.

"Help me up, will you?"

Minsky looked around. "I know this isn't legal."

"You're the one who suggested the Horowitz theory, aren't you? The killer president? What did you think we were going to do about it?"

"All right," said Minsky, lacing his fingers for Shelly's shoe. "For Lillian."

The window was unlocked—the casement kind, with a crank that turned to open it inside. Slipping his fingers between window and sill, Shelly was able to tug it open far enough to grab it higher up and put his weight behind pulling it wider. It gave with a creak of metal in need of oil, but the gap was soon broad enough for a torso to crawl through. Shelly did and, once inside, told Minsky to wait in their car—in the passenger seat, with the key in the ignition. Then he turned his attention to the room into which he had broken.

It was warm inside, with a fireplace, where an ash log still glowed. A sitting room. There was a low table in front of an Early American couch with two matching wing chairs, all done in the same orange plaid. On one side of the table was a set of carved chess pieces—each a singular handiwork of cavalry and Indians painted for war on the northern central plains. A pawn had been moved from its place in the opening arrangement, but no game had seriously begun. On the far side of the table, between the couch and one of the wing chairs, a tray of Wedgwood teacups had been set, and apparently used. Two cups bore traces of tea at their bottom—one merely a ring of brown liquid, while the other still held nearly half a cup of cold tea. Shelly sniffed it—Lipton's.

"Is anybody here?" he called out, but received no answer. The room was lined with bookcases full of hardcovers in paper sleeves, most of which seemed to have been read. There were magazines in a metal basket to one side of the fireplace, and all the utensils a poker could possibly need. And yet black flecks of burnt paper had leaped over the screen and lay on the tiles between the fire and the chess set. The light, which seemed to be the only illumination in the house, was provided by a lamp between the wing chair and the couch.

If it was intended to scare away burglars, it was a poor choice, since any of the upstairs lights would have provided as much presence and could not have been checked through the window. Why had someone left this room with its light and fire burning and turned off all other lights, inside and out? Shelly peered into the darkness of the next room, which glinted with glass surfaces—china cabinets full of dishes and a rosewood table with padded rosewood chairs. There was a telephone on the far side, sitting on a sideboard, but as Shelly tried to cross to it, his foot caught on the rug and he nearly fell forward.

Only it wasn't the rug.

It was a fireplace poker, of black iron. Except the tip, which glistened wetly in a darker shade of black, from which two drops of coagulating liquid pointed into the darkness of the dining room. Shelly moved around the back of the chair at the head of the table, where another, larger impediment blocked his path. He looked down and saw, even in that dim light, the features of David Horowitz, composed as if asleep. But he wasn't asleep, and, when Shelly bent over him, he saw the same black liquid oozing from his head.

# 16

Twelve years before, when Jimmy Carter had come to the Bronx and the Russians offered foreign aid to the citizens of the borough, plans had been made to redevelop blocks of residential housing so that new single- and double-family structures would be built, crumbling apartment buildings renovated, and several projects funded from the ground up. Tenements had been razed and foundations laid for buildings that would allow people of limited means to afford living quarters that were clean and safe and attractive.

Then the hostages were taken in Teheran, and the Carter Administration left Washington, and the office of Housing and Urban Development received a new set of funding priorities from the White House. In the Bronx several projects were suddenly short of funds required for completion. Some were able to find alternative sources, from the state or local agencies. Others simply halted in their tracks—tractors driven off the lot, subcontractors told they would be called again when new monies were available. The projects themselves were also left to wait, in whatever condition they happened to be when the construction crews packed up their gear.

At first, the local community gave these projects a wide berth, expecting their management and the security forces they had hired to return any day. But, as the weeks passed and no one returned, the projects began to take on an air of abandonment, walls of white cinder block and concrete slowly graying, until the locals were forced to admit that the promised new housing was not likely to be forthcoming. And then with a vengeance the neighborhood took its toll on the remains of yet another promise unfulfilled—bottles were smashed against the walls that rose above the level of the ground and graffiti spray painted above the glass so that the Foundation stood in its field of debris as a monument to false hope and betrayal.

Until, one night, a change had been wrought, a labor of love that transformed the angry scrawls, focusing streaks of random color in a single work of art, expressing the pride of one group instead of the disappointment of the many: FURIES, it read, giant letters in an intricate interplay of hue and form, where letters that began in a red blaze of glory rose through several shades of orange and yellow, like a dawn over the deserted lot. And the letters were shadowed, each one casting a lengthened reflection, which made them seem to rise over the landscape, to transcend the trash over which they stood as sentinels, addressing an audience passing airborne to LaGuardia, to the south and east. And beside the tribal name were two others, done in a similar style but far smaller: EL TORO, worked so that the cross stroke of the *T* looked like the horns of a bull; and, even smaller and below that, the name POQUITO 6, rendered with care and recessed so that it fell within the protection of the larger name.

And there were also, in a different hand, far less skillfully drawn, the letters: WA.

Through each of these names, a single line of red paint had been sprayed, as if the writer had wanted to cross them out but not to efface them more than necessary. A similar crimson spray made a stroke through FURIES, over which had been written in a graceful cursive DIABLOS. But the name that interested Greeley now as he studied the art on the wall was the name written above the name of the original artist. It was EL GATO, the name now linked to Rocio Lucero, who had been gunned down four nights before in an alley. And Homer flipped through the pages of his notebook to confirm his recollection that the *placas* Lucero had covered there were the same names he had covered here.

Jill Morganthal, who had parked their unmarked Reliant and crossed the lot with Greeley, was less impressed by the recurring names than she was by the state of the lot, which had been wholly trashed despite a high fence topped with razor-sharp coils of barbed wire.

"Christ!" muttered Jill, and not in prayer. "Will you look at what they did to this place?"

Considering the obstacles that had to be surmounted, it was an impressive job. In addition to the usual shards of broken glass and crushed aluminum, rubber tires had been tossed among the ailanthus trees, half hidden in the ferns; and, against the concrete wall itself, the curved pipes from the bottom of a sink lay abandoned by their fixture. Cinder blocks had been torn from the structure and piled on one another to form seats or tabletops, littered with burnt bottle caps. Underfoot and under the weeds, unseen boards lurked in puddles of mud. With every step of Jill's heels a board sank deeper, squirting brown water through cracks in the rotting wood.

"Yech! I hate when that happens," she said, wiping

the toes of her brown pumps with a tissue from her purse.

Greeley was usually meticulous about his own attire, but the sight of Morganthal fussing over her shoes made him oddly pleased with the mud stains along the edges of his own red-brown oxfords. Shelly would have brushed the dust from the concrete wall with a swipe of his corduroy jacket sleeve; Homer was not prepared to go so far, but as a gesture of abandon in the spirit of his partner, he took out his handkerchief and touched it to the paint covering the *placas*— which didn't come off on the silk.

"Have we seen enough yet?" Jill asked, looking around with suspicion. Homer understood her concern. Between their weapons, their training, and their authority, they could handle three or four, maybe five punks together, assuming they weren't surprised; but who knew how many glowering gangbangers might suddenly hurdle the fence? Tempers had been edgy on the streets since the morning, when a Fury had been blasted with a twelve-gauge shotgun outside a bodega by the el. The drive-by had timed the assault so that a train rumbling overhead confused the noise of the barrels. One moment the kid was standing, leafing through *El Diario*. Then the train roared by, cutting off the slats of sunshine through the tracks. And when it had passed he lay in a pool of his own blood on the pavement, twitching, with a hole the size of a bowling ball through his kidneys and intestines.

Jill's first words had been, "That's one less for us to worry about." But Homer kept seeing them as *kids*— and he was starting to feel sick of it.

His name had been Raoul Lopez, "The Wasp" to the Furies. Word on the street was that he had been the one who had blown away Lucero—although how the gangs learned these things was anybody's guess.

Greeley and Morganthal, with all the patrol officers working for them, could not convince a single soul to admit that anything had happened—yet someone had given the rival gang enough information to identify an individual shooter. It was galling, really, that the police found out what was happening only by carting away the pieces. But that was how they were keeping score on this one, at least: one Fury beaten inside the park, and a Diablo blown away; now a second Fury had been blasted on the street. The pressure would be on the Furies, and the younger members of their gang in particular, to even the score with more violence.

If they could reach the next shooter before he shot—that would be a way to intervene in the cycle of bloodshed. But, in order to do that, they would have to know who would be most powerfully motivated, most personally affected. That was what Shelly had meant by his question in the showroom. *Who did they overwrite?* Whoever it was had a stake in the contest, since his work was being effaced. And whoever it was would be close to the soldiers who had avenged its desecration.

The wisdom of this insight had proven itself already: Wasp was the victim of the morning. Which made it only more likely that his two colleagues, whose names had been covered along with his own, would be front-line candidates to avenge him. El Toro and Poquito 6—the two names together now twice. Who were they? Pals—a bull and a littler one. Could he find them before they made themselves known with a blast from a Celica window? Greeley placed the call to Montoya as soon as he and Morganthal returned to their parked Reliant.

And Montoya replied as Greeley expected: They would put out the word and see.

* * *

For Miguel Lopez the issue was less remote. For his beating in the park he had to show a broken nose, a fractured jaw, and a welt by his left eye. But he had also seen the enemy face to face, as one after another Diablo had struck him—and he remembered each of those faces. And their names—Torquemada had been the biggest one; his *compadre* called himself Gull, but Miguel recognized him as José Matas—they had spent a few hours dissing each other in detention at school. They had exchanged a look, in the park, but José had said nothing to Torquemada. It was true, Miguel's infraction was not only territorial but also financial, since he had crossed their turf in order to arrange a connection for cheaper crack. But when the news of Raoul's death reached him, Miguel knew who must be responsible. And if there was anyone in the world Raoul would have relied on to avenge him, it was his brother Miguel. Himself. Bandito.

Raoul would not have expected him to make a frontal assault, with a shotgun out a car window. That was Raoul's own way, his own style, and his own Celica, yellow with the black and red racing stripes. But he was also a shrewd enough judge of men to understand that each took his different approach. Miguel climbed out of his bed when the nurses were changing shifts on the ward, balled his white T-shirt and oversized dickie pants under his hospital gown, and crept down the staircase to the landing above the ground floor. There he stuffed the gown behind a fire hose, pulled his clothes painfully over his muscles, and slipped out through the front entrance into the street.

It was close to four. The air was cool, and the gusts of passing cars registered more strongly than they used to—he was not yet well, he understood, and the dizziness in his head was another token, another scar he would have to ignore in order to do what had to be done. It lent an added nobility to his task, an added dimension of suffering and tight-lipped courage. It was right that he should arise from his sickbed to avenge Raoul—how else could he demonstrate the significance of his loss? It would be a sign of their closeness, a gesture of love. He knew that Raoul would appreciate every dimension of effort and trial his murder necessitated before the departed soul could move on in peace. And Miguel was prepared to make the sacrifices gladly. But first he needed a gun.

That, as it turned out, was the easiest part of the business. For a drive-by you needed a gauge, a boo-yah—a shotgun. You didn't want to miss, from a distance, on the move. But for what Miguel had in mind, he needed something that could be concealed on his person, tucked under his shirt into his belt. If you walked up to somebody in a raincoat with a baseball bat in your pocket, you could hardly expect to find on his face that peculiar expression of surprise that was the specialty of El Bandito. Miguel did not have a big reputation, but he enjoyed imagining what someone on the other side would say one day about him, lowering his voice with respect: "That Bandito —you had to hand it to him." The way he had always felt proud when Raoul spoke of his own daring exploits as "the sting of The Wasp."

For his own sting, Miguel obtained from Paolo Wantanabe a nine-millimeter automatic handgun. The normal price was one hundred twenty dollars, but, because Paolo understood the need Raoul's death had created for Miguel, he let him have one for sixty, with cartridges. It was a gesture of sympathy on Paolo's part, and respect for the late Raoul. Miguel accepted the offer with gratitude, as he would have done a wreath of flowers for the family. It was friends like Paolo you had to depend on in times of crisis. It was good to know that when Miguel needed him he was there.

With the nine millimeter tucked in his pants, Miguel felt much better. Even his head started to clear, as it hadn't these last few days in the hospital. As he glided past the stoops of his own street, and listened to the drone of cars passing up and down the block, Miguel relaxed as he had not done since the day in the park. It was his own block, his own turf, that sustained him best and allowed his mind to work as he needed it to work. *Symbiosis* was the word Raoul had used—something he had learned, Miguel suspected, from Benito. It meant that the block depended on you, while you depended on it; your destiny was linked to the destiny of your neighbors. Raoul had restated the same idea in words Miguel believed to be his brother's own. "You've got to protect the tit that feeds you," Raoul used to say, tapping Miguel on the chest. And the tit that he meant by that was the block you lived on and the people who lived on it with you.

Revenge was just protection after the fact.

Everything depended on timing—that, too, was what Raoul had always said, and Miguel repeated the wisdom to himself to give himself confidence. Timing meant being in the right place at the right time. To do that, you had to know the right place to be. But Miguel figured he knew the place to be, since his enemies had revealed themselves to him. Each of his wounds, he now saw, and each of his sore muscles was a dear friend to him, since by their suffering he had learned the crucial information necessary to allow Raoul to rest in peace.

Every gang has its members with standing reps—*veteranos*, who have proved their courage and their effectiveness against the enemies of their gang. And every gang has its youngsters who need to prove themselves. In his beating, he had seen the leader

Torquemada urge the Gull—José—to deliver his kicks with the others. Which meant that Torquemada was doing his duty as a gang leader, trying to bring in new blood and help them understand what was required to prove themselves. A drive-by for revenge of an injury to the gang was just the sort of enterprise the Gull would be waiting for—and Torquemada would make sure he accepted the responsibility.

Which made José the best candidate for having shot Raoul, with Torquemada at the wheel. Or it might have been the other way around, José driving while the other showed him how it was done. But that didn't matter to Miguel. He felt sure that José would have been in the drive-by car—which made him a better target for reprisal than anyone else except Torquemada himself. Miguel's wounds still ached from Torquemada's boots—he didn't relish the thought of finding them again. No, José made the best target for him.

He had his weapon and his target—those made a very good start. What he needed was an opportunity to introduce one to the other. And he knew just where that was likely to arise. In the detention room, José kept talking about this girl he was going to fuck, this pussy who loved to suck his dick. He drew a picture on the desk to show what he meant—an enormous organ overwhelming the poor recipient. Miguel had asked him how he had solved the usual problem—where? Since there was never an empty apartment in any of their lives when they needed one. But José had solved that problem, he said, with a confidential grin. And he couldn't keep the answer to himself, either. There was a window with a broken pane on the ground floor in the teachers' parking lot that went into a closet in the basement, near the furnace. After dark, when the school was closed, you could crawl into there and help the girl down in after you. It was warm in there, from the furnace, and if you covered the broken pane, it was just the place for dreams to come true. José had winked at him, sharing a secret, and Miguel had felt an obligation to him.

Until he had felt his shoe in the park.

Now they were out for colors, and had chosen different sides and had to live with the consequences of those choices. Or not live with them. Miguel did not feel any special remorse for what he planned to do. It was reassuring to know that José would understand—had, in fact, demonstrated acceptance of those rules by his drive-by shooting of Raoul. It would be a rendezvous each of them was meant to keep, by the logic of the world into which they were born. If he caught up with José in the school basement closet, at least he would die a happy man, with his dick in a girl's mouth.

It did not take Miguel long to find the window—the pane was broken just as José had described it. It was a reach, from the jagged glass on the bottom row to the latch at the top of the window, but he managed it with only a little scratch to his arm. It bled a little in the warmth inside, but he staunched it with a clean rag, binding it around his biceps like a ninja. He found a blanket there, near the small space in the center of the floor between a broom cabinet and a large trash can on wheels. There was trash at the bottom of the can, some papers stuck together, but the cabinet was not filled, and Miguel managed to squeeze himself among the mop handles and the brooms. He waited there, his muscles cramping for what seemed like a year, until the medication they had pumped in his arm in the hospital caught up with him, and the heat of the furnace made his head swim. And he closed his eyes, for a second, listening.

He slept.

But he opened his eyes suddenly and almost cried

out in the darkness when something banged into the door of the cabinet. From the outside. It took him two breathless minutes before he could see again. And then the sounds started to make sense, filtering through the door.

Voices.

One female.

One not.

It was difficult to be sure it was really José out there—did all men make the same noises reassuring a woman? *Oh, yeah, baby, Esperanza, I love you . . .* Miguel had said those same words, changing only the girl's name, in just about the same order with the same inflection just a week before—but he hardened his heart to their commonality as one man to another, as two human beings with their pricks ready for action.

With incremental patience, he worked the release from the inside until the door could be opened with a push. But Miguel still did not push it, delaying the moment of surprise until he heard the desperate, regular breathing he knew would follow the pleading.

*Unh . . . huh! Unh . . . huh! Unh . . . huh! Unh . . . huh! Ohhh . . . ohhhh, baby . . .*

And then he sprang his trap, throwing open the door so that it banged and bent, while José looked up with his eyes wide and the girl screamed—muffled the first time, but it didn't take her long to get the noise level up. José's dick shriveled as if it had been splashed with cold water, and he tried to grab something in the pile of clothes on the floor.

But Miguel had the timing—that was the important thing. It felt as if he had all the time in the world. He pointed the nine millimeter directly at José's head and pulled the trigger one time and then another and another—three big booms that shook the gun in his hands. He had to aim it again each time, though he wasn't so careful now. At the head, or the neck, or the front of the chest—what difference did it make? For a moment the firing drowned out the screams of the girl who was staring at him, her face scrunched in hatred; and then she actually stopped screaming for an instant. Miguel looked at her, and tried to express a mixture of gratitude for her silence with sympathy for the horror this night had become for her. She had agreed to do a generous thing, and look where it landed her. Esperanza was her name—he almost spoke to her. But she began to shriek again, even louder than before, and she swung at him, pounding his chest with her fists, crying and crying.

He couldn't stand the crying worst of all.

Which is why he turned the gun and pulled the trigger on her. It wasn't that he had anything against her. It wasn't even to protect himself from her nails—they clawed at his face only after the first shot. It was to stop the crying that filled his ears and his memory and kept him from sleeping that night and for years to come.

# 17

On Tuesday morning, when Shelly showed up for work on the furniture floor, Stu Begelman greeted him at the elevator with a face of gleeful sympathy. "There's someone to see you," he said. He allowed Shelly a minute to review the store policy against visitors. And then he dropped the other shoe like a fur-lined slipper. "I think he's a cop. Are you in some kind of trouble, Lowenkopf?"

Shelly did not bother answering him, although he entered the floor with trepidation. And then he saw, sitting on the edge of a stretched leather sofa in the Contemporary area, Homer Greeley, in a wool suit with pinstripes. Shelly was himself wearing a silk-blend jacket with nubby flecks of pink and white against a field of black. His trousers, of blended wool, fell crisply from pleat to feet, which were shod in buttery black leather with a tassel on top. Max had chosen the outfit for him, an undercover disguise, and Shelly had the oddest sense of being better dressed than his ex-partner.

Homer stood when Shelly approached, admiring his clothing without a word.

Shelly said, "Nice to see you, Homer. Have you come for that chair?"

It took Homer a minute to remember the item. "No," he said. "I thought I could help you with some paperwork."

"What paperwork?"

"The paper trail from furniture floor to display room? Don't you remember? The last time I was here . . . you were working on a case involving stolen floor samples, weren't you?"

"Oh, yeah," said Shelly, "the case—"

"It occurred to me that this might be one of those areas you don't like to think about, Shell. Paperwork. You know, squids aren't the only things that disappear in ink."

Shelly was genuinely touched. "I'm grateful, Homer, really. But are you sure there are no more pressing crimes the city would rather you were investigating?"

"I need a break from the pressing ones, Shelly. Something like this, with a perp at one end and a collar at the other, would do me a world of good right now."

"You've been cleaning up a mess somewhere?"

"You wouldn't believe it! Two young kids . . . making love in the school basement after hours. Somebody comes along and smears them all over the dustbins."

"A crime of passion? Jealousy? A rejected suitor's reply?"

"Gangs," said Homer. And that was the end of it.

"Okay," Shelly said, "let's see if you've still got it in you." And he led the blond cop behind a wall of recliners to a hidden office, where books of sample swatches hung like salamis from hooks in a low ceiling. There was a long counter, behind which a young black woman was fixing her lipstick in the screen of her computer. From one end of the counter, Shelly reached over and brought out a tray of ticket stubs.

"This is what they fill out when they requisition a piece from the floor to complement a grouping in a display room. The blue copies go here, and the pinks go in another book, kept in the decorator's office. Inventory time, they check one against the other."

"Show me how it's done."

"Show you?"

"On the floor."

"All right," said Shelly. "Let's go find them in action."

They did not find any of the decorator's staff pulling sofas from the sofa bed floor, or even from Contemporary. But they did find a stock man penciling a stub for matching chrome lamps that had been separated to set off recliners. Sally Pinter, writing up a sale, made a sour face at the stock man hauling off the lamps, but he ignored her, accustomed to this sort of enmity. It was all one big floor—hadn't the sales manager told them that time and again? What was moved from one corner found a spot in another, adding to the appeal of the place that needed it more. Authority for those decisions had to reside somewhere, and it had been placed in the aesthetically capable hands of the designer, Harold Leming. The fact that he never seemed to get around to replacing what he had taken was a problem they had made him more aware of, and there was nothing more to do now but allow him time to correct it.

Homer watched the stock man disappear with his lamps. "He leaves the blue stubs on the tables here?"

"He's supposed to take them into the office. But, since he's got the piece with him, it's often left for the salesperson, if they're willing, to deliver."

"Like this one?"

"Which Sally will now deposit into the basket."

"As soon as I finish writing up this sale," said Sally with a snort of irritation. She gave Homer a curious look.

"From Herald Square," Shelly said with a crooked frown. "Checking out our inventory system."

She made a matching face, but said nothing to Homer. He tried to smile at her, but she cut him dead, and he turned back to Shelly.

"What happens to the yellow copy?"

"That goes into an envelope, which is dropped into a slot, then carried to the warehouse, where it is entered into a computer requisitioning a new sample for our floor."

"And the pink slips . . . ?"

"The stock man carries them along with the lamps until they're safely in place in the display room."

And Shelly led Homer after the stock man, who deposited the lamps on two end tables at either side of a Haitian couch, with rattan doilies under them. Once the lamps were centered on their doilies, the stock man initialed the pink slips and tucked them into his shirt pocket. He looked at Shelly quizzically, who was watching him with encouragement.

"Don't let us interrupt your process," Shelly said.

"My process?"

"With the slips."

He gestured toward the shirt pocket, and the stock man caught on, tucking them in more securely and then marching to the decorator's office, beyond the last display room, tacking both pink stubs to a bulletin board.

There was no one else in the office, and when the stock man left, Shelly and Homer were alone with the bulletin board.

"How often does this happen?" Homer asked.

"How often are lamps requisitioned?"

"No—how often is this bulletin board left unattended?"

"I know what you're thinking," Shelly said. "But there's no way to cheat the system. If a blue slip appears in the office basket, there had better be a pink one to match it, or the stock man who signed the blue slip on the floor is personally liable for the cost of the merchandise."

"How often are they checked? The blue against the pink?"

"Every night."

"At the end of the day?"

Shelly nodded.

"What if no blue slip is left on the floor?"

"Couldn't happen," Shelly said. "First—the stock man would run the risk of immediate dismissal if any passing salesman saw him carting off a floor sample without leaving a blue slip in its place. Second—who's going to run a scam that depends on such a whopping oversight? One bad move and the whole operation blows. That's not the way to make off with a dozen samples."

"You're convinced of it?"

"Absolutely."

"How long does a blue slip remain on the floor?"

"Until the first salesman sees it."

"Which is how long?"

"A few minutes."

"Do you think the one we just saw left is still where the lamps had been standing?"

Shelly could see Sally crossing to the phone to place

a call to the warehouse, checking stock. "I suspect she hasn't had a chance to deliver it to the office yet."

Homer strolled back to the Recliners area, where the blue stubs were indeed still on the tables. "We'll take these in for you," he said to Sally Pinter. "Shelly Lowenkopf and I will . . . since you look like your hands are full."

"Thanks," said Sally with the briefest of smiles, raising her pencil in salute.

Homer took the blue slip and carried it away. As soon as Sally turned her back, he stuck it into his jacket pocket. "Now let's go after that pink," he said.

When they returned to the decorator's office, it was no longer deserted. Harold Leming sat at a clear glass desk redrawing a set of plans—penciling in an arrangement, emitting a string of curses, and erasing whatever he had drawn.

"Not so easy this time," Shelly said.

"What's his name?" asked Homer.

"Harold Leming."

"Mr. Leming?" Homer said, louder. "Could you give me your attention, please?"

"Just a moment," replied Leming, refusing to look up. "Can't you see I'm busy?"

Homer snatched the pink stub from the board.

Shelly followed him out of the decorator's office. "Okay," he said, "so the system's got a few bugs in it. But you still haven't stolen anything from the floor."

"Oh, yes I have," said Homer, looking pleased with himself. "I've stolen a pair of lamps out of Recliners."

Shelly blinked at the lamps where they sat in the nearby display room. "What are you talking about? You haven't stolen anything! They're sitting over there, right now."

Homer shook his head. "They may look like they're still here, but they're gone—the only way the store knows that they ever arrived! A thing isn't here because you can touch it, Shell—it's here because it corresponds to a piece of paper somewhere. You and I have just eliminated the existence of those two lamps. Whether we actually take them now or leave them for later really doesn't matter at all."

Shelly looked at the two hunks of chrome gleaming on the end tables. "You mean . . . they're already stolen?"

"Already gone."

"But how do we sneak them out?"

"We don't," said Homer. "We carry them—with these." And he held up the pink transfer slips he'd lifted from the decorator's wall. "What do you say we give it a try? The two of us? With these lamps?"

Shelly didn't have any trouble imagining their success in riding down the freight elevator with the lamps in their arms. As long as they carried the pink slips too, no one would try to stop them. They could carry them down to the ground-floor bay and load them into a car.

"I think maybe we should mention this to the store manager instead," Shelly suggested.

Homer shrugged. "You know the ropes better than I do in this place."

Shelly led the way to the store manager's office one flight down from Furniture, and was surprised to discover behind the big desk Stanley Blumberg, from Max's minyan. No wonder this job had fallen to them, he realized, feeling naïve. Blumberg looked up and saw the two men standing in front of him, and reached for his suit jacket, bringing it closer to him and checking for the lump in its inside pocket.

"How can I help you gentlemen?"

Shelly explained the situation and their theory about the thefts. Blumberg listened carefully, nodding his head now and then, punctuating their account with cries of, "Those bastards!" When they had finished, he regarded Shelly with a certain respect and said, "Max was right about you. I don't know who *this* is, but he was right about you."

"This is Homer Greeley," Shelly said.

"I'm a police officer," Homer explained.

"Helping us out on the case," continued Shelly.

Blumberg studied them both for a minute. "So what now?" he said. "Who do we fire, or arrest?"

"We'll let you know," said Shelly, "just as soon as we know ourselves."

It didn't take them long to pick up the trail. Shelly showed Homer the rear freight elevator, where merchandise from the display rooms was taken downstairs when windows on the street had to be arranged. On the ground floor was a bay open to the street in which all sorts of things stood waiting, in cardboard boxes for the most part, but here and there, wrapped in clear plastic, were also large items, including pieces of furniture that had been sold off the floor. Homer propped himself on the arm of a Queen Anne chair and mused, "If only we knew which of this stuff had been hustled off the floor."

Shelly stared at a pair of items just behind the Queen Anne chair and said, "We do, Homer. We do." Easing his ex-partner out of his way, he squatted alongside the two bundles of plastic, inside which could be made out a sofa bed and loveseat in tufted rust velvet.

They sat outside in the Volkswagen squareback for most of the morning, waiting for the set to be loaded onto a truck. It was just before lunch, and just after Shelly had given up hoping, that a nondescript green van backed up to the bay and Jimmy the stock man climbed out.

The two men working the bay scowled, and started to wave him out, when a voice behind them said, "You guys go on to lunch. I'll help him out." It was Enrique Rousseau, the security guard from the furniture showroom.

One of the bay men asked Jimmy, "You got the paperwork?"

Jimmy waved a green sheet.

"I'll check it out," said Enrique quietly. "Don't worry—I got you covered."

The second bay man looked at the first, who shrugged and said, "Clams or pizza?"

His partner replied, "Clams."

Jimmy and Rousseau had the two pieces loaded in minutes and jumped in the van behind it. Jimmy was driving; Enrique closed the back of the van from inside. When it eased out from the bay, it was followed by the Volkswagen, which turned the corner after the van and followed it along the expressway. When it climbed the ramp to the Bronx River Parkway, it was followed there, too—when the men in the van must have noticed someone behind them. They increased speed, driving through the park. And the Volkswagen sped up, too. The van wound through the traffic, changing lanes three times in succession. And each time it made a change of course, the Volkswagen did the same. The van edged into the far right lane, maintaining its speed, and zoomed past the exit for Pelham Parkway—until, at the very last instant, its tires squealed, burning rubber as it crossed the white merge lines and bumped down the exit.

The Volkswagen did not catch the merge lines, but bounced over the grassway beyond the exit, doubling back toward the ramp as it swept down after the van of stolen furniture. And at that moment the rear doors of the van swung open and a heavy object thundered out, bounding on the macadam twice before toppling over and rolling down the hill into the grass of the park. As it did, its plastic unrolled, and it came to a rest in a pocket of leaves tucked away against the hill of the parkway. The plastic cover filled with air from below and blew itself across the green lawn, where it was lifted by a stronger wind and borne across the park until it caught on a streetlight at the edge of the greensward and wrapped itself around an aluminum pole. At the base of the pole a mongrel pup had been sniffing around for a place to empty his bladder. He looked up at the plastic beast snapping at the streetlight and added his own little yips to the struggle of prey and predator.

But Shelly and Homer did not stop for the couch or its wrapping. They raced after the van, its rear doors banging open, where Rousseau appeared again, struggling for his balance as he pushed a smaller object that seemed unwilling to jump. It was the matching loveseat, the only remaining evidence—but his luck did not hold. When he tried to dump it from the back of the van, its front legs cleared, but not its rear, and the little couch hung neither in nor out of the van, dragging on it, slowing its progress, kicking up bits of the road. As the van zoomed through the intersection at White Plains Road, Rousseau tried to unhinge the loveseat, forcing it to one side, and succeeded just so far—where it caught on a steel support of the el overhead. It clung to the girder, and also to the van, as its wood frame creaked and groaned but did not crack. The driver panicked and stomped on the gas, but while the engine whined, the tires whirled and skidded in place. Suddenly, the tires caught, and the van swung sideways, crashing with tremendous force into a second steel girder. That freed the loveseat of its hold on the first, but, as the driver was no longer in control, the vehicle rebounded from the girders, tilting over into the concrete base of the IRT station, where it toppled in a shower of glass.

Shelly and Homer sat in the squareback ten yards

behind the van and watched as it danced from steel partner to catastrophic contact with the concrete. It slid down the base, a few feet at a time, as its windows shattered and sides collapsed under the strain. By the time the van lay on its side, blocking two lanes of traffic, there was nothing for them to do but call for an ambulance and keep the crowd back.

The two men were extricated from the wreck still breathing, though covered in blood—unconscious, in shock, with multiple injuries. They did not look likely to be standing trial anytime soon. But they didn't look like they'd be stealing furniture, either.

# 18

Jill Morganthal had been waiting in the Allerton Avenue precinct house, wondering why her usually reliable partner had not even called in, when the telephone finally rang on her desk. *At last!* she thought, with a rush of relief she managed to restrain almost immediately. *I can just imagine the apology he's concocting.* Although the truth was she couldn't. But if her imagination failed her, so did the phone call, because the voice on the other end was rougher than Homer's and more jarring in her ear.

"We got something, amigo. Poquito—"

It was Montoya again, calling in his latest report from the barrio. Morganthal respected the man but did not like him, and cleared her throat quickly so he would hear the feminine quality in her voice before he said something he might regret.

"Officer Montoya?"

"Is this . . . Morganthal?" he said. "Okay, tell your partner we've got a line on this Poquito we saw on the wall the other night."

191

"What's the lead?"

Montoya hesitated. "It's against procedure, I know. But I met a woman the other day who teaches in the local school down there. And I asked her if she or any of her teaching pals ever came across these *placas* in the lockers, you know, or someplace like that. And she told me she'd ask around. Well, last night we go to dinner and she tells me about a friend of hers who teaches English in the same school. Writing—in those black and white notebooks with the blue lines."

"Composition."

"That's what Maria called it. Anyway, her friend remembers this one kid who turned in only one essay this term—one of the three she'd assigned. But it stuck in her mind because, she said, there was some real feeling behind it. It was about a kid who sees his name graffitied across the side of a subway car on the rails overhead—painted by his brother. And what do you think his brother calls him?"

*"Poquito?"*

"Little One. That's what it means, a nickname with love. So I check into it and find this kid lives with a foster mother in the projects. So I call the foster mom and say if she wants to keep those subsidies coming, she'd better get Poquito to drop by the community center after school today."

"And she said—"

*"Sí, sí.* He'll be there."

Morganthal approved of a little intimidation in a good cause, judiciously applied. And it seemed to her that Montoya had exercised excellent judgment. His call might have upset the foster mother, but how much unhappier would she be if the call was to inform her of the boy's demise?

She said, "We'll be there after three."

"Don't be late. Maria said she'd try to be there, too, after school. Just to try to make things smoother."

Jill wasn't anticipating a smooth encounter, but she said, "Thanks for the tip."

"Don't mention it. Except to Homer." And he rung off.

She did not get a chance to mention it to Homer until after lunch, when he called in from a telephone booth in the lobby of the municipal hospital. An infant was crying in the waiting room behind him, so it was only with difficulty that she made out his answer when she asked, "Where have you been all morning?"

"Pursuing fugitives," Homer said crisply. "Two arrests for grand theft."

"Auto?"

"Furniture. From the Parkchester Macy's. The store manager plans to write a letter to the captain commending our assistance and thanking him for our help."

"How on earth did you get involved in a . . ." Then she paused for a moment and said, "Lowenkopf."

That was why, she told herself, it made her so uncomfortable when Homer showed up at the community center at three with his old partner in the Reliant. Homer parked and locked up the doors while Jill waited on the sidewalk for him to explain himself. But all he said was, "Jill Morganthal—you've met Shelly already, haven't you?"

She did not miss the fact that he announced her last name but assumed that she would know Lowenkopf's. She did, of course, and he probably didn't know hers—but that, she felt, was beside the point. It irked her that Homer should have missed that particular point.

"I think we met when you cleaned out your desk—my desk, I suppose I should say."

She shook his hand firmly and found it was warmer and drier than she had expected.

"It looks neater than it ever did when it was mine," said Shelly. "I'll bet Homer appreciates that."

"You've . . . seen it recently?"

"I stopped by the precinct this weekend, to look in on a man in your holding cell. Thought I'd stop by the office, just to see who was in."

"Who was in?"

"Nobody."

The thought of Lowenkopf creeping around her desk made her feel even more uncomfortable. But she didn't have a chance to say anything further, because at that moment Maria Santayana appeared in the doorway of the community center building and directed herself to Homer.

"Are you here to see Alfonso?"

"Alfonso?"

"Alfonso Barreras. Poquito."

The boy was inside, in a cramped office overcrowded with desks. He was small, not short but frail, with large brown eyes that darted from Maria to the others and back again. Somehow she had won a piece of his trust since his arrival, when another boy had dropped him off at the door of the building and left him to enter alone. Maria had seen the older boy but said nothing, and her silence had impressed Alfonso as a token of sincerity and respect. But he regarded the officers with undisguised mistrust. He was there because a cop had threatened his mother, which was bound to produce a certain uneasiness at first. That was why Homer had brought along Shelly—to introduce another element into the meeting, someone who was no longer a cop yet who saw things as a cop would see them, who could talk to the cops and could talk to other people as well.

Jill Morganthal felt Shelly's presence as a rebuke to her own talents. But Homer was quite gracious about it; he ushered her into the room before either of them, and introduced her to the boy before Shelly or himself.

"Alfonso, this is Officer Morganthal, who came to see you today. My name is Sergeant Greeley. And this is Shelly Lowenkopf, a consultant with the department."

Alfonso glanced at Lowenkopf. "Nice jacket," he said.

Shelly took it off and tossed it across an unoccupied desk, where it slipped off and sagged to the floor. Homer reached over and folded it across the back of Morganthal's chair.

"Your name is Alfonso?" Homer went on. When the boy said nothing, interpreting the question as a statement of fact, Homer added, "Only sometimes you go by Poquito."

The boy's eyes slid over to him. So that's what this is about, they seemed to say. "Lots a people call their kids that name," he drawled.

"But there aren't lots of them spraying it over the walls," muttered Jill.

Homer was trying to be casual. "Are you the one that's written on the Foundation?"

Alfonso seemed to think it over. He knew it was illegal to be writing on private property, but he was proud that Benito had included him there too. He said, "I didn't write nothing on that Foundation, or anyplace else."

Homer studied him. "That wasn't you?"

The boy inspected his shoes. "I didn't say that."

"But you just said—"

Maria interrupted before Jill's tone grew impatient. "What did you mean to say, Alfonso?"

"I meant," said Alfonso slowly, "that I didn't write on no Foundation. Or on any other walls around here. I'm not a writer and don't do what I don't know how to do."

Maria listened, to see if any more was forthcoming, and then turned to Homer. "I believe him," she said emphatically. "It wasn't him."

"Just a second," said Shelly. "I believe him, too. But there's more information in what a person says than might appear at first, isn't there?"

Duh! thought Jill to herself. Who doesn't know that?

"Are you trying to tell us something more than we've heard, Alfonso?" asked Maria.

"I'm not trying to tell you anything, Maria."

Shelly nodded. "I know what you mean. You're just trying to get through our questions and get the fuck out of here."

The kid grinned. "You guessed it."

"I'll make it easy for you," said Shelly. "Twenty questions in all—yes or no. But you've got to give me straight answers. All right?"

"Yes," said Alfonso. "That's one."

"Fair enough," Shelly agreed, nodding, with a little smile that might have suggested he'd been taken for a fast one. "Here comes number two. Does that name on the Foundation wall—that *placa*, Poquito Six— does that mean you?"

"Yeah."

"But you didn't put it there."

"No."

"But someone you know did."

"Yeah."

"Your brother?"

"I haven't got a brother."

"A Fury?"

"That's right."

"Why don't you just ask him who?" asked Morganthal, and all the others looked at her.

"Because he wouldn't tell me," said Shelly. "Isn't that right, Alfonso?"

"Right," said the kid. "That's six."

"You're counting that? Don't answer that," Shelly said to him with a smile. "I don't need to waste any questions on whether or not I'm wasting any."

"Smart man."

"Thanks. But I'd rather hear that you were. So, where were we? Someone you know wrote your name on the Foundation—and on the wall where Rocio Lucero was killed. He was a Fury, but not your brother, because you don't have any brothers. Yet you wrote about one in the book you turned in to your composition teacher at school."

Alfonso sat up. "Mrs. Ramirez? She showed you that thing? Shit, that wasn't my brother anyway."

"That's what you called him."

"So what? It was just a composition, man. You know? You *compose* those things. That means make 'em up."

"So nobody wrote your name on a traveling subway car?"

He wasn't about to reveal information; but he didn't have to deny himself either. "I didn't say that."

"So somebody did. And it wasn't you. So it must have been whoever wrote your name those other places too."

"So what? You don't know who."

"El Toro."

"That's just a name, isn't it? A *placa*. You see them horns all over the place."

"No," said Shelly, "not all over the place. Just in some places. Overwritten by Rocio Lucero on the Foundation. And also on the fence where he was killed."

"That doesn't mean he did it."

"Who?"

"Anybody."

"Somebody did it."

"Yes, that's true, somebody did it. How many answers is that now?"

"I'd call it ten. Assuming everything I've been saying is on the level, and your silence is a *yes.*"

There was a long pause. "So let's get on to number eleven, already, huh?"

"All right," said Shelly, "number eleven. Now I want you to think before answering this one. Let's say you knew somebody whose graffiti was getting covered up. And then the overwriter caught it. You think the original writer blew him away?"

"I don't need to think about that. No. He didn't do it."

"You're sure?"

"No, I said, man, that's right. No. So, go on. You've got twelve."

"Somebody else did."

"That's what I said, didn't I? Thirteen."

"All right," said Shelly, musing it over. "I believe it. But the trouble is, so many people are going to find it hard to accept. Just because you said so."

"You mean like the cops, here?"

"I mean like Lucero's pals."

"Diablos? They're stupid, man. There's no reasoning with them. What does it matter what they think?"

"If they think the writer had anything to do with it, they will come after him, won't they?"

"Where you been, man?" asked Alfonso. "Don't you know they already come after Raoul?"

"Was he the drive-by shooter?"

"How should I know? But the point is, Lucero's old news."

"What about Matas?"

"Who?"

"José Matas—a Diablo—and his girlfriend Esperanza Sedillo were shot up in a closet in the high school basement at nine o'clock last night."

Alfonso didn't seem to have heard that the girl was caught in the shooting. "For Raoul," he said quietly.

"You think Esperanza had something to do with that?"

"Not her, man. But that's what happens when you hang out with a soldier."

"José was fourteen, Alfonso."

"A young soldier, man."

"Any idea who did that one?"

"No."

"Not the graffiti writer?"

"I told you already—not him! He don't make those kind of loud noises. He's a writer, man, an artist. Why're you so anxious to pin something on him?"

"Because it was his work covered up. He's either a shooter or a victim, Alfonso. We're just trying to figure out which it'll be before he figures it out."

"He's figuring already—don't worry! He figures better than you." It was delivered with enough gusto, but was all bravado—behind the boy's defiance, he was afraid, and anxious to return to the streets. He said, "How many more damned questions have you still got, man?"

"Just one," said Shelly, squatting near him. "Who is this writer, Alfonso?"

"That's not yes and no, man," said the boy. "Not part of the game."

"The game is over," Shelly replied, standing quite close to him, so that his height seemed elongated by comparison. "It's simple: They're going to kill him now. Your brother—or whoever he is to you. They're going to run out of other ideas and blow him away with a shotgun when his back is turned—while he's writing on a wall somewhere. Maybe he'll even be writing your name—Poquito—when they nail him. But it is going to happen, sooner or later, unless you help us stop them."

And Shelly didn't give him a chance to respond, moving away from the boy without looking back until he had left the room. There was a long moment of silence inside, during which Alfonso might have reached out to Maria or even to Homer. But he just slouched in his chair, examining the floorboards, until he said, "Can I go now?"

Jill knew it wasn't going to work—she could have told them that and saved them all the trouble. But there were things Homer had to learn for himself. She looked over at her partner as if to say, What'd you expect? and noticed immediately a subtle change in his demeanor. Over the last few days his detachment had seemed to be slipping away; but now, as he watched Lowenkopf try to reach the kid on his own gutter level, Greeley's eyes took on their old familiar distance and an attitude of philosophical remove. No wonder he liked having Lowenkopf around—while Shelly did all the heart-wrenching, Homer reserved his own thinking for abstract deductive reasoning.

Maria waited with Alfonso until the officers had gone. But he declined her offer of a ride home. He did not tell her, but he was sure that Benito would be waiting for him behind the center's playground, beyond the chain-link fence. He was surprised, then, to discover his cousin inside the yard, kneeling beside a huge mural on the back wall of the building. There were open tubes of paint by his feet and he worked carefully, squeezing paints from their tubes onto the pavement, mixing them there, and applying them to the outline of a playground scene that had been laid out on the wall.

Behind him, kicking a soccer ball around the basketball court, were a group of Diablos, who eyed him with contempt but said nothing directly to him, observing the rules of the center as Speedball had laid them down: no weapons in the yard and no fighting, no drugs, or even bad language. They were not cursing Benito, or dissing him, but they complained to one another that this outsider was painting on the wall that Rocio had designed—and the fact that Speedball had given him the paints didn't sit well with them either. Alfonso felt afraid, seeing Benito alone with the six of them, but they seemed unwilling to break the rules and risk access to the boxing club. Still, it was a great relief when they slipped through a hole in the fence and loped off into the streets.

Alfonso sat beside his older cousin and watched him work. His hands understood the needs of the paint so well—they squeezed the tubes gently, so that the paint came out on its own, like a turtle ready to risk extending its neck from its shell. Then he scooped it off with an ice-cream stick and lathered it onto the wall, using the stick at first, then his thumb. Before he allowed any paints to touch a new section, he ran his delicate fingertips over it, taking the feel of the surface, sensing the colors it needed to coax the image inside the concrete to reveal itself on the exterior. Children swung on the swings by the wall while their mamas talked on the benches, and Benito seemed to brush the hair of each child until he understood how the wind would play there. Along the outside of the yard fence a row of sycamores whispered how the wind appeared to them. Benito bent his head as if he heard them murmuring over his shoulder, as his long slender fingers felt each crevice in the surface of the concrete wall.

"Let's go," said Alfonso suddenly, taking a chill. Benito looked up and saw him shiver, and collected his tubes of paint, wrapping them in a handkerchief and returning them to the desk in the community center.

"This way," he told Alfonso, who had headed for the hole in the fence. He followed his cousin's instructions as soon as they were expressed. The center was a tiny island of compromise in a troubled world. There was no reason to run any risks that could be avoided with forethought.

But there are some risks that cannot be avoided, and the five Diablos and Torquemada had made sure that Benito and Alfonso could not avoid them. The cousins walked fast, crossing into the alley at the soonest opportunity and keeping to the shadows of the fire escapes, but Torquemada and his crew knew this neighborhood even better and caught up with them by the school yard. Benito did not have a chance to draw a weapon, if he had one—which Alfonso thought he did not. The Diablos were better prepared. The big one, Torquemada, called out to them, and, when they turned, five others circled around them, forcing them back toward the black iron bars of the school gate.

"An artist, eh?" Torquemada said, grinning at Benito. "And a little bird on his shoulder."

The others laughed at Alfonso, who tried to stand bravely but could not help shrinking toward his cousin.

"We are coming from the center," said Benito coldly.

"Yes," Torquemada agreed, "you are coming from there. But you are not there now. You are here, with us, now. And we make the rules here." And from under his raincoat he drew out the long barrel of a shotgun.

Alfonso struggled to keep his knees from shaking.

Benito looked at the shotgun with disdain. "This is how you fight, Torquemada? Six men are not enough? You need a boo-yah to kill me, too?"

"I'm not going to kill you," Torquemada said. His tone was not reassuring, but the words alone helped

Alfonso conquer his fear. He was not going to kill them. Then all it would mean was pain—he could handle that. But his left knee started to tremble again before he could stop it.

"Give me your hand," said Torquemada, and he held out his own as if to shake. Benito eyed it suspiciously, but could hardly refuse, and opened his own hand toward the other. But the big man did not grasp it by the palm, taking it instead by the wrist and raising it, inspecting the palm. "I see a long line of life," he said, "but a lot of suffering in it."

Benito tried to pull away his arm, but Torquemada held it, squeezing it between two black iron bars of the gate. Then he set the open end of the shotgun barrel against it.

Benito's other arm curled in a fist, but two Diablos caught him from the back and held him fast. A third held his upright arm tighter between the bars. There was barely a second in which Alfonso might have acted, but not more than that, because the fourth Diablo grabbed him too, and shoved him alongside Benito. There was no place Alfonso would rather have suffered—but did it have to be then, and there? Torquemada moved in close to them, inspecting first his face and then his cousin's with a show of fine contempt.

"An artist. And a writer?"

Benito met his gaze coolly, glaring back at him. "Only Diablos have no respect for a writer."

Torquemada raised the shotgun level with Benito's hand, so that its long barrel ran straight into it. "Is this enough respect for you?"

Benito said nothing.

"And how much did you show Rocío? Or José?"

Still nothing.

"What is your name, writer?"

## Richard Fliegel

"El Toro," said Benito, with pride.

Torquemada pulled the trigger. There was a *boom-ah* that exploded in his skull and an instant of pure horror, as directly beside Alfonso's head the delicate bones of his cousin's right hand leaped through the back of his palm.

204

# 19

Tuesday night Shelly had his chance to make up for
the weekend, when Thom had been sleeping out,
unavailable to visit with his natural father. Though
very little of substance was ever actually said between
them, Shelly and Thom each placed a great value on
these visits, though perhaps for different reasons.
Shelly carried an old anxiety that his eleven-year-old
son not suffer from the mistakes he and Ruth had
made in their marriage, that he develop a strong sense
of his personal self-worth, his right to be loved, which
can only be given to a person by loving parents early
on. If he and Ruth could no longer live under a single
roof, that was no reason why Thom should not receive
from each of them as much love as he would have had
had they managed their own emotional life more
reasonably. Shelly had resolved many years before
that Thom understand in the recesses of his spirit that
his father loved him, and not only loved him, but
valued his company more than any other that might
present itself as an alternative. It was a tall order, but

over the years Shelly had stuck by his guns, making
time for his son despite stakeouts and criminal investigations that ran around the clock for weeks on
end—never enough time, of course, to satisfy himself,
but enough to assure an unending demonstration of
paternal love.

For his part, Thom really didn't need to be reas-
sured that his father liked to see him. He wasn't sure
why, exactly, and it might have been due to the efforts
Shelly made, but he believed it, and accepted his
father's love as genuine and unstinting. Convincing
his father of those assumptions, of the effectiveness of
his campaign, was another matter entirely. Thom had
learned early on that Shelly was only convinced that
his son understood how he loved him when he was
actively demonstrating his feelings to his son. So, if
Shelly felt he had to see Thom in order to show how
much he loved him, the boy felt he had to see his
father in order to demonstrate how well he understood how much he was loved. The result was they saw
a great deal of each other, and, if neither of them had
much to say to the other, they nonetheless appreciated
what was not said, and what did not have to be said,
between them.

Conversation, however, was always less than a
sparkling art. Thom would climb through the passenger door of the Volkswagen squareback, and struggle
with the lock, which stuck, and Shelly would tell him
to tilt the knob back as he pushed it down, and Thom
would push it back, but the door would still refuse to
lock until Shelly came around the car and locked it
from the outside with his key. As they drove off, Shelly
would ask Thom where he wanted to eat, and Thom
would say he didn't know, and Shelly would ask what
he felt like eating, and Thom would say any kind of
food, and Shelly would suggest maybe lobster at City
Island, and Thom would say okay but make a face,

and Shelly would ask if he had a better idea, and they would eat at the Riverdale Diner.

But tonight was different. Shelly was not a cop anymore, and while that might have made it easier to leave his job behind, he was a partner now, which meant there was no one higher up the chain of command to tidy up unfinished business. The fact that they had taken the rabbi's case on a *pro bono* basis made not the slightest difference. David Horowitz lay in a coma in Hartsdale Memorial Hospital, the back of his head having been dented with a fireplace poker, and Shelly felt a certain obligation to look in on the man. Thom waited in the car while Shelly hustled into the visitors' room outside Intensive Care, made a polite inquiry, and was informed that, no, Mr. Horowitz had not yet woken up.

But he couldn't leave Thom sitting in the car while he made his second stop, at the synagogue, where Max had implied Dave's "accident" might leave them even shorter for a minyan, unless . . . something Max thought might happen, which would solve the problem once and for all. Shelly could not get out of him just what the solution might be, so there was a bit of curiosity mixed with his sense of obligation when he stopped by the synagogue to catch the *mincha-ma'ariv* service on the holiday of Sukkoth.

Before they entered the shul, they saw on the grass beside the front door a ten-foot structure of plain wood stakes, covered in large palm fronds. There were some men inside it, one of whom was shaking an especially large palm frond. It was called a *lulev*, whose unacknowledged origin lay in the distant past in a forgotten fertility rite.

For his part, Thom was taking in the surroundings with open eyes and mouth. He had never seen a *sukkah* erected, and the sight of these somber men shaking fronds was incomprehensible to him. Had his father taken them back through the centuries to a primitive tribal gathering? No, he understood when they entered the sanctuary, these were Jews—his own bloodline. But his blood must have been the only thing he had ever had in common with them.

And then it was Shelly's turn to be astonished. Because the *mechitzah,* the curtain that had separated the men in the front part of the sanctuary from their wives and daughters in the rear, had been moved, so that instead of dividing the room into front and back, it divided it lengthwise, into right and left. He was no less surprised to see Irene lead Julia in from the *sukkah* to a seat in the first row, on the left of the curtain as one faced the ark. To the right of the curtain, all the men were already in their seats, most with grave faces. But Max glanced backwards toward the door and stood with a broad grin.

"Shelly!" he cried, extending his arms. "Come, come, come!"

"Life goes on, I see."

"Why not? The hazzan has the keys to the cabinets, and the Torah has the keys to life. We survive one thing after another." He shook his head. "And who is this with you?"

"My son, Thomas. Thom, this is Max Pfeiffer—my partner and my friend."

"A beautiful introduction," said Max. "Come, sit with me." And he patted the seat alongside his own as if warming it up for Thom, until the boy felt an obligation to occupy it. "Have you ever been to a service before?" Max asked cordially.

"Not like this," said Thom.

"There's nothing to it, really. A few prayers from the book and a little chanting together. Normally, the hazzan would sing, but he's not here tonight."

"Tsinger's not here?" asked Shelly, who pictured the spindly old man as living inside the shul.

"Sick," said Max, shaking his head sadly. "He's older than he looks, you know."

Shelly thought he looked pretty old. And the habitual droop of his mouth toward the floor didn't minimize the years.

"And the surgery—eh!" Max made a gesture to indicate they could hardly expect more. "He's never really been the same since he came out of the hospital."

Shelly's seat was on the aisle, or where the aisle had been before the *mechitzah* was rotated ninety degrees. He felt the filmy curtain brush his shoulder.

"What's going on with the curtain, here, Max? Family night at the shul?"

"This is a new innovation," said Max, "in memory of Lillian. To tell you the absolute truth, it's a necessity now. Because of our shrinking numbers, which have only been aggravated by the loss—temporarily, thank God!—of our president, Dave Horowitz, the Ritual Committee voted tonight to adopt a recommendation the rabbi has made on behalf of our ailing president."

Zweizig, who was sitting behind them, leaned forward to set their conversation straight.

"Don't blame this on the Ritual Committee."

Shelly was impressed. "You're going to allow the women to see what's going on?"

Zweizig made a face.

"More dramatic than that! There are shuls all over the country that have begun to respond to those pressures. But here, because we cannot make a minyan night after night, and the situation is growing only worse . . ."

Zweizig seemed unable to finish. Shelly attempted to prompt him as gently as possible. "You're going to count the women in the minyan now?"

"God help us."

*"Mazeltov!"* Shelly offered a congratulatory hand, but the Ritual Committee chairman declined it.

"You don't understand how troubling this is to some of the older members."

He looked around sympathetically. But Shelly found it hard to find anybody Zweizig might comfortably consider a member older than himself.

"Change is never easy," he said, seeking comfort in inanity.

Zweizig shrugged as if there were a kernel of wisdom there. But his mind was already contemplating the implications of the policy. "Maybe we'll get some new members now. I just hope a few of them are Jews."

Shelly felt his own ethnic identity questioned by the remark. And Thom seemed to be listening now, too. "There are all kinds of Jews in this world," Shelly said. "And all kinds of ways of being Jewish."

Zweizig had heard all the arguments already. He was more interested in expounding his own views.

"Do you know what the really ironic part is? Can you guess who pushed for this hardest?"

"Horowitz?"

"He supported the idea, in principle. But he was never able to actually propose the resolution. Privately my understanding is that the rabbi's endorsed the idea for some time, convinced of it as a solution to our problem by none other than—"

"Lily Levinski," said Shelly, the answer dawning on him with a tingle at the back of his scalp.

"Now you've got it," said Zweizig.

Shelly sat for a moment in silence, looking around the room, which seemed more full of life now than it had under the old arrangement. He could picture her, in the back, all alone behind the curtain, a woman of considerable persuasive power when she set her mind to a goal. He could imagine just how she would have approached the rabbi, trundling purposefully down the aisle—just as Irene was doing now.

Max saw her, and got up from his seat. "Here's where I show all the nay sayers they were right to worry about the effects of the change."

"What was their concern?"

"That women will distract us from the spirituality of the service. They were absolutely right. I can feel my distraction growing already. Excuse me. I'll be back."

And he strolled off after Irene.

Shelly sat in his seat and watched the others fill, with men on one side and women on the other. Thom was two seats to his right, so he was afforded a view of his son at once intimate and removed, as the boy turned his head this way and that, transfixed by his surroundings. When Max returned, he carried with him two prayer books, one of which he handed to Shelly and the other to Thom, opening the boy's to the correct page, pointing.

"That's where we'll start," Max said. "Can you read any Hebrew at all?"

Thom shook his head.

"It doesn't matter," said Max. "God doesn't listen to our prayers anyway. The important thing is to be here, to take part in the worship of a community, united in the sight of God. Each of us finds God in his or her own way—the pages of the Torah are a good place to look, but they're not the only place. Just sit and listen—or stand and listen—when I do. Most of these people don't think about God too much, day to day. But they have come here for many years, and don't realize it, but can no longer tell if it's God or each other they have been coming to see. And you know what? There's no difference, either way."

The speech made Shelly's head ache but Thom seemed to follow it well enough—it was no stranger, at least, than anything else he was seeing or hearing. The rabbi came down from his office at the top of the stairs and began. Shelly didn't even try to stay with them. He stood when the other men stood, and swayed when they swayed, and sat when they took their seats. Every now and then he turned a page. But the chanting of the prayers failed to draw him in. Instead, their music eased his mind, and he found himself thinking about Lillian again, sitting alone at the back of the shul while the men sang along with the hazzan. And then he noticed that Irene had never returned from the outer room to her seat beside Julia.

He leaned over to Max. "What happened to Irene?"

"The woman is a saint," sighed Max. "When she heard that the hazzan was sick tonight, unable to join the service, she decided to bring a little of our joy to him. She couldn't wait but went home for some chicken soup, which she had to bring to him now."

"The hazzan?"

"That's right. Why?"

Shelly wasn't sure why, but a sense of alarm gripped him and he caught the lapel of Max's jacket. It was something Zweizig had been saying to him just before the service. And then another memory floated in— Max's own voice.

"Max!" he said aloud.

"What?"

"Didn't you tell me that Tsinger had the keys to these cabinets?"

"He has all the keys to this place—"

"Including the rabbi's desk drawer?"

Max tried to remember.

Shelly remained standing by his seat when everyone else sat down, and Max rose slowly beside him.

"I think she's in terrible danger—"

# 20

Hazzan Itzak Tsinger lived in a two-bedroom apartment on the sixth floor of a walk-up—an apartment building built before the war, without an elevator. A flight of incredibly steep white marble stairs rose from inside the lobby door, zigzagging from one poorly lit landing to the next. Irene looked up at that staircase from the lobby floor with a pot of chicken soup in her hands, and her resolve nearly faltered. But the old hazzan had no one else to look after him except the women from the shul—not that he had ever done much to reward them for their efforts in the past. He was a strange man, Itzak Tsinger—even stranger after his surgery. But there was nothing to an act of *tzedakah* if it was done for the reward; what made it a mitzvah was that a person gave of herself to another for the sake of the gift alone. Irene took a deep breath, gripped the handles of her soup pot more securely, and began her ascent.

Climbing up and down those stairs had kept old Itzak healthy all the years of his residency in that dark brick building. He had moved into the place in

1933—which Irene thought must have been the last time anyone had painted his apartment. He couldn't blame the landlord for that, she recognized; the painters were kept out by the same thing that had kept him in his apartment for so long—not finances or memories, or even a sense of belonging there. It was records. Eight thousand of them.

She had heard his side of the story.

It had started simply enough. Tsinger was a simple man. To help him with his studies of melodies and harmonies, he scraped together money for a record player and a few special records to play on it. And over the years he had bought a few more, expanding his interests from the European folk melodies of his first few disks to the classical repertoire that developed on its fringes—instrumentals, of course, but also vocals. From opera he learned many valuable lessons, which he applied to his own work in the shul. In his free time there was nothing he enjoyed more than spending a couple of hours in the record store, talking with the clerks behind the counter about their latest acquisitions, and whether a new one was as good as the ones on a shelf over his living room console.

That shelf didn't suffice to support his collection for long and Itzak moved the bulk of them to the linen closet one day—which held them for nearly two years. He was a single man. His expenses were limited, since he lived a life of God, taking few pleasures. When he awoke in the morning, he said the blessing of awakening and wrapped the leather *tfillin* straps around his head and left arm—close, as it should have been, to his heart. When he had crossed a street and arrived on the other side, he murmured a blessing of arrival. So what was the evil in collecting a few more albums—a hazzan, whose music was his way of expressing his thanks to God?

After operas, he collected individual voice recitals.

Then operettas. He remembered the day, in 1938, when he bought his first musical. *Showboat.* He had stood in the aisle of the record store with the cardboard sleeve in his hands, conscious of the step he was about to take—the risk he was about to run. Who would fall into temptation were it not pleasing to the eye—and in his case the ear? But the lyrics of "Old Man River" kept ringing in his head, as Robeson had rendered it: "You and me, we sweat and strain, body all achin' and racked with pain. . . ." Who could have missed the living spirituality expressed in that song? It broadened and deepened his own religious awareness, and made him a better Jew. He determined never to play it on the Sabbath, of course, or even when he was thinking about the Sabbath on other days. But he loved to have it there on the shelf, where he could reach up whenever he liked to fill the house with music that moved him so powerfully.

Then, of course, came *Oklahoma!* with an entirely different message about the world. That was America —everything he could not understand about it. When he listened to the radio during the war, and could not figure out who Roosevelt was talking to, he played the album of *Oklahoma!* and recognized a difference in point of view between Rivington and Essex streets and that of the rest of the country. Album by album, he constructed a sense of the world beyond the sheltered community in which he lived his life. When his linen closet overflowed, he built shelves near the ceiling on every wall in every room of his flat. There was a built-in bookcase in the living room, which he filled, of course, with albums, as well as several wooden cases that dominated his study. At one point he realized he no longer had the strength to move them, or to take them down from their shelves to box them for moving. So he was stuck there, in the sixth-floor apartment, by his record collection, the weight of which his landlord said kept that end of the building on the ground.

Hah! Some joke.

As Irene reached the sixth-floor landing, she stopped to rest on the banister. From the narrow end of the hall where the hazzan's door was hidden, she heard music: the stirring strains of a klezmer band playing East European melodies.

Itzak Tsinger was aware that his record playing disturbed his neighbors sometimes—just as the noise of their arguments and their children and their love-making disturbed him. One had to put up with all sorts of inconveniences in the close quarters of an apartment building. He was an old man, sick enough, who would soon pass away. Then the landlord could rent out the apartment to a new tenant, at twice the cost, and the neighbors could find something else to complain about. He was not the most patient man, himself, and was a little hard of hearing. He kept to himself, and didn't waste smiles as if he had an endless supply. He would snap at the children in the courtyard when they came running into him, chasing a ball. Didn't the sign forbid ball playing? They did not care for him, and he returned their opinion, but only God is perfect. A little shortness of temper, an occasional lapse in politeness—these were not the worst sins.

And that was the list of his imperfections, as he had counted them on Yom Kippur. He was lonely, but never chose to address that need by adjusting his life in any way to the likely needs of another. When the rabbi said, "Life is compromise, Itzak—why don't you find someone to argue about it with?" Tsinger would shake his head in wonder and say nothing. Oh, he knew all about the rabbi's indiscretions, as he called them—the Levinski woman was only the most flagrant. Hadn't the rabbi allowed himself to flick off the lights in the sanctuary after the Sabbath service had concluded? There was no end to the list of similar affronts—of sins, when you came down to it, and tolerance of sins. They had worked together for thirty years, and Itzak had said nothing, but kept his thoughts and his counsel to himself.

To be fair, the rabbi would probably have married her, if she had not been an *agunah*. It was not a casual liaison. But the point was, she was not free, and the rabbi should have stayed away from her completely. What was so important, that he hug and kiss that woman? What was so special about her?

There came a knock at his door, and on his way to answer it, he stopped at the record player to turn over the album, which had come to an end. Then he went to see to the door. Peering through the peephole, which made the entire hallway look like a horror movie, he saw a woman standing close to his door, ringing the bell. What did she want?

"Yes?"

"It's Irene. Open up. I brought you some soup."

She stepped back so he could see the pot in her hands. So he undid the locks, one at a time, and opened the door for her. She was wearing a blue dress, very nice, as if for services. He was wearing his bathrobe over pajamas and a sleeveless white undershirt, with slippers he knew he had to replace. She looked at his outfit and pinched her mouth to one side.

"How long have you been wearing those clothes?"

The question did not strike him as rude, but as an inquiry after his state of mind, which implied an offer of assistance if any was necessary. He dismissed the implicit offer with a tilt of his hand.

"I've been doing my own laundry for sixty years now. I can keep myself in underwear, thank you."

"Let me heat this up for you, at least."

Itzak climbed back into his bed and listened to the sounds from the kitchen as she opened cabinets, looking for a bowl, and drawers, for a *fleishidik* spoon. His head was aching again today—when had it not since the surgery that had put him into the hospital for a week, where they pumped him full of poisons and left him lying, alone and disoriented, under a tight sheet in a narrow bed by the window?

And then, when he came back to find that plans had been laid to desecrate the shul in his absence . . .

He did not like to think of it. But he could not forget the conversation they had shared—himself, the rabbi, and that woman. With her plan to make a minyan! As if God could not count the men for Himself!

He allowed his mind to drift to the music, which was sad and sweet and reminded him of a world now dead. He had come to this country from Galicia, in Eastern Europe, where he had spent his boyhood during the First World War stealing potatoes off the army trucks so that his mother and sisters could eat. After the war, they had sent him to the States, on a ticket paid for by an uncle in Detroit, where he would earn the money to bring over the rest. But he had not been able to earn enough to send for them in time; when the Nazis came through, they all perished— women and young girls! It was the music that brought them back to him, the music he used to sing while his mother listened appreciatively as she washed his clothes for the morning. Only the culture he kept alive still linked him to the world he had left in Galicia, with his mother and sisters alive in it.

Irene came into the bedroom with her soup in his porcelain bowl. She brought a long, heavy spoon with her, a paper napkin, and a telephone book. She set the book on the comforter, placed the folded napkin on the book, and the bowl of soup at its center of gravity.

"Now," she said. "What else?"

## A MINYAN FOR THE DEAD

The hazzan murmured a blessing and took a long slurp of soup. Good and salty. He scooped up a piece of floating chicken and said, "Bread?"

"Do you have any?"

"In the box on the counter by the toaster oven."

She went to get it—very proficient, this one. A lot like her friend Lillian . . .

She had presented it all so thoughtfully. Certain changes in our membership, and changes in the world—our contract with the Eternal One to be decided by a vote! Renegotiated with the Lord! It was laughable, really—or at least it should have been, if Sholem had been able to see her for what she was, and to recognize blasphemy when he heard it. But he had sat there, in her apartment, and listened to her plan as if it were the most sensible thing in the world. She was sure the Ritual Committee would accept it, with the rabbi's support and his own; Horowitz had already indicated he would follow the clerical lead. And all the while the two of them, the rabbi and that woman, had been planning what they would do to each other once the old man went along! But he wasn't about to be taken in—not Itzak Tsinger. He listened politely, of course, and said he would think about it—to make Sholem happy! But the only thing he really had to think about was how to get rid of her. When Sholem made an excuse to stay behind with her, he had supplied an answer to that one too.

From the kitchen, through the other rooms, Irene called in, "None of it's sliced yet?"

"There's a bread knife in the second drawer," Itzak shouted back. "Just bring it in and I'll cut it. Just bring the whole thing."

And he heard the utensils slide as she opened the cutlery drawer, until the rising strains from the record player drowned her out.

His mind drifted back to Lillian.

He had left her apartment to think about the *mechitzah,* but thought about the gun in the drawer instead. He had never liked it there, himself, but Sholem was a practical man. A noisemaker he called it, to frighten off spooks in the night. Itzak had seen his own share of spooks, even if he had never spent any time where the men dressed up in sheets with pointy hats in the night and splashed walls with swastikas, and burnt down synagogues. If Sholem chose to protect his books with a noisemaker, who could blame him? And, once the terrible idea was accepted, what was the difference, really, between protecting the House of God from an assault that came from without and an invidious kind that came from within?

There was a point in his reasoning here that caused him trouble, irritating him in spite of himself. Itzak turned his mind to the music again as the violin faded. Since the surgery, deep thinking required too much effort. But he couldn't help thinking of Lillian . . .

He had meant to scare her with the gun. He waited outside until Sholem came out, and he went back in to see her alone. She was surprised, he thought, to see him again—and he was shocked at her attitude. Because the sweetness of her presentation, that had so affected the rabbi, was gone now—completely disappeared! A display for Sholem's sake alone.

First he had tried to convince her.

She said she understood his concerns, but simply disagreed: Women were different today. She did not intend to distract men, if the *mechitzah* was moved, any more than she expected them to be distracting her. She would not listen to his explanation of the difference between the sexes, or his citations of the verses that supported his view. The One God was her God, too, and she felt that He should hardly object to being worshiped by women as well as by men. That was what really got him mad—as if it were up to any of them to decide how He should choose to be worshiped! He tried to raise this point with her, to help her see the problem, but she was never really interested in learning.

She asked him to excuse her—she said she had to dress—and left him alone in the living room, where he stood for two full minutes expecting her to return. But she never did. And then he heard her through the rooms.

Irene came back with his bread and his knife, and he sawed off a thick slab of rye. She watched with approval as he dragged it along the edge of the bowl, picking up stray carrots and bits of celery and onion there. He tilted the bowl so that his spoon could reach the last broth, and dropped the spoon back into the bowl with whatever else remained.

She took the bowl but left him the bread and knife, standing over him as he wiped his chin on the napkin. "Thank you," he said at last.

"That's all right."

"Did you come straight from the shul?"

"The Sukkoth service."

"Do they have enough for a service tonight? Without me and David Horowitz?"

Irene hesitated. "The Ritual Committee adopted a new policy on that."

"On what?" asked Tsinger as she carried out his bowl. She didn't reply so he asked again more loudly. "On what?"

He heard the tap run in the kitchen.

And turned his mind to the music.

What a stupid thing a gun is! The only way to use it to scare a little sense into someone is to threaten to do a great harm. So he had taken it out and pointed it at her, when he went into the bedroom. She was inside, with her blouse off, sitting at a mirror in a satin thing with shoulder straps, rubbing ointment on her shoulders. But she didn't even turn around and look at him. She had chutzpah, that woman!

He couldn't recall what he said about that—it couldn't have been too rude. Her reply was certainly uncalled for. What was it now? Something, watching him in her mirror . . . about lying down to die. She hadn't meant Itzak personally, of course—she'd meant the shul, if they couldn't adapt to the world of the future. But what about the past, he had wanted to know—should they abandon all their loved ones to the fires?

She told him she'd had enough of the past—she was thinking about what life still had to offer. So full of high spirits—she started to sing! What did she think he would make of that? he wondered. It was so easy to pull the trigger. He thought it would break the glass. That would have frightened her, if it had struck the glass. . . .

He tried to turn his mind back to the music, but he couldn't help hearing Irene instead, coming back to his room.

He had expected them to come for him, once the police took Sholem away, but they never did, and he thought he understood why. This was Sholem's way of repentance, of acknowledging his insight—he refused to free himself at Itzak's expense. There was no way for Horowitz to understand that, of course, though he had worked out the rest for himself. Lillian must have spoken to him, winning over the president's support for her proposal. He had urged Itzak to turn himself in, and then threatened to do it for him. That was when Itzak had clarified the situation with the poker from the fireplace.

And now they were starting again—a new "policy" from the Ritual Committee! He knew what that must entail. So the rabbi let her have her way in death.

Because women like this one here continued the cause. Lillian and Irene did not speak for all women —for his mother, and sisters, and the women who had died with them. So how many more would repudiate the past if something happened to these?

His head throbbed. He held it.

Sholem would be angry at him. He wouldn't understand it all followed from his first acquiescence. Like the apple in the Garden—you took a single bite and all the evil rushed through the skin. Well, it hadn't been Tsinger who took the first bite: It was she who had offered it and Sholem who accepted it. But he would wait for that revelation to dawn on his rabbi. If he was forced to bleed another lamb, he would make that sacrifice, too. God would understand and forgive.

"Are you finished with that bread now?" Irene asked.

Tsinger lay back on his pillows.

She picked up the chunk of rye bread and looked around the comforter. "Whatever has happened to the knife, now?" She knelt and peered under the bed.

When Shelly Lowenkopf found the sixth-floor walk-up Max had supplied as the address of the ailing hazzan, his heart sank at the pitch of the staircase. These were deep steps and lots of them, and he was nearly out of breath already after running the five blocks from the shul at breakneck speed. But there was no faster way to the rooms at the top. He drew a deep breath and leaped for the first flight, tackling the marble steps two at a time. By the third floor his lungs were pounding, but he kept up his speed, in the best tradition of New York's Finest.

On the fifth floor, it occurred to him that he could stop and call for help. He pounded on one door but received no answer and jangled the bell of another; the tiny peephole lightened and darkened, but no one responded. He stood in the center of the floor by the stairs and shouted at the top of his lungs, "Someone call the police!" It was an odd thing to hear himself say, but it made him feel better. He caught his breath and bounded up the last flight.

Tsinger's apartment was buried in the corner, like a rabbit hole on a riverbank. There was a buzzer, which made no sound when he pressed it. So he knocked on the door itself. There was no answer specifically to him, but he heard a shriek from inside and beat his fist on the door.

"Open up!" he cried. "Police!"

He could explain the situation later, if it helped get the door opened. But there was still no direct response. Instead, another shriek followed, louder than the first, and he put his shoulder to the door. It was metal, aluminum, but by the way it gave he suspected it was only locked once, by the knob—a lucky break, in this building. He squatted by the doorknob, rolled his shoulder, and let his weight do the heavy work. Once, twice, three times—and still the doorjamb held. And then, as he braced himself for a more reckless assault, the door suddenly opened in front of him.

On the other side was Irene, utterly shaken. Her eyes were large as coat buttons, and her mouth was slack, the lower lip trembling as she stared back into the apartment. She pointed a tremulous finger toward the bedroom in the rear.

"In there," she said hoarsely. "With a bread knife."

"Call the police," said Shelly.

She turned toward the bedroom, then stopped, and looked back at Shelly. "The phone's in there with him."

He stepped in from the door. "Try a neighbor."

She did not have to be told twice. But she shivered

224

as she passed him at the doorframe, and not from a chill.

Shelly did not have his gun in his coat. He never liked to wear it when he was out with Thom. So he edged along the hallway carefully toward the open bedroom door. No lights were lit in the hall, so that the illumination of the small lamp on the table beside the bed worked to protect his approach from whatever real danger lay ahead.

"Lay down your weapon!" he cried out, turning the corner with both arms outstretched as if there had been a gun in them. He heard a whizz, as of a knife flying. But nothing struck him, and he looked down to see the hazzan Itzak Tsinger lying on a stack of pillows in his bed, under a lumpy comforter. He sat up, smiling, happy to see a visitor.

But there was a nine-inch bread knife sticking out of the front of the bureau across the room in front of him.

# 21

On Wednesday, David Horowitz awoke from the worst dream of his life to find himself on a life-support machine in a hospital he could not remember having entered. Chronically worrying over his health, Horowitz saw the nurse and listened to the beeps of his heart on the monitor, and nearly gave out in shock at the long-dreaded heart attack. He had no memory of the blow that had cracked his skull and left him unconscious for twenty-four hours. Once prompted, however, with the details of his injury, he was able to supply a few frames of the story Lowenkopf had only surmised.

Lillian Levinski had indeed approached him with a proposal to count women among the minyan at services. He was aware that other shuls had begun to alter seating arrangements so that the *mechitzah* separated men from women without relegating women to the back of the hall. And he understood that Conservative and Reform temples included women among their minyans. On Friday afternoons in particular the proposal would prove useful—perhaps even, as she called it, an inescapable adaptation to the modern world. But there were members of their congregation whose faith amounted to the way things always had been done, and they could hardly afford to *lose* congregants, could they? He would not take the dramatic step and support the idea. But—if she could win the rabbi and the hazzan over to the idea, Horowitz wouldn't block it, either.

That had been the extent of their discussion on the matter. But he had heard from Sholem Pirski, who believed Lily's idea might present the only solution to their problem. Their roster of members had fallen below the necessary point, and none of the names were spring chickens. Their minyan would grow more and more difficult to collect, until they would be unable to hold services at all. And the rabbi was intrigued with the suggestion of Lillian's that the policy might attract new members—young people, whose ideas about men and women were quite different than the old ones'.

The problem, the rabbi had felt, would be winning the hearts of the oldest men, who would turn to Tsinger for support. And the hazzan himself would encourage them to refuse to participate under such conditions. Unless they could reach him before the issue was addressed by the Ritual Committee. Pirski was planning a private meeting with Tsinger, himself, and Lillian Levinski, at which he hoped she might charm the old man as she had charmed himself.

Riordan had stopped Horowitz at this point, to clarify a question. Hadn't they noticed anything unusual in the hazzan's behavior to that point?

Horowitz had replied that the hazzan was in every respect an unusual man. His connection to the everyday world had never been absolutely solid. And his surgical relief for an aneurysm had loosened the link still further.

"Nuts?" Riordan asked.

"Not before," replied Horowitz.

"Well," said the veteran detective, regarding the man in his bed, "he certainly is now, isn't he?"

There was no denying that, but there was little likelihood of a trial. His heart was not long for this world, and the home in which he would be placed would see him to the end.

Irene had wept at the news, and Shelly was unable to tell how many of her tears were for her own trauma and how many were for the man in the bed.

At the shul, however, where Max joined them, the mood was considerably brighter. The rabbi was sorry for old Tsinger, of course, but it was a tragedy he had supported alone for a long time. The news proved a double release to him—a personal relief from the burden of an increasingly disturbed old friend, and a gratifying vindication from the complications of legal charges. How much he had been able to guess about the hazzan's role in Lillian Levinski's murder, Shelly was unable to determine. His silence, which he had clung to for five long days of suspicion, confirmed to Shelly that he was unwilling to free himself by breaking faith with the hazzan. Having somebody else do it for him, however, was another story entirely.

"What a partner you have here, Max—what a detective!" the rabbi said, sharing the joy of his release with the two men most responsible for it.

"What did I tell you, Sholem?" replied Max with evident pride. "Trust yourself in our hands."

Trust was the last thing the rabbi had shown Shelly during his interview in the precinct cell, but neither of them were in a mood to remember that.

"You were right, you were absolutely right! And it paid off in spades! Thank you, gentlemen, both of you."

"You're welcome," said Max.

Shelly was unaccustomed to receiving any praise for doing his job—Madagascar's usual comment was a constipated scowl. But he didn't mind the feel of it at all, really.

"There's nothing to thank me for—"

"Oh, but there is! I couldn't say anything about poor Itzak to the police, and couldn't even break his confidence with you. But you figured it out for yourself! Remarkable!"

"It was nothing, really," Shelly mumbled.

"You should've seen the job he did for Blumberg," said Max.

"For Blumberg too? At the store?"

"Caught the thieves red-handed."

"No!"

"With the goods in their truck."

"Remarkable!" said the rabbi. "What a *kep* on him!"

Shelly turned to Max with a serious expression. "Max," he said, "I don't want to stir up trouble, but I can't believe those two in the truck managed it all alone."

"Of course they did."

"A stock man and a security guard? I don't think so. The paperwork alone was confusing enough to require my old partner to sort it out. And the choice of merchandise . . . and the timing . . . they must have had some guidance from above."

"Don't worry about it."

"Don't worry? But the thieves behind the scam are probably still at large."

Max took him around the shoulders. "Don't you think Stanley thought of that, too? So who are we talking about now? The sales manager? Or the decorator? I spoke to Stanley about it. He would rather straighten this matter out privately. In house."

"And let them off?"

"Maybe . . . if they make good on all the stolen merchandise. Whatever deal he chooses to make is all right with me. He's the client, Shelly. You're not on the force anymore."

"So we catch the bad guys just so our clients can set them free again?"

"We're not in the business of catching bad guys. We're in the business of pleasing clients. Look at the rabbi here, and how happy you've made him."

The rabbi was certainly beaming.

"What I especially appreciated," Pirski said, "is that you never lost faith in me. Never doubted my innocence for a minute! I know the evidence looked pretty bad there, for a while."

Shelly didn't have the heart to tell the man that he'd thought he was guilty for sure, but that their function as his advocates kept them plugging away in his corner.

"Thank you," he said, taking Shelly by both arms.

"You're welcome," said Shelly.

The rabbi gave him a bear hug, which flustered Shelly for a moment. Not that he didn't enjoy it.

Afterwards, when Max and Shelly were walking to their cars, the senior partner turned to the junior and said, "There is an item of business I'd like to discuss with you, Shell. Is this a good time?"

"Good enough," Shelly said. "What's up?"

"You may have noticed," began Max, "that Irene and I have struck up an interest between us. This is not a new thing, Shelly. I have been after this woman for years. But, at the funeral the other day, she started to thaw, and at her brother's house even to flirt. But you have no idea what her encounter with Tsinger did to her."

"Shook her up, eh?"

"You could say that," said Max. "Maybe 'loosened her up' is a better description, or even 'warmed' her up. We had a long talk last night, which lasted well into this morning. And by the end, she agreed to go to Miami with me."

"Miami? Max, you old beach dog! How long do you plan to be away?"

"No, you don't understand," said Max carefully. "She agreed to *move* there with me, on a permanent basis. I have a bungalow near the beach in Hallandale that should make a lovely little honeymoon cottage."

Shelly patted his partner's slender arm with real affection. *"Mazeltov,* then."

Max looked uncomfortable. "I'm afraid I'm going to have to ask more of you than that."

"What do you need?"

"You remember, when I took you in and made you my partner, I said one day you might buy out my end of the business?"

"When I had learned how to run it from you. And you were ready to retire."

"From your work on the rabbi's case today, and the Stanley Blumberg affair, I'd say you could run it just fine. And Irene's acceptance of my proposal means it's time for me to retire."

Shelly said, "How much do you need?"

"I'll take less than it's worth, whatever it is," said Max, "but how do you figure these things? I have clients, like Stan, who've always called me with their problems, and will no doubt continue to call you now. I know you haven't had time to collect any cash yet—other than furniture commissions and your share of the Blumberg account."

"To tell you the truth," said Shelly, "I was planning to use that money to send my son to Hebrew school. When I saw how he watched the service, it occurred to me that there was nothing a father could give his son that might prove more important in the end than a line back to his own heritage—how his grandfathers put the world together, and what they valued in it. I don't know what he'll make of it, but I want to give him a chance to figure it out."

"Absolutely," said Max, clapping his hands. "That's the best first use of your money. But you could find a partner, couldn't you? I'll settle for ten thousand dollars."

Shelly counted in his head and realized, setting aside enough for Thom, he could still meet about half. He promised to see what he could do—but before leaving, he sat down on the hood of the Continental next to his senior partner. "Tell me one thing, first," he said. "Why would a man give up a business he had spent his life building to run off to Miami with a woman like Irene? She's very nice, and spirited, but it's hard to believe you're in the grip of a passion in your blood."

"Is that really so hard to believe?" asked Max, with a kind, patient smile.

"At her age?"

"Ah-ha," said Max. "Now I understand. You don't see how sexy an older woman can be."

Shelly's first thought was Mordred. But he said, "When I think of an older woman, I think forty-five—"

"In their forties, they're just getting the hang of it," Max said. "What does a woman in her thirties need to know about how to please a man? Just to take off her blouse is usually enough to drive him to distraction! It's only afterwards, when nature's gifts start to slip, that they have to learn to invent, and to respond, and to anticipate pleasure."

"You mean—"

"I mean a woman in her forties begins to understand how to please herself, and you. And a woman in her fifties has had the time to learn how to do those things a little bit better. When sex is an act of desperation, you never get the chance to settle into it. But when the fires burn lower, they burn more evenly, and longer, too, for that matter."

"Have you and Irene had a chance yet to—"

"You can see it in their eyes, Shelly. You can distinguish the ones who really enjoy it from those who play by the numbers. And when you see a woman who really enjoys it, grab her! Because she'll see to it that you really enjoy it too."

At that moment, two white-haired women came walking down the sidewalk on their way to the market, their baskets rolling behind them. As they approached, Max took Shelly by the arm and pulled him out of the women's way, taking off his hat and bowing slightly to them as they passed. The woman on the left refused to acknowledge him, staring straight ahead. But the one on the right glanced their way, and gave him a brilliant smile. It was sweetly grateful, and warm, and wonderfully inviting, too. For an instant, Shelly felt an urge to fall into step behind her. Max returned her smile but said nothing until they had passed.

"So which one do you think would be giving and kind in the sack?" he asked Shelly.

"The one on the right?"

"You got it. Now go forth and appreciate the beauties of God's creation."

# 22

It was eleven o'clock in the morning, and already Homer was standing over a teenage corpse, in a coffee shop near the school. It seemed that an hour before two adolescents, having ditched their academic programs for the day, occupied the plastic booth just inside the plate-glass window and ordered two plates of scrambled eggs with bacon and toast and coffee. The manager of the place was uncertain whether to serve them until the bigger of the two placed a ten-dollar bill on the table and said, "You can eat a lot of breakfast for ten dollars, no?" And the manager had motioned the waiter to their table.

"Were you their waiter?" asked Jill Morganthal of a pale, thin man in a white cotton T-shirt and black trousers.

He nodded.

"Had you ever seen these particular boys in here before?"

"*Sí.*"

"Did they act differently this time?"

"Differently?"

234

"In any way at all? You never know what might prove to be significant later."

The waiter thought it over. "Usually the big one orders sausage, I think, with his eggs."

Morganthal jotted it down in her pad. "Thank you."

"Was that what you meant?"

"We'll see."

Homer did not interfere with her questioning, not because there was so little to be learned, but because there was so much. The restaurant had been half full of customers when a young boy had approached the picture window from the street, extended a gun in both hands, and blasted away through the glass, which had fallen away in panes, attracting the attention of everyone within a fifty-foot radius of the spot on a crowded street. Which meant they had more than twenty witnesses, all of whom agreed on the many fine details, including a description of the kid who fired the gun. They were waiting now to make their statements, one by one. He and Jill would have to sit down with each of them, asking them for their name and address, and for an account of the event in their own words. Except Homer already knew what had happened, and who had made it happen. He knew it would happen the night before, though not where and when. And the last thing he wanted to hear again was a description of the shooter.

"Oh, yes, I saw him quite clearly," one woman reported. "He was about this high"—raising her palm in the air—"and wore a clean white T-shirt, just like his"—indicating the waiter—"and had a round head with curly black hair and eyes like a rabbit in a hutch."

HUTCH EYES, wrote Jill in her pad. "And you would say about a hundred and twenty pounds?"

Homer nodded before the woman could answer. He *knew*.

Jill looked up brightly, thanking the woman for her report and eyeing the waiting line eagerly. "Who's next?"

Homer went outside to smoke a cigarette offered him by the waiter when that slender man stuck one between his own trembling lips. Homer had given them up years before, but now for the first time in a long time he felt a need for the kick in the back of his throat when the nicotine burned in. There was an entrance to the elevated subway not far from the coffee shop—that must have been where he waited, the big gun tucked under his sweater, for Torquemada and his pal to make their morning breakfast stop. He would have sat on the fourth or fifth step up, out of sight of people on the street until he ducked his head under the stairway roof for a view of the coffee shop entrance. He must have planned to go inside, to find them at their table, until he saw them sit at the table inside the front window. That would have made it easier for him, since he wouldn't have to hear their voices until the bullets broke the glass. He just pointed his gun, like you do to hunt ducks on Nintendo video games, and pulled the trigger five times: *blam, blam, blam, blam, blam!* Then he just ran, because he didn't have to go inside, and it occurred to him that maybe there was a chance he could get away after all.

But there wasn't, of course. Because he had voluntarily obliged the police and stopped by the community center. If he hadn't, this would never have happened. But Homer had asked Montoya to find the kid, and Montoya had made sure he would answer their summons. So Homer knew the face well enough to fit it to the first description he had heard of the shooter.

Alfonso Barreras. Case closed.

Jill was having the time of her life—finally one they

could solve! They could find this kid, and put him away, and make all the people feel they were solving the problem. But the arrest of eleven-year-old Alfonso, for the murder of the man who had blown away the hand of his talented cousin Benito, did not strike Homer as much of a solution to anything they had learned the past few days. Rocio Lucero had killed himself, grieving for his mother's return to the streets; his friends had avenged that death on the instrument instead of the cause, and the pendulum of violence had swung back and forth ever since that sad day. Now they could bust one, the youngest, weakest, and gentlest of all, whose crime was an act of love, and an act of fear, and an act of horror at the cruelty of his life.

But they could identify him, and make a case, and send him off to the farm. That was the happy note in Jill's voice as she asked her questions and jotted down the answers, preparing for their day in court. All they had to do to wrap it up was drive over to Alfonso's foster mother's place and wait in their car out front. He would have to show, sooner or later—where could an eleven-year-old hide? Finally they had someone to show for them all, for Rocio Lucero, Raoul Lopez, and the couple in the closet in the school basement— Homer could not remember their names—José and Esperanza something or other. Now was their chance: They could lock up Alfonso and close the case, forgetting all the rest.

Except Homer was having trouble forgetting them. Where was Shelly when you needed him? Homer wondered. When his former partner was around to feel for these kids, Homer didn't feel the need to do so. But now, with Jill greedily writing down every last line of testimony, someone had to remember that there were two or three sides to every story, and the papers would only carry one of them in the caption under the photograph of the fractured window with the two gangbangers in its glass.

And then, as if in response to Homer's unspoken wish, Shelly came strolling down the avenue.

"Hey, there," he said, matter-of-factly. "The precinct told me you were down here."

"Another gang killing," said Homer with a shrug.

"Who did it?"

"An eleven-year-old wanna-be, trying to protect his cousin."

"Who's going to protect him, now?"

That was it, thought Homer, that was the very question in his mind—who was supposed to protect Alfonso? It seemed as if no one had ever protected him, unless it was the boy in a room at the Bronx municipal hospital with the remains of his right hand wrapped in several layers of gauze.

"I don't know," said Homer. "We were supposed to."

"Too bad," Shelly said.

"Yeah."

An awkward silence hung between them.

"This isn't a personal visit," Shelly said.

"No?"

"I'm here on business."

Homer looked at the corpses in the glass, which were still being studied by the Crime Scene Unit. "They didn't hire you. Don't tell me the coffee shop."

"Nobody hired me," Shelly said. "I just wanted to tell you why I quit the force."

"I know why," said Homer. "Because the money is so much better. And the hours, too. And because you don't have to watch this shit anymore, with nothing that you can do."

Those were pretty good reasons for someone to quit; but they weren't Shelly's reasons. "Nope."

"Because you'd seen enough suffering here to last you a lifetime."

There was plenty of suffering, Shelly thought, on both sides of the street. "Wrong again."

"So tell me."

"I couldn't stand putting the bad guys away."

Homer knew just what he meant. "It's not getting any easier to do that, is it?"

"Let me ask you a question, Homer."

"Go ahead."

"Have you got five thousand dollars socked away anywhere?"

"Why?"

"An opportunity has come up," Shelly said, "for you to leave all this behind."

"And go private?"

"Uh-huh."

Homer shook his head. "What's it like?"

"I'll tell you something—when I started, I had no idea. But I'm learning, case by case. I had a rabbi for a client on a case recently, and spent a lot of time in his shul. And the more time I spent there, the more I was convinced that I had nothing Jewish about me. I mean, I don't know the language, or the prayers, or what the wise men have said about anything, Homer. I felt like a little boy who hasn't yet learned how to act in a world of adults."

"I'm not too religious, either."

"But that's where I was wrong, Homer. I'm pretty Jewish after all. You see, the difference between what I'm doing now and what we did together is the difference between punishment and compassion. We used to go after the guys who did bad things, Homer, to make them pay for their crimes. Now I look for reasons to believe my clients are honest people. Instead of incriminating, I've been exonerating. And that, as it turns out, is a Jewish way to approach things. Which is why I think I've discovered I'm Jewish after all."

"I'm happy for you," said Homer.

"No, you're not very happy," said Shelly, "and for the same reason. When it comes to crime and redemption, you're pretty Jewish yourself."

It was the first time anyone had accused the blond detective of any such thing. He suspected Shelly meant it as a compliment, the way a Native American chief bestows honor on a favored guest by declaring him a member of the tribe. But Homer wasn't sure he was ready to join any tribe that counted Shelly Lowenkopf among its warriors.

"I've put in eleven years already," he said.

"Which means," said Shelly, "you've got only nine more years of this to go."

At that moment Jill Morganthal came out, sliding her pad into her purse. "Ready to pull out," she reported to Homer. "We've got a solid I.D. on the kid when we need it. If we run over now, and lean on the foster mom, we ought to be able to pull him in before lunchtime."

Homer said, "Are we sure we want this kid?"

"I want him," said Jill. "Don't you?"

Homer imagined the scene awaiting them. They would knock on the door of the foster home and explain that Alfonso had gotten himself into trouble. The foster mom might cry a little or might pretend she didn't care. They could slink down in the Reliant for a couple of hours, lying in wait for an eleven-year-old kid. Then they could spring their trap. The kid would try to run into the house, where the foster mom would either try to protect him, and they would have to haul him out from under her, or else she would shrug and tell him she couldn't interfere, in which case they would have to watch the kid disintegrate. It was more than a job—it was tearing the kid up, and tearing a fragile family apart at the seams.

Shelly was waiting for an answer.

Jill was waiting too, with eager eyes.

Homer said, "All right," to no one in particular.

"Ready to roll?" asked Jill.

Homer turned to Shelly. "I've got five thousand dollars. I'm ready to try my hand in the private sector."

Shelly shook his hand. "Glad to have you, partner."

Homer picked a nit off Shelly's woolen lapel. "Nice suit," he said.

Morganthal groaned.

# 23

Mordred groaned, too, when Shelly invited her over that night, cooked her a dinner of veal scaloppine with a dry white wine, and finished the evening efficiently with affectionate, generous lovemaking. When they had finished, and lay in each other's arms and the covering sheet, she threw herself backwards, stretching her muscles, and asked him, "What happened?"

"We made love."

"But how? I mean, why? Why was it so easy tonight?"

"You know what the problem was?"

"You didn't want me anymore."

"No . . . I wanted you badly enough. Just the way you are. But every time we got under way, a memory came back to me, of lying in the hospital parking lot after the accident, floating away from my body."

Mordred shrugged. "They say love and death are two sides of a coin."

"Yes—and it kept flipping over. I relived my experience in the netherworld, where I saw all the souls that were close to my own, life after life after life."

"And I wasn't one of them?"

"Yes, you were—the central one in the picture, as a matter of fact."

"The picture?"

"They keep these family portraits in heaven. So people will know their relations."

"And we're related?"

"Linked souls. In one life, brother and sister. In another we're husband and wife."

"I like the second one better."

"So did I. But I kept seeing this picture of you, as a very old lady."

"In my forties?"

"Old."

"Uh-oh."

"That's what I thought. And every time I did—no surprises. But Max was talking to me today, and I started to imagine it in a very different light."

"He helped you to see me as young again?"

"He helped me desire you old."

"Oh, my. How kinky."

"That's what Max was trying to tell me. And what do you think happened when I embraced you as an old lady?"

She wrapped her arms around him. "I became young again."

"How did you know?"

"I was there, wasn't I?"

She looked up at him, and he kissed her on the mouth, and he saw her in all her ages. And she was beautifully sexy in all of them.

Benito Durazo lay awake that night in his hospital bed, trying to see if anything at all was left of his right

243

hand, which was wrapped in gauze so thickly one digit was indistinguishable from the next. He thought he could make out three remaining, the thumb and the two nearest to it, although the mass of wadding beyond the third finger did not look promising at all. Motion was incredibly painful, but he kept trying to flex, unwilling to believe that the ring finger and pinky were no longer part of his hand. He still felt them there, for Christ's sake—although the doctor had told him he would, even though. The doctor had called him a lucky guy—if the barrel had not shifted off center when the trigger was pulled, the blast might have amputated everything below the wrist. They could reconnect hands that had been sliced cleanly off in industrial accidents, but the mess a shotgun left was another story entirely.

The pinky he had known was gone—he had seen it explode. But the ring finger still had been dangling—they had to cut it off in Emergency to save what they could of the rest. Three was all he really needed, Benito observed in consolation, the thumb and middle finger to grip the can and the pointer to press the button on top. The doctor said the odds were fifty-fifty he would be painting again—there was some question about the bone structure, if it would heal properly, or if the shock had done some damage to the remaining joints. But Benito was hopeful. They had not taken his life on the street, and that was a turn for which he was genuinely thankful. He thought of Raoul, who had not been so fortunate, and Miguel, who was hiding now in the basement of their mother's building, afraid of reprisals for his own act of vengeance.

And he thought of his cousin, Poquito, the Little One—Alfonso—who had poked death in the eye to avenge the wreck of his hand. Torquemada was gone, and with him the greatest threat to Benito's own life. Without him, they could make peace with the

Diablos. Benito was anxious to do that now, since he planned to return to the community center and resume work on the mural. He understood the composition had been laid out by Rocio Lucero, and intended to be faithful to it. The final result would be a collaboration between the two of them, a Fury and a Diablo, which reflected beautifully the message of the design. He had spent most of the last few hours thinking about the colors that would bring out the relationships between the figures. Lucero had a good eye for shapes, but no sense of color at all, of how it affected the viewer's heart. Benito felt confident that between them, they could produce one hell of a vision of the world in which they should live.

Only where was Alfonso tonight? Benito thought of all the places they had hidden together. He might be with Miguel, who had given him the gun he had used to shoot Torquemada. But, no, Alfonso did not like Miguel, and would not have stayed with him. So where had he gone on this cold night? The police would be waiting at Clemencia's—Alfonso would certainly know that, too. Benito loved his cousin, and he hoped he had taught him enough to take care of himself out on the streets alone. He promised to do whatever he could to heal himself quickly and protect Alfonso again. All he could do from his hospital bed was say a brief prayer for him. But he did that.

"Dear God," he said aloud in the darkened hospital room, "find my brother Alfonso, and send an angel to look over him this night. Protect him from the cold wind, and from the cruelty of the streets into which he was born. Let him feel, even where he is, that he is not alone in this world, that someone loves him and knows why he has done what he has done. Let him know that he is forgiven, Lord, for the life that he has taken. And let him also forgive me, for requiring it of him."

Benito was not given to prayer, but the sound of his voice in the silent room comforted him. And hadn't Clemencia said that the prayers of children, when they are unselfishly offered, travel with a special grace and are listened to in heaven?

Alfonso, for his part, was thinking of Benito—of everything his cousin had taught him. He knew until peace was made between Furies and Diablos the blocks of their own neighborhood might be fatal for him. So he spent the day in the Bronx Zoo, sticking to the crowds, trying to keep in sight of a policeman at all times. The police were no friends of his, but their presence might scare off his enemies for a while. After the first couple of hours, though, he forgot about his own troubles and began enjoying the exhibits along with the rest of the visitors. He liked the great apes, with the mirror behind the bars in an exhibit marked: THE MOST FEARED ANIMAL IN THE JUNGLE. He liked the bears in their open pit, and the Reptile House nearby with its snakes behind the glass and the alligators, too. The House of Darkness, where all the nocturnal animals were fooled into believing it was nighttime already, was full of bats and geckos and funny-looking beasts. And it was pitch dark inside, so no one could see well enough to risk taking a shot.

He did not want Clemencia to worry about him, but he did not want to tell her where he was, either. He made a fast call to say he wouldn't be coming home for a while. She cried over the telephone, which broke his heart, and all he could do was to keep repeating, "Don't cry . . . I'll be back . . . right now, it's for the best. . . ." She wept over him and complained about the foster care agency, who would take everything away from her.

Closing time presented a problem of its own. He decided not to risk hiding out in the zoo. If they found him, as they would probably do while he slept, the police would return him home—and then take him away from his home again. He had to find a place to sleep where no one from his neighborhood might happen upon him before he could tell who they were. Which meant no place in his neighborhood was really safe for him. And if he had to look for a spot to sleep in a strange neighborhood, the only place he felt at all safe was in the park.

There was a rear entrance to the zoo, near Pelham Parkway, where cars could leave the Bronx River Parkway and weave around to the zoo. He left by that exit, following the steep hill that ran alongside the parkway for a while. He was thinking about Benito spending the night alone in the hospital when a peculiar thing reared itself up in his path.

At first he was afraid of the hulking shape in the darkness. But then he gathered his courage and moved closer and found it was nothing but a sofa—in rust-colored velvet, still wrapped in the cords that bound it new, lying on its side. He pushed it up, and collected the pillows, and arranged them where they belonged. Then he sat on it, feeling very strange in the open air, while the cars whizzed by on the parkway behind him and the black grass whispered in front of him. The sofa must have fallen from a car, he imagined, into the little depression where the ground sunk below the level of the park grass, cutting the night wind. He climbed off and pushed it closer against the hillside of the parkway, and turned it around so the back of the couch blocked the wind even more. Then he stretched out on it, full length—and the pillows were soft and comfortable, a gift from heaven.

No—not from heaven.

In the morning he would find Benito at the hospital and the two of them would take off together, protecting each other from all the world. He thought of Clemencia, too, all alone in her apartment for the night, and he thought of Raoul, even lonelier in his grave. He heard the wind whistling across the park above him, but he gathered his collar around his throat and the sofa kept him warm. He watched the headlights of the cars turning off the parkway as they swept the grass, away from him. And he said a final prayer for his dear cousin Benito—for his wounded hand, and his mind, and his heart. He thanked him for the sofa, which he understood in the crawl spaces of his own heart that his cousin had somehow provided.

Then Alfonso closed his eyes and went to sleep, dreaming a dream of peace.